# THE
# BLAME

# BOOKS BY KERRY WILKINSON

## Standalone Novels

*Ten Birthdays*
*Two Sisters*
*The Girl Who Came Back*
*Last Night*
*The Death and Life of Eleanor Parker*
*The Wife's Secret*
*A Face in the Crowd*
*Close to You*
*After the Accident*
*The Child Across the Street*
*What My Husband Did*

## The Jessica Daniel series

*The Killer Inside* (also published as *Locked In*)
*Vigilante*
*The Woman in Black*
*Think of the Children*
*Playing with Fire*
*The Missing Dead* (also published as *Thicker than Water*)
*Behind Closed Doors*
*Crossing the Line*
*Scarred for Life*
*For Richer, For Poorer*

*Nothing But Trouble*
*Eye for an Eye*
*Silent Suspect*
*The Unlucky Ones*
*A Cry in the Night*

## The Jessica Daniel Short Stories

*January*
*February*
*March*
*April*

## Silver Blackthorn

*Reckoning*
*Renegade*
*Resurgence*

## The Andrew Hunter series

*Something Wicked*
*Something Hidden*
*Something Buried*

## Other

*Down Among the Dead Men*
*No Place Like Home*
*Watched*

# THE
# BLAME

## KERRY WILKINSON

Bookouture

Published by Bookouture in 2021

An imprint of Storyfire Ltd.
Carmelite House
50 Victoria Embankment
London EC4Y 0DZ

www.bookouture.com

ISBN: 978-1-80019-502-8
eBook ISBN: 978-1-80019-501-1

# ONE

SUNDAY

I'm not exactly sure when it happened but it was somewhat recently that I realised I had become a brunch person. I'm one of those people who spends large amounts of my life banging on about how important my time is, and yet I will willingly devote forty-five minutes on a Sunday morning to standing in a line outside Yolkely Dokely.

And why?

Because some underpaid, overworked, sweaty bloke in an apron knows how to poach a couple of eggs and then dump them on an English muffin.

I've embraced avocado. I've had *actual* conversations with *actual* people about sourdough starters.

It's crystal meth for the middle classes and I have somehow become everything I would've hated back in the day.

As I continue to wait in line by myself, it is impossible to avoid overhearing the conversation of the couple behind about how their Little Jessie has a flute exam this week. How their Little Jessie got a gold star from his or her teacher for helping carry some books. How their Little Jessie is already semi-fluent in French. How their Little Jessie is a know-it-all pain in the arse who is likely the most unpopular kid in his or her class who will likely…

Anyway.

It is likely the endless talk of Little Jessie growing up is why my mind drifts to thoughts of Paige… and Richard… and… *home*.

Aside from when I was a kid, I've never believed in premonitions or anything like that. Stories of the supernatural are fairy tales that adults tell themselves to make life a little more understandable, or bearable.

Except… those thoughts of childhood and Macklebury appear from nowhere and then, seconds later, my phone starts to buzz. It's a WhatsApp call and Paige's name is on the screen.

I feel a chill tickle my spine, even though I'm bundled up in a winter coat and hat. I try to remember the last time Paige and I spoke to each other but there's no specific occasion that springs to mind. It would be at least five years. There have been messages back and forth in that time – but never anything more substantial than a brief 'happy new year', or 'happy birthday'. I doubt there would have even been that if it wasn't for Facebook's know-all algorithms spewing out notifications every time someone gets a bit older.

I do the mental arithmetic without thinking: it's a little after ten in the morning here in a chilly Toronto, which means it's three in the afternoon back in the UK.

Even seeing her name after all this time somehow lets me know that the reason she's calling won't be anything good. I could ignore it and go on with my life… except I don't.

Paige sounds hesitant when I answer the phone and say her name. She replies with a 'Harry' but there's a croak to her voice and then a second or two of quiet.

'Are you okay?' I ask.

There are a good twenty people waiting in line along the front of the restaurant and it feels as if everyone has fallen silent as my question goes momentarily unanswered.

'Are you still in Canada?'

'Yes. Where are you?'

Another pause. I'm a few blocks from the public square of Yonge–Dundas, with its huge billboard on one side and mall entrance on the other. There should be a buzz of traffic and people, even on a Sunday morning, and yet everything is silent. Even the scrapes of cutlery on plate from inside the restaurant have shrunk to nothing.

'When did you last talk to Richard?'

I puff out a breath and the cold spirals away into nothingness.

'A few months back? Maybe a year? He texted after they announced the World Cup was going to be over here. We said something about sorting out tickets if England end up playing in the city but left it at that.'

There's another hesitation, perhaps because football has never been something in which Richard or I was interested. I thought it was a strange message at the time and it was a couple of weeks later when I wondered if he was simply after someone to talk to.

'He's been arrested,' Paige says.

'*Arrested?*'

The 'Little Jessie' couple behind are definitely listening in now. The guy inclines his head towards me, while the woman leans in a little. I sense it, rather than see it.

'I know you're busy and everything…' Paige says. 'I probably shouldn't ask… I suppose I was just wondering if, um… maybe you could come home…?'

I turn away from the eavesdropping couple and lower my voice.

'What do you mean *arrested*?'

'For murder.'

I hear what she says but it's as if it's in another language. It makes sense, except that it doesn't.

I step out of the line and there's a second where I wonder whether I'll be able to get back in if the couple move forward to swallow up my spot.

Nobody likes a queue-jumper.

I take a few more steps along the street, past the door to the restaurant and into the alley that runs along the side. There are overflowing wheelie bins here and a scattered pile of plastics from where someone has gone through to fish out the cans for the recycling refund.

Paige hasn't spoken again but I can hear her gentle breaths through the phone.

'What do you mean murder?' I ask.

'I don't know. It's just happened.'

'There has to be a mistake…?'

I want an instant 'of course', except it doesn't come. It's like there's a delay on the line with an old-fashioned transatlantic phone call, except there isn't.

'I'm kinda busy with work, um…' I tail off, unwilling to complete the lie.

There's something about a childhood best friend that never leaves a person. We move on with new relationships, friends, work colleagues, flings, deep conversations, soulmates. We can get married, divorced and remarried. We have kids and pets. We travel the world and see things we'll never forget.

And yet, beyond that, those connections we make when we're kids feel fixed and permanent.

'Murder…' The word sounds unreal from my mouth. 'Who do they say he killed?'

Paige doesn't reply right away, as if she's weighing up the word too. *Murder…*

'It's complicated,' she replies eventually. 'I didn't know who else to call…'

There's another little falter to her voice and I'm a teenager again.

I sigh and look up through the small gap between buildings to the hint of the beautiful blue Canadian sky.

I tell her I'll see what I can do but, in my mind, I'm already on that plane.

# TWO

It's around twenty-three hours later that I clamber out of the taxi and breathe Macklebury's air for the first time in a decade or so. There are no towers here, no life to be lived in perpetual shadow.

There's sky.

The buildings are no more than a couple of floors high and the blue from above stretches deep into the distance, offering an openness that I'd somehow forgotten existed.

The driver grimaces when I tell him I'll have to pay on a card. I show him the inside of my wallet, which contains the rainbow of Canadian dollar notes, and say I have no English cash. His frown deepens as he bashes the card machine with the side of his hand and mutters something under his breath. I push in my card and enter my PIN, before waiting for a sputtered receipt. Then I turn and take in the nearly deserted High Street.

It's the same but different.

The buildings are all in the place I remember but there's something off. The Lloyds Bank, where I opened my first account when I was sixteen, is now a betting shop. Green's Newsagent, where I used to eye the top-shelf magazines while pretending to look at comics, has been replaced by a juice bar.

I stare along the street, before spotting the cash machine that's attached to the nearest Co-Op supermarket. A homeless man is sitting against the wall, with a sleeping bag tucked under his chin. I almost leave my suitcase abandoned on the street before remembering it when I'm already a step away. As I near the machine, he smiles up to me with glazed, unfocused eyes and I do the thing that I think everyone does. I acknowledge him with the merest of nods before ignoring his silent plea as I feed the machine my card. There's a message about fees and exchange rates but there's little alternative as I use my credit card to withdraw a wad of notes that I try to hide from the homeless man when I fold them into my wallet.

There are no messages or calls on my phone and it's only when I look closer that I realise roaming is turned off. It will cost half a house deposit to switch it on but it doesn't feel as if I have much choice as I toggle the option and then wait for the data bars to appear.

When I call, Paige answers before the phone even rings at my end. She asks where I am and, when I say I'm outside the Co-Op, she says she'll find me.

I've barely been waiting a couple of minutes when there's the sound of scuffing feet and then I turn to see Paige bustling towards me. She's in tight jeans and a thin, short jacket, with her hands jammed into the pockets. I blink and we could be teenagers once more. There are a few more lines in the face, perhaps – but she wouldn't be the only one.

'You're going grey,' she says, as a whisper of a smile flitters across her face.

'We can't all dye our hair black.'

The smirk spreads into a grin. 'I forgot how annoying you are.' She takes a breath, the smile fading as she adds: 'I didn't know if you'd come…'

'You caught me at a good time with work and everything...'

She waits a beat, wondering if there's more to come.

'How was the flight?' she adds.

A shrug: 'Long. I can't sleep on planes; then it was either three trains and a bus to get here, or a taxi. I took the taxi.'

She nods but there's a part of me that wonders if she's ever flown that far before. Whenever I think of Paige, I think of this town. It's hard to picture her anywhere else. Thinking of someone as a small-town guy or girl sounds overbearingly patronising and yet…

We watch one another for a moment before she spins and starts walking along the street. I slot in at her side, the wheels of my suitcase making a steady *doof-doof-doof* as it bumps across the divots in the pavement.

'Who are they saying he killed?' I ask.

'Mr Wilson.'

It takes me a few seconds to process. It's a name I've not heard, or thought about, for fifteen years or more.

'Our old head of year?'

'It was outside The Pines on Saturday night. It was all so messy at first. It's why I said I'd tell you properly when you got here. I didn't know at the time.'

It's a lot of information in one go. I've heard of The Pines but it's misty and distant, a disjointed name, and then the fuzz clears. 'The hotel?'

'Right.'

We keep walking for a few more steps and the only sound is my suitcase.

'What happened?' I ask.

'I don't know. I saw on Facebook that someone had been killed outside the hotel. You know what it's like around here – nothing ever happens, so everyone was going crazy. Then people started *naming names*. Someone said Richard had been arrested. I texted him and didn't get a reply. I messaged Ollie and he said it was true. That's when I called you.'

She speaks so quickly and there's a lot to take in. Meanings within meanings.

When I lived in Macklebury, Facebook wasn't a thing. Rumours would get around but it was all in hushed tones, with a *you'll never guess what?* snidey-ness. Nothing was ever in the open. I'd never considered the clash of twenty-first-century communication with a small-town mentality, but I can feel it in Paige's clenched-teeth tone. This was no way for her to find out.

The other thing is that Paige *messaged* Richard's brother Oliver. Not asked him, she *messaged* him.

We pass the pub at the end of the High Street and take the corner. It used to be called the Duke of York but is now the Prince of Wales. The scratched window frames have been replaced by shiny, new double-glazing and there's a board outside advertising that tonight is curry night. We're past the pub as I remember this is where I bought my first underage drink. I ordered a cider and black because, in my mind, it was more of a grown-up drink than straight cider. Richard got served directly before me and went for a lager-top, because it's what his dad drank. If our squeaky voices didn't give our age away, then the fact the landlord knew Richard's parents should have done. Either that, or the fact we ordered individual drinks and paid with coins.

'Where are we going?' I ask.

'I didn't know what time you were getting to town,' Paige replies. 'Ollie said he'd tell me what happened in person. I was hoping you'd get here before then – and here you are.'

I bite my lip to stop myself from asking the obvious question and we walk for five minutes or so until we reach the gates to Albert Park. A man is leaning against the fence, thumbing his phone before he looks up and notices us. He cranes his neck a fraction when he spots me, then his eyes narrow into a squint.

Some older brothers fit the role almost too well – and Richard's sibling is definitely one of those. Back at school, Oliver was taller, fitter and stronger than either Richard or me. He was the type who would delight in having more knowledge about almost everything compared to us. Regardless of anything we might have ever experienced, he either did it first, or did it better.

He's in a big puffy coat, with a navy beanie that's pulled down over his ears. Despite the padding of his jacket, the way he's standing tall makes it feel as if he's still that same athletic know-it-all that he always was.

Oliver looks down, glancing between Paige and me – then he takes in my suitcase – before silently asking for an explanation that sort of comes from Paige.

'Harry's back for a bit,' she says, as if that clarifies everything.

Oliver chews the corner of his mouth, sucking in his cheek, and I can't read what he's thinking. Either way, it's a welcome that befits the bristling, crisp wind.

'Is it true?' Paige asks.

'Mum's at the police station,' Oliver replies, looking only at her. 'Richard's got some solicitor that Dad knows and they're trying to straighten it all out.'

'I don't understand any of this. Have you seen what people are saying on Facebook?'

Oliver's features harden. When he speaks, his lips barely move. 'I told you to stay off that nonsense.'

'I was only trying to find out what was going on.'

He pauses a second, still not happy. 'The police got permission to keep Rich for longer, so they can hold him for up to four days now. We thought he might've been released tonight without that.'

'What actually happened?'

'I only know what Mum says. Apparently, Wilson was stabbed in that alley at the side of The Pines. It was a single wound to the heart and he died instantly.'

'But why do they think it's Richard?'

'I don't know. Mum said the police arrested him at his flat yesterday. He let them in to do a search, which she reckons will look good because he was cooperating. She thinks they might have to go back again.'

'What did the police take?'

'No idea. I've never been in his flat. You know what he's like: I don't think even Mum has a key for the place.'

Paige opens her mouth but then closes it, before glancing away. It's only a moment – but it's more than enough.

When we were young, Paige would say that her best clothes were in the wash to explain the rips in her school tights. The bruises on her arms would be countertops she walked into. That glance away would always tell its own story.

Oliver sees it, too. He leans in, lowering himself slightly so that he's closer to our height.

'You have a key…?'

Paige shrugs. 'It was for emergencies.'

Creases carve their way into Oliver's forehead, which says more than his words. Paige seems emboldened.

'You don't have to make that face,' she adds forcefully.

'What face?'

'Just because we broke up, it doesn't mean I'm shagging your brother.'

Oliver's eyes dart towards me and then away again. He steps backwards, the conversation seemingly over.

'You're still my wife,' he says firmly.

Paige doesn't hesitate before firing back. 'Not for much longer.'

# THREE

Paige quickens her pace as we walk away from the park and head towards the outskirts of Macklebury. If a faster speed means a darker mood, then she's furious.

I keep close, unsure where we're going until I see the sign for The Pines. When it was built, the hotel would have been majestic and luxurious. I can't say for sure but it's likely it would have been the grandest building in the town. There are wide, stone pillars, with a long bank of windows that stretch across the front of the stone walls. At its best, it would have been a sandy-coloured version of the White House.

Now, after years of neglect, the bricks have turned a grimy grey and there's a string of unkempt ivy eating at one of the corners. A section of guttering has slipped from the roof and is hanging diagonally. Perhaps worse than any of that, the lettering on the sign has been scratched away, meaning we're now standing in front of The Pies.

'What are we doing here?' I ask. They're the first words I've said since Oliver climbed into his car and Paige set off at speed.

Paige puffs a deep breath, which is when I realise I'm gasping, too. The air is stiff and my face is tingling.

'Thinking,' she says, cryptically. She stands on the spot near the sign for a few seconds before turning in a full circle and then heading back the way we came.

I follow her around towards the alley at the side, where there is blue and white police tape stretched across the entrance. There is no one else in sight and, for a moment, I think Paige is going to duck under. Instead, she retraces our steps for a little longer and then follows a network of cut-throughs until we end up in a crumbling car park at the back of the hotel. Spindly, bare tree branches sway low to the ground, with a dusting of frost clinging to the shadows as Paige walks with purpose towards the side of the hotel that's closest to the taped-off alley.

The wheels on my suitcase bump angrily across the potholes, making so much of a rumble that I feel certain everyone within a half-mile radius must be aware of my presence.

Paige stops to wait for me as she nears a small pagoda that sits near a back door to the hotel. There's a sense that she's been here before as she folds her arms, before nodding across to a guy in an apron who's smoking underneath the cover. He's flicking ash with one hand, while scrolling on his phone with the other. Smokers have always been the ultimate multi-taskers.

'Minimum-wage smokers are *always* the people who know what's going on,' she says, making it sound so obvious that it's as if this fact is something we learned in school.

'Do you know him?' I ask.

Paige shakes her head with a disdain I'd forgotten she could have. The sort of expression that could – and seemingly *can* – make me feel as if I'm a raging idiot of Piers Morgan proportions.

I hadn't realised it was such a silly question but, as they start talking, I quickly remember the difference between living in a big city and living in a small town. There's a paradox in that cities are crammed with people – and yet anonymity is the default. Nobody particularly wants to be bothered by anyone else, even though there's a constant parade of people who could do the bothering.

In a place like Macklebury, there's more space and much fewer people – but there's a shared life. Everyone went to the same school. Everyone takes the same buses and shops in the same places. We were taught by the same people, got drunk in the same pubs, and grew up hanging around the same market square in town.

A person doesn't have to be known to be *known*.

Paige is already in the process of lighting a bummed cigarette as I sidle up and hang around like a husband standing outside a shoe shop.

'…should've seen the state of them,' the guy in the apron says. He can't be much older than his early twenties. At least ten years younger than Paige or me.

'The teachers?' Paige replies.

'Aye. I'd rather be dead than that embarrassing. Imagine getting that pissed when you're that old.'

Paige angles the cigarette across to me. 'This is Harry,' she says, before nodding to the guy in the apron. 'Luke says there was a teachers' reunion party at the hotel on Saturday night.'

Luke gives the merest of head bobs and then continues. 'They were doing karaoke pretty much all night. Old farts getting up and singing these songs you've never heard of before. Really ancient stuff.'

'Like what?'

A puff of smoke swirls into the air. 'I dunno. Someone said it was stuff from the *eighties*.'

I see the smile appear and disappear from Paige's face with such speed that it's as if it was never there. Luke sees it too. He coughs a laugh and then has another puff on the cigarette. He knows what he's doing.

'What happened with the guy who died?' she asks.

Luke takes a couple of seconds, eyeing up the pair of us before apparently deciding he has nothing to lose.

'Some sort of barney,' he says. 'I was carrying trays and this teacher guy – the one who was killed – was arguing with this other bloke. It's the one they arrested. The teacher guy was laughing in the other one's face – and then the younger one threw a punch that missed. A whole bunch of people rushed in to separate them after that. The younger guy was shouting threats, saying he was gonna kill him – and then the manager threw him out.' Luke takes a breath and then adds: 'Big bloke, my boss. If he throws you out, you stay thrown.'

Paige nods along, taking it in as she has a couple of puffs on the cigarette. There's a moment when I think she might offer it to me but, instead, she simply switches it from one hand to the other. I might as well not be here.

'What were they arguing about?' she asks.

A shake of the head. 'No idea. I think they'd both been drinking – the younger one especially. Bit mad, though, innit? What's the point of yelling that you're gonna kill someone – and then actually doing it?'

'Do you think he did it?'

A shrug. 'Dunno. My mate reckons he saw that guy hanging around out there.' He nods towards the car park we've just crossed. 'Next thing anyone knows, there's a dead guy in the alley where we usually put the bins.'

'Did you know the teacher?'

Luke shakes his head. 'Before my time. Heard he was a head of year, or something like that.' He sucks the cigarette and blows out the smoke before stubbing the remains into the top of a bin. 'You know him?'

'He was *my* head of year,' Paige says.

Luke pouts a lip. 'Why are you bothered?'

'They reckon it was my mate who killed him.'

That gets a slight frown, although nothing more until a blink resets Luke's face. 'You reckon your mate did it?'

'I doubt it.'

Luke looks between us and nods slightly, as if he was weighing up whether to tell us what comes next. 'The police came and talked to us all yesterday. Everyone had to give statements. My mate told them about your friend being in the car park after he'd been chucked out and they seemed really interested in that.' He shuffles on the spot and then adds a 'sorry', although he doesn't sound it.

Paige finishes her cigarette and then mashes what's left into the same spot as Luke's.

'Cheers for the smoke,' she says, before motioning past Luke towards the hotel beyond. 'Who've you got in tonight?'

'Christmas party for a load of people who work in insurance. To see 'em, you'd think they'd be an uptight lot in their suits and everything – but there were some mad bastards last year. Set off the fire alarms, broke two windows. Couple of 'em got caught shagging in the stairwell.' He stops and looks at me: 'You're not one of 'em, are you?'

Paige laughs and slaps me playfully on the shoulder. 'He might as well be an insurer,' she says. The slap turns into the gentlest of pushes as I take the hint and step backwards towards the car park. She calls a 'see ya around' towards Luke, adding that she owes him a cigarette, before we cross the tarmac and exit the hotel's grounds.

I wait until we're back on the pavement before I ask her how long she's smoked. Paige either doesn't hear the question, or doesn't *want* to hear it. When we reach the front of the hotel again, she looks both ways along the street. The sun has set so quickly that a string of orangey street lights are now providing the majority of the light. I pull down my sleeves to cover my hands and clamp my mouth together to stop my teeth from chattering.

Paige seems unaffected by the drop in temperature as she stands and squints into the dusk. 'Where are you staying?' she asks.

'I've not thought about that. After you called, I got online and booked a ticket – then I had to be at the airport. I've barely stopped since my phone rang.'

She turns and looks up into my eyes. Her pale skin glows in the orange of the lights and I feel myself shrinking under her stare.

'I'm sorry,' she says, looking away.

'Don't be.'

'I've been… *It's* been difficult.'

I'm not sure how to reply but it's like there are two girls I used to know. The one who doesn't feel cold in the middle of winter, who'll march up to an apparent stranger and get information she shouldn't have. Then there's the one whose voice croaks mid-word, the same as it did when she told me her mother had ripped up her maths textbook because she hadn't eaten all her tea.

'The only people who know I'm back are you and Oliver,' I say. 'I'm not sure where I'm staying.'

'Didn't you tell your sister?'

I blink at Paige and the name 'Evie' slips from my mouth before I know it's there. It's only now that I realise how odd it is that I hadn't let Evie know I was coming home. It would have only taken a message.

'I was worried about Richard,' I say.

A nod, though I'm not sure she was listening. 'D'you reckon your sister will have you?'

'It's technically half my house.'

Paige raises an eyebrow, letting me know that she's as aware as I am that the chances of me using this argument with my sister are zero. If I wanted my share, I would have come home to take it years ago.

'Shall we go see…?'

Paige motions in the vague direction of the house and then sets off without waiting for a proper answer.

I hurry to catch her and there's so much we could say as we walk together but conversation doesn't come. I've not slept properly in well over a day and everything feels sluggish, even thoughts.

The night has closed in at an alarming rate, with frost already beginning to crisp the verges as we rattle past. The clouds feel low and a mist is starting to swirl around the tops of the street lights.

There's a familiarity as we walk; comfort, too. Like the first night back in a person's own bed after time away.

Macklebury is a succession of housing estates that were all built at different times. Closest to the hotel are the tight red-brick terraces that surround the railway lines. Factory workers used to live in this area, with the men piling out of the houses and all heading to the same place for what they thought would be a job for life.

I was in my first years at school, maybe five or six years old, when news came out that the factory was closing. Even at such a young age, it felt as if the world was ending. Adults would talk quietly to one another and then go silent when any of us kids got near. My dad didn't even work at the factory but I still thought everyone was going to starve.

Paige and I skirt around that estate and cut through a series of suddenly memorable lanes until we emerge onto a newer road that's lined with two-up, two-down semi-detacheds that were put up at some point after the war. I can remember playing in the road when I was young – but there'd be no chance of that now. Cars are parked nose to tail along both sides of the street, leaving a narrow path that's barely a car's width along the centre.

The two of us walk with almost telepathic levels of communication for where to cross and where to find the shortcuts between streets. This is the reverse of the route that Paige and I would've taken thousands of times when we were teenagers.

Before I know it, we're standing in front of our adjoined houses: Paige's on one side, mine on the other.

Except they're not ours any longer – and haven't been for a long time.

'How's your mum?' I ask.

The curtains are open and there are lights on inside Paige's house, although there's no sign of movement. Next door, the blinds are down and the lights are off. It looks like nobody's home.

'Same as ever.'

'Do you ever—?'

'She lives by herself.'

I take in the two houses for a moment. They are mirror images of one another, identical in many ways, except that seeing the pair together is like looking at them through one dirty glass lens and one clean. Everything about the house in which Paige grew up is slightly tattier, from the grimy windows, to the blackened brickwork, to the weeds growing through the path.

Paige sets off towards the house that isn't hers.

'It's cold out here,' she says, as she rubs her hands together. The sideways glance towards her mum's house is a better indication of why she wants to get away from the pavement outside the two houses.

I catch her again and then knock on the door and ring the bell. After twenty seconds or so, nothing has happened, so I try again. When there's no answer the second time, Paige starts bobbing from foot to foot. I dig into the top pocket of my suitcase, fumbling around until I find my keys.

'I think I have a key,' I say. 'I've had it since I was ten or eleven. I've carried it around all these years.'

'Do you think Evie's changed the locks?'

I flip through the keys, finding the faded silver one and running my finger along the grooves. I couldn't guess the last time I let myself into this house. Even if the key were to fit, I'm not sure I can justify letting myself in, regardless of whether the place is technically half mine.

Paige flicks another glance towards her mum's house and again bobs from one foot to the other.

'Maybe Evie's on holiday?' she says.

'Maybe…'

'We can't stand out here all night.'

I take another step towards the door, thinking about how unhappy I'd be if someone let themselves into where I live back in Toronto. It wouldn't matter if it was a family member with a key. There are lines.

'I doubt she'll mind,' Paige adds, although I doubt she's kidding herself.

I can't do it. Not yet.

It's as I start to scroll through the contacts list on my phone that the headlights swing across us and then flicker to black. There's a clunk of a door, footsteps, and then, out of the shadows, my sister steps onto the path.

She's smart in a suit, with shorter hair than I've ever known her have. When we were kids, she would take great delight in telling people the last time she'd had her hair cut. There was a time when it was past her waist and she screamed at our mother, saying she'd never have it cut.

Now, it barely touches her shoulders.

We stand in the mixed light from the street lamps and next door, sizing up one another. With her heels, we're the same height and it feels so strange to see this grown woman as anything other than my little sister.

'What are you doing here?' she asks.

'Home for Christmas.'

She sniffs the air, probably smelling the bull. 'I hope you're not expecting a present.'

# FOUR

Brothers and sisters who call each other best friends are truly some of the weirdest people on the planet. They should be locked up. Siblings were never meant to offer loving support to one another. They were meant to argue and torment – and then one day learn to just about tolerate the other's existence, as long as there's a healthy distance between them of, say, a few hundred miles at the absolute minimum.

Evie and I never fell out with each other – but we were never close either. Some families drum into one another the importance of sticking together but our parents never did that. If anything, we were encouraged to be independent and make our own futures.

When they died, there was no will and everything passed jointly to Evie and me. She wanted to move into the house where we grew up and it was fine by me. Technically, she should probably be paying me half the going rent – or she should have half a mortgage to pay off – but life's too short for all that.

We're not close but we're not at war. I think those two are closer than most realise when it comes to family.

Evie continues to stand a couple of steps away from me, her house keys dangling from her finger, bags in the other hand.

'Are you going to invite me in?' I ask.

Her eyes flicker towards Paige and then back to me. She steps past us and heads to the door. 'I thought you'd have more of an accent.'

'What sort of accent?'

'Don't Canadians sound like Americans?'

'The same as the English sound like Scots.'

Paige stands aside and Evie slips her key into the lock before opening the door. She drags a large shoulder bag over the threshold and keeps walking along the hall as Paige and I follow her in.

The last few hours seem to have been lived in a perpetual déjà vu, where everything's the same and yet nothing is. This hall used to be lined with movie posters from the 1950s. They were originals that Mum had found in the back of an old cinema where she worked as a young woman. The manager had let her take them and we'd grown up walking past prints from *Cinderella*, *Around the World in 80 Days*, *Rear Window*, *The Bridge on the River Kwai* and *Ben Hur*. The walls are bare now, aside from a patterned border that runs the length of the hall.

Into the kitchen and there's more of Evie's minimalistic taste on show. Instead of the various utensils and small appliances that covered the countertops when this was Mum and Dad's house, everything is clear. The walls are white and it's like a quarantine hospital room.

It's Paige who speaks first. She shuffles onto one of the stools that sit underneath the newly installed breakfast bar that runs along one of the walls.

'I like what you've done with the place,' she says.

Evie glances to her as she puts down her bags – but she doesn't respond directly.

'Why are you really back?' she asks, talking to me.

'Richard's been arrested for murder.'

Her pencil-thin eyebrows crease towards one another. 'Your old friend?'

'Right.'

'Is it to do with that guy who was killed over by The Pines? I heard it might be a teacher.'

'It was our old head of year.'

Evie's frown deepens. 'Wilson?'

'Yes.'

'Why would Richard kill your old head of year?'

'I have no idea.'

My sister watches me for a moment, though there's little more I can add. She then stretches for the chrome fridge and opens the door, before pulling out a clear plastic bottle that's full of some dark green juice. She gives it a shake before offering it to me.

'What's in it?' I ask.

'Cucumber, kale, spinach, parsley, celery, lime, apple and ginger.' She unscrews the lid and then adds: 'I made it myself. You'd be surprised how much money you can save by buying your own fruit and using a juicer, instead of getting something store-bought.'

It takes me a moment to reply. 'We are *such* different people,' I say.

There's a hint of a smile and she says, 'That's funny,' even though she doesn't laugh. She swigs the juice, re-screws the cap, and then puts it on the side. 'How's Liane?' she asks.

'Fine.'

'Is she happy enough for you to fly home for this?'

I can feel Paige watching me from the side but ignore the stare. 'Happy enough.'

Evie doesn't push but, even though we've not seen each other in a while, there's still enough of a bond that she can read between the lines. In case she wants to torment me a little, I get in first.

'I was hoping I could stay a few nights,' I say.

'How many is "a few"?'

'I'm not sure. A week? I didn't book a return.'

That gets a gentle wrinkling of the forehead. 'It's your house, too.'

I glance around, taking in the kitchen that is most definitely my sister's. This time, I even spot her juicer nestled in at the side of the fridge. There's a stainless-steel press handle sticking out high above the rest of the contraption. It looks expensive.

'It's not *really* my house,' I say. 'That's why I'm asking.'

Evie has another sip of her juice and she swills the liquid around her mouth, possibly weighing up the request.

'I've done hardly anything with your old room,' she says. 'You're welcome to that – but I'm up early and sometimes out late. I'll need first dibs on the bathroom and I hope you've learned how to flush a toilet in the time you've been away.'

'I *always* flushed the toilet.'

'It would help if you could pee in a straight line, too. I'm not cleaning up after you.'

I start to reply but then stop myself as I realise Evie is saying all this for Paige's benefit, not mine.

Evie hauls one of her bags up from the floor and says she has work to do. She motions through to the living room and then stands in the doorway for a second too long, making it about as clear as she can without saying as much that the bedroom upstairs is my space, while this is hers.

'We'll catch up later,' she says, which sums up our relationship about as well as anything could. We've not seen one another in years, we can tolerate each other's presence, and yet any catching up can be done at an indeterminate time in the future.

Evie closes the door to the living room with a very deliberate click and, moments later, the sound of some sort of new music I don't recognise begins to seep from beyond.

Paige nods towards the door. 'She seems fun.'

'Evie's always been driven.'

'What does she do for a job now?'

I stare towards the closed door and then can't meet Paige's stare. 'I have no idea.'

Evie's music continues to bleed through the walls. It's the sort of song that might be played in an advert. An inoffensive, pleasant woman's voice singing something that's equally safe. Dad would have hated it. He was a seventies rock and roller, all leather jacket and impossibly tight trousers back in his day. There were plenty of mornings where I'd be woken up by Led Zep riffs pulsing through the floor of my room.

'Where are you living now?' I ask.

Paige avoids my stare and instead focuses on the door, arms crossed. 'I've got a flat off the High Street, near where I met you.'

'Is your mum still next door?'

'Yeah.'

'How is she?'

'Fine.'

The reply snaps back and then Paige steps across to the fridge and opens the door. When I lived here, my parents' old fridge used to buzz like a swarm of furious wasps. There's none of that now – and I can imagine Evie calling round a contractor or two to empty everything from the house in one go before she built the place back up in her own image.

'There's a lot of juice in here,' Paige says.

'Any real food?'

'Eggs.'

I wasn't hungry before but my belly grumbles now. In terms of my body clock, it's around lunchtime – but I've not eaten a proper meal in the best part of two days. Eggs and juice aren't going to do the job.

'What do you want to do?' Paige asks.

'I saw there was a curry night on at the Duke of York.'

'It's not called that now.'

'You know where I mean.'

Paige is already re-zipping her jacket as she closes the fridge door. 'Let's go.'

The Duke of York used to be full of battered booths, with chewing gum stuck under the tables and cigarette burn marks through most of the furniture. Even after the smoking ban, the stale smell of cigarettes would cling to the walls. That would accompany the steady thump of darts into a board and the clink of pool balls. It was a place for men, with one choice each of lager, cider and ale. Anyone wanting anything beyond that would have been viewed with suspicion, if not outright hostility.

It's not like that now.

The Prince of Wales is full of high tables, with trendy, uncomfortable stools. The dartboard and pool table have been replaced by a pair of quiz machines, which have attracted a small semicircle of twenty-somethings who are seemingly happy to feed pound coins in one after the other.

At the other end, there are big screens, showing Sky Sports News as a separate group of young men chat underneath.

There are signs about coffee, breakfast, a quiz night and a Christmas dinner – all of which would have likely had the ghosts of this pub's old working-class clientele turning in their graves.

Not only that, this new iteration serves three different types of lager – plus a range of cocktails.

I dip a spoon into the curry as Paige and I listen to the sounds of the new Macklebury around us. This might be normal for her but, for me, it's like an invading force has taken over. It's not bad but it's different. It feels like someone else's home town.

'When were you last in here?' I ask.

'Months ago. Maybe longer.'

'I bet you can't get a pound a pint any more.'

'You can't get much at all for a pound now.'

'Do you remember Richard and his lager-top, just because his dad used to drink it?'

Paige shakes her head a fraction and watches the dribble of food slip from my fork. She said she wasn't hungry. 'I don't remember.'

'I used to get cider black because I thought it was more adult than a straight cider.'

'Did you...?'

Paige's attention slides towards the door of the pub as it opens and closes. A pair of women head inside and begin unwrapping their scarves, before moving towards a table close to the bar.

'What's really going on with Liane?' she asks.

I take a bite of the naan to give myself a second. 'It's complicated.' Another gap and then: 'How about you and Oliver?'

She doesn't reply at first, instead reaching for her glass of water and having a mouthful before returning it to the table. 'That's complicated, too.'

I carry on eating as Paige continues to watch. She's here but she's not – and I can't figure out what's changed from earlier. When we talked to Luke at the back of the hotel, she was focused and direct... but that's now gone. She scratches her arm and then, when she realises she's been doing it for an uncomfortable length of time, she pulls down her sleeve and folds her arms.

'We can go somewhere else,' I say.

'I think I'm just tired.'

'Are you working tomorrow?'

A shake of the head.

'We can maybe meet up again then...?'

Paige nods slowly but it's only now that I realise I've flown home with no plan. My friend... *our* friend has been arrested for murder and, even though I flew for eight hours to get back – plus navigated various other transport methods – I did so without putting in any thought about what I could do to help. There's an odd sense of not being myself. Logic trumps emotion for me and yet... apparently it doesn't. Not now.

'There's something I've not told you,' Paige says, her voice only a little above a whisper.

'What?'

She leans in closer. 'There have been rumours on Facebook ever since someone named Richard as the suspect for killing

Wilson. People remembered what he did. They remembered what *you* did.'

The hairs rise on the back of my neck. Perhaps, deep down, *this* is why I came back. It's why I'd always come running for Richard.

'What?'

'You know,' she says.

'Tell me.'

'It's Graham,' she says. 'They're saying Richard might've killed Graham, too.'

# FIVE

It's Evie who wakes me the next morning. Perhaps she's being deliberately loud, or maybe going in and out of the bathroom a dozen times is part of her routine. I lie in bed and listen to the sounds of the house. So much has changed – but the hot water pipes creaking is as comforting now as it was frightening to my younger self.

Not everything is different.

I wait until I hear Evie head down the stairs and then visit the bathroom myself. It's as clean as I'd have expected, with a new shower unit built into the corner, plus black tiles and pristine white grouting, as if it's never been used.

When I head downstairs, Evie is sitting at the breakfast bar, sipping one of her juices. She momentarily looks up from her phone and then speaks while staring at the screen.

'You got in late.'

'We were at the pub and got talking.'

'Must have had a lot to say…'

'We've not seen each other in a long time.'

Evie screws the cap back onto her bottle, before she locks her phone screen and puts it down. 'Why are you *really* back?'

Her stare clasps onto me and it's hard not to wilt under it. It feels like *she's* the older sibling.

'Because of Richard.'

'You've barely been friends since you went to uni years ago. Even if you were still best mates, what do you think you can do for him?'

'Offer support.'

'Isn't he with the police? You won't be allowed to visit him – and, even if you were, it's not like you're any sort of witness. You were in Canada.' She pauses and then adds: 'Weren't you?'

I hate it when she's right. Neither of us speak for a moment but it's as if her sheer force of will compels me to answer the question.

'Liane and I have separated,' I say. 'I was thinking about leaving my job and coming back to England. I was standing on the side of the road, queuing to get into a breakfast place – and, when the call came, it felt like it was the right time.'

Evie takes this in with no emotion. There's no reaction about the separation, or Liane in general. It's almost as if she didn't hear.

'Does that mean you're back for good?'

'I don't know.'

Her juice is red this morning and she gulps down another mouthful. 'No offence, but we can't live like this forever.'

'I agree.'

'Do we need to talk about me buying you out, or…?'

'Let's give it a few days and see what happens with Richard. I'll get a hotel if need be, else maybe I'll end up going home if things settle.'

She purses her lips. 'Does that mean Toronto is still "home"?'

I start a reply and then stop. I'd not said 'home' consciously.

'I don't know that either.'

Evie finishes her drink and then opens the cupboard under the sink before tossing the empty bottle into a recycling tub.

'What about you and Paige?'

'What *about* me and Paige?'

Evie tilts her head in the way Mum used to. The *you're-not-kidding-anyone* look. I don't add anything else, so she replies with a sigh. 'C'mon… you didn't fly all this way because *I* called you. It was because *she* did.'

'Actually, it's because Richard was in trouble.'

My sister rolls her eyes with a derisive mix of annoyance and ambivalence. I try to match this with a defiant stare of my own – but fate has had too much of a part to play in my life over the past couple of days.

The doorbell sounds and I know who it is before either of us move. We both know.

I head along the hall and take in the shape of the caller through the rippled glass. It's another moment of falling through time. Back then, Paige would've crossed the short distance from next door to ring the bell and ask if I was ready to walk to school, or head out for the summer's day.

Now, she has her arms wrapped across herself and is seemingly wearing the same clothes from yesterday. She has her back facing her mum's house and her body angled away.

'Do you wanna come in?' I ask.

A slim smile emerges from nowhere: 'Are you allowed out to play?'

'I'll have to ask Mum.'

'Wrap up warm,' Paige says, 'we don't want you catching a cold.'

# SIX

I allow Paige to lead me through the streets of Macklebury. We head along the High Street and there are more people sleeping in the doorways than I noticed yesterday. Flattened cardboard boxes and sleeping bags are packed into the small spaces, with various limbs poking out onto the street.

Homeless people are common in a city but I don't remember anything like this from when I grew up here. Nobody is causing any bother and Paige is walking too quickly for me to stop even if I was going to. We follow the length of the High Street and then turn in the direction that we would have taken to school back in the day.

There's an entirely new district that's popped up since I left, with tidy, identikit red-brick apartment blocks now lining the banks close to the river. We slow as we reach a large sign advertising Macklebury's 'vibrant' river district.

'Richard lives on the docks,' Paige says. 'He's got a little one-bed flat. It's quite nice. Very accountanty.'

'How long has he had that?'

'I can't remember. I think he bought it off-plan when everything was still being built. There was a big thing about how much people could make if they bought and then sold once everything was finished. People thought they were going to get rich – but then nobody wanted to move here, so half the places are empty.'

We pause next to the sign and stare down towards the Christmas tree that's on the towpath alongside the river. Even though the sun is up, it's still dark enough for the tree lights to be on and winking through the grey.

'Bleak, isn't it?' Paige says.

'It's not *that* bad.'

'Sometimes no decorations are better than something on its own like this.'

The tree lights continue to flash on and off, the blinking doubled by the reflection in the black water of the river. Paige is right: this is bleak.

'C'mon…'

I follow her away from the river and we're on autopilot, still heading towards the school we haven't attended in almost two decades.

Since we spoke about Graham the night before, I suppose I knew we'd end up here sooner or later.

There's a trail that leads down a bank towards an abandoned set of railway tracks and the arch that towers over the small valley below. When we were walking to school, heading along the tracks would take almost ten minutes off our journey compared to following the road. If we were running late – which we always were – this was the only way we could get to registration on time and avoid a morning detention.

So much of the town has changed since I was last around – but the arch and the tracks below are unburdened by progress. A slimy green moss coats the lower half of the crumbling arch, while the gangly leafless bushes and trees are still growing wild and untouched along the length of the tracks. The ground is hard in the shadows, crusted with a dusting of frost – but there are footprints in the soggier sections of soil. Once a shortcut, always a shortcut.

Paige and I stop a short distance from the arch and, without a word, she slips her hand into mine and squeezes. Her fingers are slender and cool, though not explicitly chilly. She always said she didn't feel the cold.

'You okay?' she asks.

'I guess I didn't expect to be back here.'

'We can keep walking…'

I don't reply. Instead, I stare towards the bush that sits against the wall of the arch. It's grey and sparse now – but I'll always see it as thick, leafy and green. A person likely never thinks their dreams will forever be haunted by a bush. I can go months, maybe a year or more, and then I'll be back in this spot.

'How many years?' Paige asks softly.

'Eighteen.'

More than half a lifetime ago.

'People are going to talk about it again,' she says. 'Everything will come back out.'

'I know.'

'I won't mind if you fly home again. I didn't know any of this would happen.'

Her fingers squeeze mine once more and then she unlocks them and puts her hand back in her pocket.

'I think I knew I'd end up back here sooner or later.'

Paige doesn't reply to that. Maybe we all knew? That's what happens when big questions go unanswered. Paige seems happy to wait for me.

'Did Richard ever talk to you about it?' I ask.

'Neither of you did.' She takes a breath and then adds: 'Where did you find him?'

I point towards the bush. Someone should have dug up the whole thing, or burnt it until there was nothing left.

It's still there, though.

'Under there. The grass was this reddy-black colour but I didn't notice it at first. Sometimes people would fly-tip stuff down here and there'd be oil stains, or other muck. Graham's arm was sticking out of the bush and then… I guess everything changed.'

'I sometimes wonder what it might've been like if I was with you.'

Paige's voice is soft and haunting; her words echoing around the archway and back again.

'It's not like the three of us spent every moment together,' I reply.

'We walked to and from school together more days than not.'

She's right – but finding Graham's body isn't something I'd have wanted for someone I hated, let alone someone I didn't.

'I wish it could have been someone else completely,' I say. 'I wish we'd walked the long way home. I wish… I just wish it wasn't me.'

Paige steps closer to me and rests her head on my shoulder. We stand together for a minute or two, maybe more, until she edges away.

'Let's go,' she says – and I'm not about to argue.

We head underneath the arch and keep walking until we reach the trail on the other side that leads up the bank. We emerge onto the road adjacent to the school, where the abandoned house that used to be over the road has been replaced by Betty's Butties. There's a small line of people queuing through the door and a pair of builder's vans parked along the side.

'You hungry?' I ask.

'Not yet.'

'Mind if I get something?'

'Be my guest.'

We cross the road and then I slot into line while scanning the bewilderingly large menu of sandwich choices. Inside, there are three tables along the edge of the single room, plus a long counter. There's little space for anything else. Radio Two is the soundtrack, while smouldering fatty bacon lingers on the air. Among the health-conscious array of acai bowls and quinoa lunches that pervade the centre of a huge city, this is something that's as alien as it is beautifully familiar. There's nothing quite like spending years out of the country to make a person realise how two crusty slices of bread filled with Branston Pickle on top of a chunky cut of Cheddar is truly the food of kings.

We're heading back outside when Paige stops in front of me. I bump into her back and start to mumble an apology before I see why she halted. On his way in, as we're on our way out, stands Oliver. There is a blinking moment of confusion as he eyes his wife and me, before he steps aside to let us past.

'Have you heard anything from Richard?' Paige asks.

'Mum got to see him last night but we're waiting on the solicitor. Nobody seems to know what's going on.'

'How's he doing?'

A shrug: 'How d'you think?'

He sounds annoyed – though Paige doesn't seem ready to leave. Someone squeezes past us to get into line but she remains standing in front of Oliver.

'We heard, um…'

'What?'

'People are saying that the police are linking Richard to what happened with Graham.'

Oliver's eyes narrow: '*Who's* saying that?'

'Lots of people. In the pub last night, on Facebook…'

She tails off, perhaps aware that she's essentially just told her husband that she was in the pub with someone else the night before. I half expect Oliver to be angry but his shoulders slump slightly and he steps away from the door, edging us towards an alcove next to a blazing radiator and a steamed-up window.

'It's been a long night,' he says, more quietly than before. 'Mum and Dad were shuffling around and I don't think anybody slept much.'

'You still at your parents'?'

A nod, although his eyes flicker towards me. It's that small action that seems to trigger the memory. He turns and looks at me properly. 'It was you, wasn't it?'

'What was me?'

'You and Rich found the body by the arch. You were together.'

'Yes.'

Paige coughs an interjection and then says she needs the toilet. She disappears around the side of the counter and through the door at the end as Oliver and I watch. I take a quarter-step away, conscious that we're in an enclosed space and that Oliver is between me and the door. He stands over me and it's impossible not to be aware that things could be very awkward. There is tension, as if he's weighing up what to say.

When it comes, it's not what I expected. 'How's the sandwich?' he asks, nodding down to the packet in my hand.

'Good. I've only had a bite.'

'D'you get much like this out in Canada, or wherever?'

I presume he means the sandwich. I can do food-based small talk. 'Not *specifically* like this.'

Oliver bobs on his heels and takes a long breath. 'Mum says the police seem to think Rich is some sort of serial killer. Not just that teacher fella out at the hotel – but your mate, too. They've specifically been asking him about the body you found.'

'That's… crazy.'

He looks down to me, fixed and firm. 'Can you think of anything important from the time? Anything at all?'

'It was such a long time ago.'

'Not the sort of thing you'd forget…'

'I spoke to the police at the time – Rich and I both did. That was the best I'll ever remember things.'

Oliver nods at this and then turns towards the still-closed door through which Paige headed. The shop is beginning to feel full as a pair of men in jeans and huge fleece tops bustle in and join the queue. They blow into their hands and then start to talk loudly about 'some old dear' who 'couldn't park a bike in an empty car park'.

Oliver motions towards the far side of the counter. 'You and her a thing?'

'Paige?'

A nod.

The question is so direct and out of the blue that I feel my mouth bobbing like a goldfish. 'Of course not,' I say automatically. 'I'm married.'

Oliver looks down towards my hand. At first I think it's because of the sandwich I'm holding but then I realise it's to take in my ring-less ring finger.

'So's she,' he says.

It feels almost like a challenge.

'It's not like that,' I reply. 'We've been friends for ages. She lived next door when we were teenagers. The two of us and Richard used to be together all the time. You must remember?'

It's his turn now. Oliver sucks the corner of his mouth, the way he did when he was talking to Paige the day before.

'It was a long time ago.'

His gaze flips to the closed door once more and then he leans in closely enough that I can smell the coffee on his breath.

'Do you know what she did?'

Oliver angles away, lips pressed together, weighing me up.

I don't know how to reply – but get no opportunity anyway because there's a click and then Paige emerges from the bathroom. She slides around the waiting line and then slots in between Oliver and me. If there's tension in the air, then she doesn't seem to notice.

'I'm glad I ran into you,' Oliver says, suddenly with a chirp to his voice. 'I was going to message but now you're both here anyway...' He turns to Paige. 'Do you remember I once said there were loads of clippings about Graham in my parents' attic?'

Paige seems surprised at this, blinking back at him. 'Did you?'

'I was wondering if they might jog Harry's memory? Perhaps he'd be able to read them through and it would help him think of something to help Richard?'

Paige turns to me and shrugs a little. 'I don't have anything on this morning. You?'

I'm not sure I want to do this but, with both Oliver and Paige looking to me, it doesn't feel as if 'no' is an option.

'I suppose I could go through them…'

'Excellent,' Oliver says, with a clap of the hands. 'Just gimme a minute. I almost forgot the reason I came in.'

# SEVEN

Here's the thing about Richard, Paige and me. We were unquestionably a trio of friends – but Richard literally came from the other side of the tracks. Paige and I lived next door to one another in those houses that ended up being sold off under Thatcher. It wasn't a sink estate or a particularly rough area – but it was, and is, on the poorer side of town.

Richard's parents lived on the other side of the railway line, where the houses are bigger and newer. Even now, perhaps three decades after the estate was built, it feels fresh, with the neat lawns, large driveways and carports. There are signs up advertising the local am-dram pantomime, plus small posters in windows offering things like badminton coaching and piano lessons. When we take the turn onto the street where Richard's parents live, it's impossible to miss the boat that's parked in the driveway of the first house.

Oliver lets us into his parents' house and then gets us to take off our shoes before leading the way up the stairs.

'Mum and Dad are out,' he says, more to Paige than me.

There's a hatch in the ceiling next to one of the closed bedroom doors – and he pulls a cord to drag down a set of in-built steps that lead up to the attic. Minutes later and Paige and I are sitting on the carpet at the top of the stairs searching through two boxes of browning newspapers. Oliver said he'd be downstairs if we need him but I have the sense he'd rather leave us to it.

There's a mix of local, regional and national newspapers in the boxes, from a time before the internet dominated everything.

'It looks like everything's in date order,' Paige says. She holds up a cutting from the *Daily Mirror* that's dated from early May. I check the one at the top of my box, which is a full copy of the *Macklebury Gazette* that was printed a little under three weeks earlier.

'The *Gazette* shut down about five years ago,' Paige says, as I hold up the paper. 'There was a big drive to save it but their office got turned into a pizza place.'

### BODY OF SCHOOLBOY FOUND
#### Discovery made by classmates

Police have confirmed that a body found close to Macklebury High School yesterday afternoon is that of a student from the school.

The unnamed 15-year-old was discovered in undergrowth close to the school by two of his classmates who were on their way home.

Officers have so far refused to confirm any details relating to the death, other than to say that enquiries are ongoing.

Detective Constable Ian Jones said that anyone who would have passed by the old railway arch at the back of Greenwich Lane yesterday should contact the non-emergency line.

I pass the paper across to Paige, who scans the front. There are no further details inside and I imagine it was hastily put together on the same night that Richard and I found Graham's body. There would have been few details at the time, mainly because nobody was quite sure what had gone on.

The next paper in the box is also a copy of the *Gazette*, from the day after.

### SCHOOLBOY NAMED AS
### MURDER HUNT BEGINS
#### Police appeal for witnesses

Police have named the 15-year-old whose body was found in undergrowth close to Macklebury High School.

Graham Boyes never arrived at school on Wednesday morning – and his body was later found by two classmates who were on their way home.

Officers have confirmed that a murder inquiry is now under way.

Detective Constable Ian Jones said: 'Graham sustained significant injuries to the back of his head. This is a serious crime and we believe someone must have seen something.'

DC Jones added that the post-mortem examination would be carried out in due course and said that police were looking for 'a blunt object, likely a rock, that is roughly the size of a fist'.

Police are examining footprints from the area, although they stress that the recent spate of dry weather has hampered those efforts.

The body was discovered in undergrowth close to the abandoned railway arch at the back of Greenwich Lane, which is a popular cut-through for students heading to and from the school.

Anyone with possible information has been urged to contact the police's non-emergency line.


I had forgotten the period of time in which Richard and I knew Graham's identity, even though nothing had been confirmed officially. The papers were wrong that he was our *class*mate – but he was in our year and we both recognised the body. Graham's name rippled through school the day after the discovery and it felt as if everyone knew it was his body that had been found, long before anything was announced officially. That was the way things were before social media.

Paige reads the second article and then passes me back the paper for the pile. 'I thought he was skiving,' she says.

'Graham?'

'He was in my science class but hadn't shown up on that day. I always thought anyone not at school was having a skive.'

I skip through the next few papers as they largely repeat the information. There is day after day of coverage, with only small details being added each issue. It's about a week later that the *Guardian* ran a piece full of background, with photos of Graham playing Dr Frank-N-Furter in a school production of *The Rocky Horror Picture Show* a few months before he died. That play became a controversial *Gazette* front page at the time, with boys in drag and *think-of-the-children* types worrying about the message being sent to young people.

It feels like such an innocent storm, a relic, given what was to come.

There are pictures of Graham in the choir and from the time he captained the school's quiz team at a county competition in which they finished last but one. We did a mock election and Graham put himself forward as the Green candidate back when it was far more of a joke movement. He's shown with a large green rosette pinned to his school uniform.

Paige scans the article and then puts the paper down on the others. She sighs long and loud. 'It makes him sound so real,' she says.

In isolation, it would be a silly observation – but she's right. If I ever knew all these things about that murdered teenager, then I'd forgotten them. For years, he's been a boy without a face in *my* story – but now, in front of me, it's *his* story.

## NO LEADS IN HUNT FOR SCHOOLBOY KILLER
### Victim's brother appeals for witnesses

Police say they are still looking for clues in the hunt for the person who murdered a 15-year-old student close to Macklebury High School.

Graham Boyes was found in undergrowth almost a month ago – but police are yet to make an arrest and say they've been struggling with a lack of leads.

Detective Constable Ian Jones said: 'Graham did not arrive at school on the morning of Wednesday 17 April. We believe he took the popular shortcut underneath the railway arch at the back of Greenwich Lane and would like to talk to anyone who might have passed along that route on that day.'

The post-mortem revealed that Graham was killed by a blow from a blunt object to the back of the head, likely a rock or stone. The murder weapon has never been found.

The victim's brother, Martin, 17, said: 'Graham was well-liked among his friends and family and we've not been able to come up with anyone who might have a motive for this. I miss watching wrestling with my little brother and beating him at *Mario Party*. I miss arguing about the length of time he spends in the bathroom and trying to get him to do my homework, even though I'm older.

'If anyone knows anything, then I beg you to come forward. We just want to know what happened to my brother.'

There's more but I pass the article across and Paige reads it before replacing it in the pile.

'Martin's still friends with Oliver,' she says.

'He still lives here?'

'I'm not exactly sure where – but yes. He was best man at the wedding.'

I almost ask an obvious question before I realise she's talking about *her* wedding.

'Out of everyone, I'd have thought that Martin would be the one who wanted to get away after what happened with his brother.'

In the time after Richard and I found Graham's body, we never walked to or from school that same way again. Even if the rain was hard or the wind was strong, even if we were running late, we'd go the long way around. I find it hard to understand how Martin could continue living in a place so close to where his brother was murdered… but maybe that's because I left.

Paige doesn't reply. Instead, she leans back against the wall and scratches at her arms. 'Do you remember when we stayed up for *WrestleMania* that year? You, me and Richard were up all night.'

'Richard fell asleep when the main event was coming on but that was the first time I stayed awake all night.' I glance back to the paper. 'I forgot we were into wrestling…'

'Everyone at school was back then. We—'

Paige cuts herself off because the front door sounds. We wait at the top of the stairs, listening to the noise from below as Oliver comes into the hall and greets his parents. Their voices are muffled, the words unintelligible; but, even with that, the pauses in her speech makes his mother sounds exhausted.

Before I can move, Paige stands and starts to head down the stairs. I find myself following until we emerge at the bottom.

Richard's mother is mid-word when she spots Paige and stops herself. She used to be one of those women who'd never be outside unless she'd spent an hour getting ready. Times and circumstances have changed, though. She looks her age now, with wiry grey hair and pale, sallow skin.

She also has a death stare for Paige.

'What are *you* doing here?'

Her teeth are clenched, eyes narrow.

'It's okay,' Oliver says. 'Do you remember Richard's friend, Harry? He's here with Paige. They're going through the old articles you kept. Harry was there, remember? With Rich when they found Graham…'

I step out from behind Paige, offering a small wave that immediately feels inappropriate. It's seemingly not taken that way, because Richard's mother's features soften as she steps towards me and then pulls me into a hug. It's so out of nothing that by the time I've patted her on the back, she's already pulling away.

'How are you, love?' she asks. 'I thought you moved away?'

'I heard Richard was in trouble and, well… here I am.'

Richard's father steps around Paige, ignoring her as he offers his hand and then squeezes mine firmly as we shake. I remember very little about him from when I was young. He always seemed to be working, or somewhere that wasn't home. Even on the occasions he was around, I'm not sure I ever remember him speaking. Perhaps that's why it's such a surprise that it's him who speaks next.

'I didn't know Ollie called you,' he says.

'It wasn't Oliver.'

There's a long, awkward silence as Paige stands with her hands tucked under her opposite armpits.

It's Oliver who breaks the impasse. 'Did you find anything?' he asks.

It takes me a second to realise he's talking about the box of articles still on the upstairs landing.

'Not yet,' I reply. 'I don't remember reading anything at the time. I think Mum and Dad must've kept a lot of it back. We're not even halfway through.'

Richard's mum lets out a long breath. 'You won't believe what they're saying about him,' she says. 'Awful things. Terrible. I keep telling his lawyer that it's all a big misunderstanding – but now they're saying he's got a history. They're talking about Graham. I don't understand what's going on…'

She looks to me as someone new who might be able to help explain – but I have fewer answers than she does.

'What are they saying?' I ask.

She takes a breath, readies herself. 'That he killed his old teacher outside the hotel. Why would he? It can't be true but they're now saying he must've led you to find Graham back when you were kids.' She gasps for breath, as if she's been running. 'It's not true, is it? That's not what happened?'

I don't have a reply – and, luckily, Oliver realises what's happening because he jumps in for me.

'It's not the time, Mum,' he says. 'It was a long time ago. Harry's here because he wants to help. That's why he's been looking through all the articles you kept.'

She accepts this with a slow nod and a hand on the shoulder from her husband.

'Do you want something to eat?' she asks. 'I've got some lamb shanks in the freezer and—'

'You don't have to do that, Mrs Whiteside.'

'It's Veronica, love – and it's no trouble.'

I tell her that I ate not long ago – but I'm not convinced it's enough to stop her putting the oven on. She's definitely the sort who'll attempt to cook or clean her way out of anything she doesn't want to think about. Not that that's a bad thing.

'How is Richard?' I ask.

I blink and almost miss it, though Richard's dad gives the merest of nods to his wife before she answers.

'As well as you could expect,' she says. 'You know what he's like. Always tries to look on the bright side. His lawyer is confident he'll be able to sort it out. It's all a misunderstanding. Wrong place, wrong time. That sort of thing.'

She speaks quickly, rattling out the clichés I suspect she's been repeating ever since her son was arrested. It's hard to blame her.

Her husband motions towards the stairs. 'Why don't you go and have a lie-down?' he says to his wife. 'I'll come get you if anything happens.'

She takes a step towards the stairs but then stops and turns between Paige and Oliver.

'We're not back together,' Oliver says pointedly.

His mother gives another very deliberate glare towards Paige, who is looking at her own feet. After that, his mother turns and starts to make her way upstairs.

Paige rams her hands deep into her pockets and twists on the spot, still not looking up. I consider suggesting we should leave but Oliver doesn't give me the chance.

'Did you want to finish checking those articles?'

It's a question that sounds more like a demand and I find myself agreeing that I do want to finish – even though I'd far rather get myself out of the house.

Paige leads the way up the stairs and the opened boxes are where we left them on the landing. It's only now that I realise how odd it was that neither of us thought to ask for a chair, or to go into a different room. Oliver put the boxes on the floor, Paige sat, and so did I.

She sits again, folding her legs underneath herself and arching backwards gymnastically until she's resting on her heels. She does it in a way I doubt I could've managed even when my body didn't creak every time I have to haul myself out of bed in the middle of the night for a wee.

Paige picks up the next article from the pile and scans it. I watch her for a few seconds, perhaps too long, considering the best way to ask why she and Oliver are no longer together. He asked if I knew what she'd done – and his parents don't seem remotely happy that she's potentially still on the scene.

I almost ask. *Almost.*

Then I remember that there are things about my life abroad that I'd rather she didn't ask about.

Instead, I flip through a few more articles and keep going until I'm almost at the bottom of the second box.

## CRIMEWATCH TO
## AIR STUDENT RECONSTRUCTION
### One year since body of 15-year-old found

BBC One will tonight air a reconstruction that shows the events leading up to last year's murder of schoolboy Graham Boyes.

The Macklebury High pupil was found in April last year by two fellow students in undergrowth close to the railway arch at the back of Greenwich Lane.

Police have so far struggled to find witnesses or a motive for what led to the brutal killing.

*Crimewatch*, which airs at 9 p.m., will show Graham leaving his house at approximately 8.05 a.m. on the morning of Wednesday 17 April. He said goodbye to his mother, Jean, and was not seen again until his body was found a little after 3.15 p.m. on the same day.

Brother Martin Boyes, 18, said: 'The family are hoping this will help spur someone's memory from the morning Graham went missing. It's inconceivable that he could have simply disappeared. Someone must have seen something.'

Graham's head of year, Keith Wilson, said: 'The entire Macklebury High community has been devastated by this. It is a close-knit school and we have been offering counselling to any students who require it.'

The *Crimewatch* piece was filmed last month and required the High Street to be shut to traffic for three hours. The actor playing Graham was described as 'incredibly accurate' by his family.

Detective Constable Ian Jones said that a specific phone number has been set up to accommodate any potential leads. He added: 'We would implore anyone who was in the area at the time to rack their memories for anything they might have seen. Anything you believe to be trivial could turn out to be important and we value every tip.'

I read the piece twice, focusing on the quotes from Mr Wilson and only now realising that, in everything that's happened, I didn't know his first name until now. There's something about teachers that means students see them as 'Mr', 'Miss', 'Sir', or whatever, long past leaving the school.

Paige takes the article and reads it through before looking up and echoing my thoughts. 'Keith…?' she says quizzically.

We were thinking the same thing about his first name, which makes me stop for a moment.

'Do you ever remember counselling?' I ask.

'Nothing. Surely you'd have been the one they offered it to before anyone?'

She's right – but I don't remember anybody at the school ever saying there was someone I could talk to if need be. Even if there was, I know I'd have turned it down. People talk about their feelings and mental health now but, even twenty years ago, that wasn't the case – especially for boys. Our PE teacher would regularly shout at us to 'stop acting like girls' because we were shivering in the rain.

'I remember the reconstruction,' Paige says.

'Do you?'

'I was working at the pub and they decided to stay closed because some of it was being filmed outside.'

'You can't have been old enough to work there.'

She shakes her head. 'I was old enough to collect glasses and wash up.'

'I don't remember that.'

'You were doing your A-levels with Richard...' She tapers off, even though it's the end of a sentence and I realise what she's actually saying.

My reply feels temporarily stuck as the simple act of her voice drifting away makes me realise something I never saw in the past twenty years.

'I was always going to go to university,' I say. 'If I got the grades, that was. I didn't want to stop being friends.'

Paige doesn't respond to that.

'I didn't realise the reconstruction was happening,' she continues. 'I'd gone to work as usual but everything was closed. I ended up watching it as they filmed him walking along the street and heading towards the bank that goes down to the railway arch. I remember thinking that they had to be guessing he went that way, because nobody knew. That's where you found him – but nobody had ever actually said that's where he was killed.'

I find myself rocking back until I'm resting against the wall. Until Paige pointed it out, I'd always assumed that Graham was killed close to where we found the body. Chances are, he probably was – but it feels odd that she's thought about it more than me. I wonder how much more I've simply blocked out.

'The actor really did look like Graham,' she adds. 'They had him with Graham's school bag and the uniform. It was like it was actually him.'

'Did you watch the show?'

'I don't think so. You?'

'We had an assembly on the morning it was due to be shown. They said that police would be around the next day in case anyone remembered anything.'

'But did you watch it?'

'I don't know. I remember the police being there the next day and that a few people went to talk to them… but that's it.'

I pick up the article and scan it a third time. Mr Wilson was our head of year at the time Graham was killed, so it's normal that he would have been quoted. His name springs from the page now, with everything that's happened in the past few days.

The thought drifts because Oliver appears on the stairs in front of us. He's midway, looking up, and he points to the boxes.

'Found anything?'

'Not yet,' I reply.

He gulps and then climbs up two steps. 'I need to wake Mum,' he says.

'What's happened?'

Another gulp. 'Rich has formally been charged with Wilson's murder.'

# EIGHT

There is a burst of activity as Richard's parents rush to their car to head off and meet the solicitor. Oliver says he needs to leave as well, which is a not very subtle hint that we should go, too. Not that remaining in the empty house would be something I wanted either way.

The sun is already on its way down as Paige and I get back onto Macklebury's High Street. Mist is beginning to descend once more, clinging to the tops of the street lights and swirling towards the ground. The only people we see are bundled up in mounds of coats, scarves, gloves and hats. In my haste to pack, despite Toronto's winter being more brutal than here, I somehow forgot anything to fight the cold, other than my coat. Paige isn't even wearing that and I wonder how she can possibly be comfortable given I'm having to clench my fists to stop my fingers from freezing.

She's walking quickly again, hammering along the pavements as if in a race. If she could master the silly walk, she'd surely be in with a shot at the Olympics.

As we move, I realise there are more homeless people in the doorways than I'd noticed during the day. More sleeping bags and pillows poking onto the street.

We eventually stop at a pedestrian crossing, although from the way Paige springs on her heels, I suspect that she would have simply crossed if I wasn't around.

'Do you want to get something to eat?' I ask.

'I'm not that hungry. You can, though... but there won't be much open.'

I glance backwards towards the direction from which we've come – and realise that I'd missed what should have been obvious. The reason homeless people are shuffling into the doorways is because so many shops have already closed for the day. In a city, places will stay open late but not here.

We cross the street but Paige's pace slows as she pulls her phone from her pocket. 'I need to send a text,' she says.

Without waiting for a reply, she drifts into a small space close to a postbox and turns her back to me as she taps something into her phone.

I move away, giving her space, and then a few seconds later she's back at my side and we're walking once more. Paige's speed is noticeably slower, though I think little of it until a boy on a BMX pedals directly towards us. We're in between street lamps, swallowed by shadows, and I jump backwards, thinking he's about to crash into either of us. Instead, he slides to a halt a metre or so away.

I'm about to say something when he chirps an upbeat 'y'right?'. He holds out a brown paper bag with a McDonald's logo on the side and, in a flash, Paige has taken it and crammed it into her own bag.

It happens so quickly and in such gloom that I almost miss the exchange. The boy is slight and slender, plus his voice is yet to break. As Paige tries to pass, he holds out a hand and yips a high-pitched 'oi!' at her.

Paige ignores him, instead turning to me and muttering a sharp 'come on'. I have to jog to catch her as she marches away without bothering to look over her shoulder. If she had, then she'd have seen the boy pulling a phone from his jacket pocket.

'What was that?' I ask.

I check over my shoulder again, where the boy is pedalling in the opposite direction with one hand on the bars, while holding his phone to his ear with the other.

'Nothing,' Paige says.

'What did he give you?'

Paige doesn't answer, instead upping her pace towards the next crossing, where the light turns red moments before she gets there. If it wasn't for the turning car, she would have definitely kept going.

'Two Big Macs,' she says.

'I thought you weren't hungry.'

Paige puffs a long breath, sending a plume of steam up to join the falling mist. The green man starts to flash but she doesn't move.

'It's hard to get doctor appointments round here,' she says. 'You have to phone at exactly half-eight but the lines are always busy. Then, when you get through, everything's already been taken.'

I wait, not completely clear where this is going.

'Even when you do get in, they're sniffy about giving out prescriptions – plus things are expensive anyway. So I found an alternate source…'

'Alternate source for what?'

'Stuff that helps.'

'Drugs?'

She bumps my shoulder with hers. 'Don't be so dramatic. We're not at school now, having to watch all those videos that make it look like smoking a joint will mean you end up homeless and jobless.' She pauses and then adds: 'They're not *drugs*-drugs.'

'So what is it?'

'Nothing. Just let it go.'

Paige starts walking again and I trail her across the road as we reach the final stretch of shops before we hit the first of the housing estates.

'How old was that kid?' I ask.

'Stop worrying.'

'He can't have been older than nine or ten…'

'You can't be charged with a crime if you're under ten.'

Paige speaks so matter-of-factly that I pause for a step and suddenly realise I'm behind her.

'I was made redundant last month,' Paige says, unprompted. 'I was working at the Co-Op but there was a last one in, first one out thing. I've been a bit short since then. I'll sort it all out soon enough, then I'll be able to afford proper prescriptions again.'

She slows slightly as we reach the front of a kebab shop that has a spinning browny-grey cylinder of what I assume to be meat in the steamy window. It looks like it might be edible but there's also a sense that it could be some sort of roadkill that's been dragged off the road the night before. The smell drifting through the open door is something close to socks after a workout.

'We're not eating here, are we?' I say.

Paige is digging into her bag and mutters a 'not again' under her breath.

'What?'

'I can't find my keys.'

She has another riffle through the bag before shaking her head and adding a quick 'come on', before she sets off around the side of the building.

The alley at the back of the kebab shop is lined with bins against the wall and a general smell of a portaloo on the final day at a festival. Paige seems unconcerned by this as she speeds along the cobbles and then crouches next to a grate in the ground. She reaches to the nearest wall and pulls a narrow twig from a gap between the bricks, before she uses that to lever up the grate.

After retrieving a key from underneath, she then nudges the grate back into place, before returning the stick to the wall.

'You look like you've done that before,' I say.

'It's not the first time I've locked myself out.'

I follow Paige back around to the front, where she stops in front of the door that's next to the kebab shop. I had been so taken by the shop itself that I didn't realise there was a second door.

Paige slips her key into the lock and turns, before twisting back to me. 'You coming up?'

# NINE

The stairs beyond the door lead up to a long corridor that runs the length of the row of shops. The tight, enclosed area smells of cheap meat, stale pizza and dried urine. Only one of the overhead spotlights is working, leaving almost the entire hall shrouded in a grim, clinging darkness.

None of that affects Paige, who passes three or four doors as she strides towards the end and then opens the final door with the same key as before. She reaches around the frame and flicks a switch that sends light cascading into the corridor. The main thing that achieves is to showcase the grubby, stained carpet and the pile of ash opposite her door that was previously hidden.

'Home sweet home,' she says as she pushes the door wider. I have no idea if she's being ironic.

I head through the door and my worst fears – perhaps prejudices – are not realised. The inside isn't too bad. There is a sofa and a matching brown armchair on a tufty cream rug, which sits close to a kitchen counter.

As well as the overhead light, Paige goes around the room switching on three separate lamps, before she disappears through a door. She returns moments later without her coat but wearing a pair of slippers that have a giant Scooby-Doo head bobbing from side to side. She slumps onto the sofa, curling her feet under herself as she puts her bag on the glass coffee table. She then looks to where I'm standing next to the kitchenette.

'You're allowed to sit down.'

I take off my coat and then sit in the other chair as Paige angles her phone towards me to show a photograph.

'There's a betting shop downstairs and they have their Wi-Fi password on a whiteboard next to the counter. You get perfect reception up here. Do you want it?'

'Sure.'

Paige reads out the string of letters and I log on to the same network that she apparently uses. I figure, if nothing else, it'll save me something in roaming fees.

The flat is the type of place that an estate agent might say 'has potential'. It's small – but because Paige only has a sofa and a table, there's a lot of space. The built-in kitchen is like something out of a documentary on East Germany but I've seen worse. Paige notices me looking around, though she says nothing.

Oliver must have had money – his family certainly does – and it's hard not to wonder how Paige ended up here by herself.

Any thoughts of that are extinguished as she reaches across and pulls out the McDonald's bag, which she places on the table.

'Look if you want.'

It feels like a challenge. If I'm a good enough friend, then I won't need to.

Except that I do.

There are two items in the bottom of the paper bag. The see-through baggie contains a couple of tablespoons of greeny-brown tea-like shreds.

'It's just weed,' Paige says, as I return it to the bag and remove a small white tub. It rattles as I twist it around, looking for a label that doesn't exist. I struggle with the cap – childproof is seemingly me-proof, too – but, when I get it off, there are four circular green pills inside.

'What are they?' I ask, as I return them to the tub and re-screw the lid.

'Do you really want to know?'

I don't reply, figuring that I probably don't. Paige must take this as confirmation, because she answers anyway.

'Oxy,' she says.

I slide the McDonald's bag back onto the table, thinking that I was expecting worse, which probably says more about me than her. If Paige were to say it, she wouldn't be the first person to tell me I'm a negative influence on their life.

'Who was writing you a prescription for that?' I ask, knowing I shouldn't have said it.

Paige turns away. 'We used to drink when we were fifteen,' she says. 'We all tried smoking when we were about thirteen. Where are you drawing a line? There's no difference. You're no better than me.'

There's fire and venom. This is the Paige who I used to hear raging back and forth with her mum through the wall of our adjoining houses.

'Sorry,' I say, not really sure if I mean it. I don't know *that* much about prescription painkillers – but I do know there's something not right buying dodgy pills off nine-year-olds.

She sits and stews, staring at the wall for at least a minute before she angles back towards me.

'What do you want to eat?' Her tone is quieter now. Calmer. It's as if the mini argument didn't happen. 'There's kebab downstairs, or noodles and soup in the cupboard.'

'I don't think my stomach could take that kebab meat.'

I eye the cupboards but am not brave enough to say that I'm also not in the mood for noodles or soup. I feel like that brunch snob of a few days before.

'Shall we go to the supermarket?' I say. 'We can get some stuff to last the next few days.'

If she's annoyed by the implication I might be eating here then she doesn't show it.

'I don't have the money for that.'

'I can—'

'I don't want *charity*.'

The spite is close again.

'You used to give me lunch money all the time when we were at school,' I say. 'I'd only be paying you back.'

'I used to *nick* money from Mum – then buy you a Crunchie at lunch because I felt guilty.'

I let that sit. I suppose I suspected as much at the time, if not outright knew it. There's little point in replying specifically to that. I've walked myself into a minefield and would rather escape unscathed.

'I'm banned from the Co-Op.'

Paige says this unprompted while staring at the floor in the way she did with Richard and Oliver's parents.

'Why? They can't have banned you just because they made you redundant…'

She looks up to me, with a stare that's a pure *really?* – and I know what happened before she has to say it.

'I wasn't made redundant,' she says, quietly and slowly. 'It was more of a firing.'

From nowhere, she makes eye contact and then holds it.

'I was having a bad week and just sort of… stole some things. There were cameras and my manager knew it was me anyway. It's not like I denied it. They said they wouldn't call the police but that I was fired and banned for life.'

She doesn't look away and neither do I.

'You can leave if you want,' she says.

'Why would I go?'

'Why would you hang around with a thief?'

I try to think of something smart about how companies who don't pay tax are also thieves but nothing quite comes out.

'I once nicked a porno mag,' I say.

'Huh?'

'I was about fourteen. I went into Green's Newsagent and Mr Green had to go and do something in the back. There was no one else around, so I grabbed a mag from the top shelf and made a run for it.'

Paige glances away and then a slender smile ripples across her face.

'You dirty get.'

'I was a teenage boy!'

The smile spreads: 'We used to hang around together almost every day – and there you were nicking filthy mags and doing god knows what with them.'

'It only happened once.'

'Sure it did.'

The awkwardness has gone, so I stand and reach for the coat I've deposited over the back of the chair.

'I'm going to the Co-Op,' I say. 'You might be banned but I'm not. I'm actually a decent cook, so I'll make you something.'

'I don't—'

'Just let me do this.'

Paige huffs a breath and, even though we've not spent much time together recently, I know her well enough to know this is more for show.

'Fine,' she says. 'But don't go nicking any porno mags. No point in us both getting banned.'


I pull the tub of Ben & Jerry's Salted Caramel Brownie Topped from the shopping bag and show it to Paige.

'You can't get this in Canada,' I say.

'You've bought so much food.'

She starts pulling items out of the bag and naming them as everything goes on the countertop.

'Teabags, bran flakes, milk, porridge oats, carrots, frozen peas, apples, Rice Krispies…'

'Don't forget the four-packs of Crunchies. Why are they so small nowadays?'

Paige ignores me: 'Why did you buy so much?'

I start putting things into the fridge. 'Because you only had noodles and soup.'

'I told you I don't need—'

'I've already bought it now – and I'm living with my sister, remember. I can't store stuff there, so let's just put it all away here and if you don't want to eat it, then you don't have to eat it.'

There's stomped-feet reluctance but Paige starts to help. When she gets to the tub of Ben & Jerry's Caramel Chew Chew, she stops and stares at the ingredient list.

'Do you remember when this stuff first came out?' she asks.

'You ate a whole tub of Phish Food.'

'It was so worth it…'

'I've been to the original factory.'

Her eyes widen. 'Where is it?'

'Vermont. It's amazing. I was going to send you some pictures but then…'

I don't know how to finish the sentence but Paige lets me off. 'What are you cooking?' she asks.

'Risotto?'

She smiles wider than I've seen in a very long time. 'I think I'd rather have kebab…'

'How about I make the risotto and then, if you don't like it, we'll have a kebab each?'

Paige stretches out a hand towards me to shake. 'Deal.'


I overcook the rice slightly but Paige is nice enough to claim that it's the best meal she's had in months. She's on the sofa and I'm in the armchair, eating off our laps.

'This is good,' Paige says.

'You already said that.'

'Not the food. *This.*' She blows on a forkful of rice and then lets it hover close to her mouth. 'Do you remember when we used to go back to your house after school? Your parents would be working and your sister was out somewhere. We'd do fish fingers under the grill and then microwave some beans. Then we'd sit on the floor and eat off our laps while we watched TV.'

She swallows a mouthful and I realise I've been watching her for a good minute or so. I hastily eat a forkful of my own and then go back to staring at the wall. There's no television in Paige's flat, so no central point on which to focus.

'It was good then, wasn't it?' she adds.

'What was?'

'Everything. Before Graham, before uni, before Oliver. Just… before.'

I don't know what to say to that. I think most people have a few golden years around their mid-teens. People are old enough to go places without their parents, while having few or none of the pressures, such as money or a job.

'What about you?' she asks.

'What d'you mean?'

'What happened with you and Liane?'

It's so direct, so out of nothing, that I find myself staring towards Paige, who is scooping the last of the rice into her mouth.

'We separated,' I say. 'We're probably going to divorce.'

'Why?'

'She was spending more and more time at work. When we met, she wasn't a big careerist. She grew into it as she was offered promotions and became better known in her industry. I went the other way, finding myself less interested in work and big cities. It was all shiny and new at one point… then that went away and I wanted to have space. I wanted to be able to look out the window and see fields and be able to sleep through a night without sirens raging past at least once…'

Paige doesn't reply instantly. She takes a moment and then says: 'You can take the boy out of Macklebury…'

She scrapes at her plate and glances across towards me. It could be a mean comment – but it isn't. There's a sad crease to her lips that's perhaps more knowing than I feel comfortable with.

'People change,' she adds. 'Then they change again.'

I think about her and the painkillers. Whether it matters.

'Is that what happened with you and Oliver?'

Paige stands and heads across to the kitchen, where she rinses her plate, before coming back to take mine. I wait as she runs the tap across it and then leaves both on a draining rack.

I don't expect an answer but, when she returns to her chair, she angles away so that I can't see her face.

'Oliver didn't want me to work,' she says. 'He wanted a good little housewife, just like his mum. He was after someone to cook, clean and pop out a football team of babies.'

'That… doesn't sound like you…'

Paige makes a sound that's something close to a tut. 'People change,' she says, repeating herself. 'Then they change again. I thought it might be all right at first. I was only working in pubs and shops. I didn't want to be my mum – and the last thing she could be accused of being is a good little housewife.'

'True…'

Paige takes a deep breath and starts to tug at her hair. 'I couldn't have kids. It took us years to figure that out. Oliver and I were never, um… regular.' She wriggles in the chair. 'I assumed it was because of that – but then I ended up going for tests and they said… well, you don't need to know the details. I'll never have children, though.'

'You could've adopted…'

A shake of the head. 'Oliver didn't want kids just to have kids.'

She leaves that hanging and I almost ask what it means. It's not clear… except maybe it is. Some people see their children as extensions of themselves. They're accessories, like an expensive bag or car. A mini-me to live out the goals and dreams at which an adult has already failed. That's easier if the child literally comes from a part of them. Adopting a child is far more of a selfless act.

'His mum made me sign a pre-nup,' Paige says. 'It wasn't actually his idea. We're not quite divorced yet but, even when it's done, I won't get anything.' A pause. 'Not that I'm saying I *want* anything but that's how things were. She had no faith in us, in *me*, before we'd even said the vows.'

'Why?'

Paige spins to face me, her features a twisted mix of anger and confusion. 'You've not been away *that* long.'

'I don't—'

I stop myself mid-sentence because I *do* know why. Lots of things have changed in Macklebury but those railway tracks still bisect the town. We come from one side, while Richard and Oliver come from the other. To people like Richard and Oliver's parents, that sort of thing matters. It's more important than anything. It's who they are and it's who *we* are.

She must see the realisation because Paige's face softens once more. 'The thing is, I actually think Oliver believes we'll get back together at some point.'

I don't ask the stupid question this time.

'Marriage is fun, isn't it?' she adds.

'A right laugh.'

Paige nods towards the kitchen. 'What else did you buy?' she asks.

I stand and cross to the bag I left next to the front door and produce a bottle of whisky and another of vodka.

'Have you got glasses?' I ask.

'Coffee mugs.'

'That'll do.'

# TEN

I know what everyone must be thinking because I'd be thinking it, too.

We didn't, though.

Paige and I might be many things. We're really old friends and we were next-door neighbours as kids. We were teenage wrestling fans and fell in with neither the sporty kids, nor the geeky ones. She was the first person to whom I ever sent a text message, back when mobile phones first came out. I did her maths homework for most of a year and it's almost certain our teachers knew. We cooked each other fish fingers and beans more than a hundred times. I once said something that made her laugh so much that she accidentally sneezed in my face. Or, more to the point, she *said* the sneeze was an accident.

We're all those things but we're not clichés.

We didn't then and we don't now.

I doubt it occurred to Paige and it certainly didn't to me, not until the morning after when I woke up in the armchair and spotted the text from Evie asking if I was OK.

I make the mistake of moving, which sends something raging through me that splits my head into two – but I don't reply to tell my sister that. Instead, I say that I stayed with a mate.

My creaking body sends twinges across my back, neck and thighs to indicate its displeasure as I heave myself up from the chair. The most surprising thing is that I seemingly made it through the night without needing to use the toilet. I thought that particular luxury was long gone once I hit about thirty.

There's a single window in Paige's flat, with a view that looks across the bottom end of the High Street. There's no curtain or blind, and a gentle white light is sending a porthole onto the rug.

It's snowing.

My first thought is that ploughs will be out… then I remember this is Macklebury, not Toronto.

I cross to the bedroom and knock on the door. A few seconds later and there's a mumbled 'yeah', followed by padded footsteps, and then the shape of a bedraggled Paige. She's in a T-shirt that's a good five sizes too big and her hair is shooting off at all angles.

She stares up to me through half-closed eyes. 'You're not a pretty picture, either,' she says.

'It's snowing.'

Paige dissolves into a little girl in front of me as a smile spreads and she races across to the window to take in the view.

'It's sticking…' she says.

'If I was in Toronto and there was snow in the forecast, I'd be fuming.'

'Why?'

'Because I'd have to get to work and all the side streets would be messy. They plough the main roads but there are still mounds everywhere. It's a nuisance to get anywhere.'

'It's so pretty,' she says.

'This would barely even count as snow in Ontario. It's more of an icing sugar dusting.'

'You're such a grump.'

'Don't get me wrong. I'm not in Toronto and I don't have work. This is all fine by me.'

Paige and I stand side by side, watching as a bus attempts to stop at the stand opposite. The wheels lock and it skids forward a good few metres, before crunching to a halt.

'Buses have these pillowcase things in Toronto,' I say.

'Are you winding me up?'

'They're called tyre socks. If the weather is really bad, they wrap them around the wheels to keep everything moving.'

The bus across the road tries to pull away but the wheels slide sideways, before gripping and allowing the vehicle to move.

Paige heads across to the bathroom and closes the door behind her. I continue to watch the street as a pair of boys and a girl in school uniform scuff their way along the pavement. They stop next to an electricity box and one of them slides his hand across the top, creating a small snowball. He threatens to hurl it at both of his friends, before changing his mind and lobbing it at a passing car.

It's clearly bad behaviour – and there's a solid thump as it connects with the roof – but it's hard not to see the trio as Richard, Paige and myself. Things change… but they really don't.

When the bathroom door goes again, Paige emerges and heads for the kitchen. She fills the kettle and then flicks it on.

'Richard's in court this morning,' she says.

'How'd you know that?'

'Text from Oliver. Shall we go?'

I take a few steps towards the kitchen, which is when I spot the flecks of greeny-white powder sitting on her top lip. I'm not sure what it is at first – and then it occurs to me that she might have crushed her pills. It takes me a second to click back into the moment.

'What time?' I ask.

'From ten.' She fishes into the sink and rinses out our mugs from the previous night. 'Do you want a tea?' she asks, looking up to me for an answer.

I brush my top lip and she takes the hint all too quickly, rubbing away at her own until it's clear.

'Milk?' she asks. 'Sugar?'

'It's already twenty past nine,' I reply.

Paige picks up her phone from the counter and lights up the screen. 'We better get going.'

The snow crunches under our feet as we hurry through the streets of Macklebury towards the magistrates' court. The flakes drift weightlessly through the air and it's hard to be sure they're even heading towards the ground. Life in the town continues as normal, although with more layers and thicker hats, coats and scarves. That's true of everyone except Paige, who is in the same light jacket as she has been since we met on the street where the taxi dropped me off. Her hands are clamped into her pockets and she tears along, on a mission.

I'm in the same clothes as the day before. If we had more time, I'd have gone to the court via Evie's to get a change of clothes. I'm a dirty stop-out, I guess.

We're close to the court with minutes to spare when Paige allows the pace to drop. We slot in at one another's side and she motions up towards Hail Hill, which is just about visible in the distance.

'Remember when we went up there with tea-trays from your kitchen cupboard?' she asks.

It's another one of those moments lost to the fog of time until she mentioned it. Now she has, it's right there, burning bright and so clear that it could have happened the day before.

'It was like the whole school was out,' I reply.

'I think it was the first snow day we ever had. We were maybe fourteen or fifteen.'

'We went up and down the hill so many times, I ended up soaked through. It was like I'd been swimming with my clothes on. Mum was furious.'

'Didn't someone break their arm?'

Paige and I stop at the bottom of the court steps and stare quizzically at one another. Her cheeks are a pinky-red from the cold.

'Wasn't that… *Graham*?' I say.

Her eyes flare wide. 'I think it was.'

'He was off school for a week or so – then came back in a cast.'

'I remember seeing it now you've said. He was sledging down but hit a rock, or something like that. His sledge went sideways and then he came off and landed on his arm. When he stood up, it was bent the wrong way.'

'I don't think I saw it.'

'You'd have been at the top. People were freaking out at the bottom. I remember this girl screaming – and then one of the older kids took Graham off to the phone box in town, where they called an ambulance.'

I look up to the hill again. The squalling snow has mixed with a soggy mist, making the outline barely visible. I wonder if there will be children up there today, making memories they will still talk about in twenty years' time.

Paige starts up the steps and I follow. Beyond the doors, the wall of warmth is like a firm hug from a trusted friend. I immediately start unbundling clothes but Paige doesn't acknowledge the temperature change.

'Didn't we have a school trip here once?' I ask.

Paige either doesn't hear or doesn't acknowledge it. Instead, she pushes herself onto tiptoes and scans through the crowds. That's when I realise there actually *is* a crowd. A magistrates' court on a Wednesday morning would normally have the liveliness of a graveyard – but not today.

There must be at least fifty people mingling close to the doors that lead into the main court. People are talking quietly but it makes little difference because the cold, hard floor and the high ceilings send the noise spiralling up and around, creating a cacophony of sound.

'How many of these d'you reckon are journalists?' I ask – but Paige still isn't listening. She bobs onto her toes a second time, before muttering a sharp 'come on' – and then weaving her way through the crowd. I follow as closely as I can, allowing her to make space between people and then slotting into it before it's gone.

We quickly emerge into a small clearing next to a pair of benches that are adjacent to the doors for court one. Oliver and his mum are sitting alongside a man in a tidy dark suit, who is wearing a pair of rimless glasses. The three reactions to Paige's appearance could not be more different. The man blinks up and then back down, clearly with no idea who she is. Oliver mutters a whispered 'hi', while his mum's face creases into a wrinkled, wordless frown.

Luckily, there's no chance for anything more to be said because, from behind, the doors open and then an usher beckons Oliver across. The trio from the bench head into the court, with Paige and me tucked so closely behind that, to an untrained eye, we must look like extra siblings.

The court has a huge painted seal at the front, next to a clock. There is beech wood panelling around all four sides, with an aisle along the centre and rows of benches on both sides, set across a couple of levels.

The man in the suit must be Richard's solicitor, because he takes a seat on the bench at the front – and is quickly followed by a young woman carrying an armful of folders.

While that's happening, the usher shows the four of us across to the front of the public gallery, which is on a slightly elevated level.

The next few minutes are pure organised chaos. People cram into the benches behind us, while the press gallery is so full that someone ends up sitting on the steps at the side. Solicitors enter to represent the prosecution and then have a brief conversation with Richard's lawyer, which ends with a smile and a laugh.

The usher continues to hurry around the court, stopping at various points to talk to someone along one of the benches. I lean in and whisper to Paige that his step count is going to be high tonight but she isn't listening.

Moments later and there's a muffled call of something I don't catch, followed by the sound of a packed court standing as one.

I was expecting magistrates but, instead, a single district judge appears, who swiftly beckons for everyone to sit.

There's a buzz to the room as the clerk runs through a list of proceedings. 'Richard Whiteside' is noticeable as the first name on the list.

Oliver's mum reaches into his lap and grips his hand. She squeezes so hard that I watch her knuckles turn white.

One more minute and there's a loud clunk as the door behind the dock opens.

It's been a long time since I've seen Richard in anything other than a photo. It's not like something from the US, where someone's in ankle cuffs and an orange jumpsuit. He's wearing a suit that's cut tight to his trim frame. His hair is very short at the sides, with the rest brushed forward on top. It is a world away from when he refused to have it cut for the best part of a year when we were in sixth form.

He could be the same clean-cut, anonymous businessman that saturates every city centre on the planet. That's not meant to be an insult but I suppose it is. I wonder if I'd have recognised him if we were to pass one another on a train platform, or the street.

Richard is flanked by a security guard in a stretched white shirt and black trousers. He blinks his way towards the dock and then looks up towards the public gallery. His mum waves, which he acknowledges with the merest of nods. I expect him to turn away but he doesn't. Instead he focuses on me, his eyes squinting slightly. It takes a second for me to realise that, of everyone he might have expected to see in court, I would have been low on the list.

He fractionally bows his head a second time, recognising my presence, before he turns towards the front.

That's when his mum bursts into tears.

# ELEVEN

It's only as Oliver, his mum, Paige and me are ushered into a small side office close to the courtroom that I realise Richard's dad isn't at the court. The other thing that's unclear is how Paige and I have managed to get away with tagging along to something that is – essentially – nothing to do with us. Paige is still Richard's sister-in-law, so I guess there's a connection there, but I'm a true interloper.

Nobody says anything, however, as Richard's solicitor closes the door behind us. The room is small as it is – and the clutter of three chairs and a table doesn't help as the five of us arrange ourselves around the walls.

'That went more or less as expected,' the solicitor says, while cleaning his glasses on his suit pocket.

It's Richard's mum who answers: 'When will he be let out?'

'Bail cannot be granted at magistrates' court for murder any longer. Used to be, back in the old days. This was only ever going to be a hearing to send everything up to Crown Court.'

'How long does he have to stay in prison?'

The solicitor replaces his glasses and then tilts his head and puffs out his cheeks. 'I'd hope to get a bail hearing on Friday, possibly Saturday depending on the schedules. Maybe Monday at the latest.'

'Will they let him out then?'

There's a hint of a wince this time. 'Maybe. I can't believe anyone would see him as a threat to the public and they could easily impose conditions that would have him living with a tag to monitor his movements. They might not let him live somewhere on his own but—'

'He could come back with us.' She's hopeful, almost pleading.

'Indeed – but that's a bridge to cross if and when it appears. For now, we'll have to wait. I'll stay in contact.'

He picks up his briefcase, apparently ready to head out, but Oliver speaks before the solicitor can reach for the door.

'What about the other thing I asked you?' he says.

The solicitor reaches for his glasses once more but this time resists the urge to clean them. 'Your brother hasn't been charged with anything in relation to the body that was found when he was a teenager. How many years ago was it?'

'Eighteen.'

He clucks his tongue. 'I know you were concerned about social media rumours but I would advise against listening too much to those. The police will be aware, of course, but it's not a good strategy to bring them up from our end. For now, your brother has been charged with one thing – and that's what we need to focus on.'

The solicitor rattles his case and scans across Paige and me, either wondering who we are, or waiting to see if there are any further questions.

'I'm going to head down and have a word with Richard,' he says. 'You've got my numbers and everything – but I wouldn't expect to hear anything today. I'll let you know when we have a date and time for the bail hearing.'

He clicks the door open and closed, leaving an awkwardness hanging like a crooked picture on a wall.

Nobody speaks for a good ten seconds until Oliver's mum reaches for the door. 'Let's get off,' she says to her son, before nodding towards me and offering a polite: 'Thank you very much for your support.'

She ignores Paige and then Oliver and his mum disappear. We leave it a few seconds before Paige follows without a word.

I trail her through the dwindling number of people now in the main reception area and we are out the doors at the front before I realise an impromptu press conference is happening at the bottom.

The snow continues to fall gently, which, if anything, sets a better backdrop for the cameras that are facing towards a man in a suit who is standing on the steps. I have no idea who he is – but the pair of uniformed police officers at his side means he's likely someone senior to them.

He's mid-sentence as we slot in at the side of the crowd, saying how he can't talk about specific details relating to the murder case. It's hard not to think of those articles about Graham as the man says that any witnesses who were at, or around, The Pines when Mr Wilson was murdered should come forward. Every one of those articles seemed to be punctuated by a sense that the police had no idea what had gone on.

There are five or six journalists and two TV cameras – plus around a dozen hangers-on with nothing better to do. As I peer up towards the senior officer asking for questions, I realise how much more official and serious this will appear on someone's screen. Whether it's on a television or through a news webpage, nobody watching will see the scattering of journalists; they'll see the steps and the court; the snow and the suits. It feels a little tinpot in person but it will come over as grave.

Someone asks whether the accused – Richard – was one of the students who found the body of Graham Boyes eighteen years ago. Paige tenses at my side and I feel a chill that I don't think has anything to do with the cold. I half expect the officer to glance over the small crowd and point towards me, saying that one of the boys is right here. He doesn't, though. He acknowledges the question with a gentle nod and then offers a short: 'That is correct.'

'Do you have anything to say about links being made from the killing of Keith Wilson to the killing of Graham Boyes?'

He must have expected the question because there's no hesitation as he replies with an even sharper 'Not at this time.'

After that, he holds up his hands and says there will be a later update – but then the uniformed officers lead him off towards the side of the court as the crowd begin murmuring to themselves.

Paige is pale now as she grips my hand and tugs me in the opposite direction to the one in which the police went. She doesn't need to say it because I already know. That was the moment where the officer could have shut down all the rumours. He could have said there was no link. He could have said they weren't looking into that.

Instead, the 'not at this time' will only fan the speculation.

'What do we do?' I ask, as Paige lets go of my hand.

She takes a breath and then turns towards the High Street. 'Let's find out who really killed Mr Wilson.'

# TWELVE

I find myself doing the same thing I've seemingly been doing since getting out of the taxi: following Paige. She makes it sound so obvious that we'll find the real killer and that will be that. No hint at the fact we have no resources and no idea. It's hard not to picture the powder under her nose a few hours before and wonder if this is what somehow emboldens her.

That's what's in my mind as I bump into Paige's shoulder. Without warning, she's stopped dead, like she did in the sandwich shop yesterday morning. We've not even made it as far as the High Street but Paige is frozen on the pavement. In a flash, she turns to head back the way we've just come.

I ask what she's doing as she spins indecisively on the spot, which is when I spot the man hurrying towards us. The door of his souped-up GTi orange shit-mobile hangs open as he bundles his way along the street. He's squat and wide, with no discernible neck. An English bulldog in human form. The sort who'd follow England to a World Cup and then start throwing restaurant chairs at waiters as local police fire up the water cannons.

Paige is now standing and facing him – and it's only when he's upon us that I realise I know who it is.

'What was that last night?' the man says angrily to Paige.

'A misunderstanding.'

'Pay me now then.'

They stare at one another and Paige doesn't flinch, even though the man is at least twice as wide as she is. He's the sort of bloke where it's difficult to know if the aggressive front is all bluster, or if there could be something genuinely frightening behind it all.

I glance backwards, to where the court steps and police are just about in sight. There is no one else around us.

'Are you Pete Baker?' I ask.

His head spins towards me and he breaks into a curious smile. There's something charismatically dangerous about the way he eyes me. I can see him helping an old lady over the road with a cheery bluster, before he goes around the corner to give a right kicking to someone wearing a football shirt he doesn't like.

'Who are you?'

'Harry,' I say. 'Harry Curtis. We were in the same year at school.'

'So?' Pete shrugs and turns back to Paige. 'Let's have it then.'

'I don't have the money right now.'

'So get it.'

'It's not that simple.'

'You want something, you pay for it.'

'I can't give you what I don't have.'

Pete takes a step backwards and digs into his pockets. 'There'll be consequences,' he says.

There's no reply and Pete is about to head towards his car when I call after him. 'How much does she owe?'

Paige gasps a quick *shush* but Pete is now looking towards me. It's as he does this that I realise what's different about him, compared to when we were at school. Or, perhaps, what's different about me.

Pete no longer looks down on me because we're the same height.

'About ninety quid,' Pete says.

Paige grabs my arm and hisses a harsh *'Don't'* but I ignore her and take out my wallet. The English notes feel so alien now; no longer the paper ones of my youth. I pull out five twenties and offer them to Pete.

'Does that cover it?'

Paige reaches for it but Pete gets there first, snatching the money from my hand and stuffing it into his pocket. He pokes a podgy finger towards Paige's face. 'You're on thin ice,' he says.

'I don't—'

Pete doesn't let her finish as he turns and heads back to his car, where the door is still hanging open. There's little surprise as the suspension drops when he gets in – and then the blaring exhaust sounds. A moment later and he's done a U-turn and is heading off towards the town centre.

I take a couple of steps but Paige doesn't move. I can hardly bring myself to look at her, knowing what will be there.

'You're such an arsehole,' she says.

'What did he mean by consequences?'

'Nothing. He's all talk. I know how to handle him and don't need you.'

'I was trying to help.'

A sharp shake of the head. 'I don't *want* your help.'

'I live three thousand miles away – and you literally called me for help.'

'For Richard, not *me*!'

We stand at an impasse. Her fists are balled, her shoulders tight and arched forward.

'Funny how some things never change,' I say, trying to calm the mood.

'Like what?'

'Like Pete. He was always the school bully, along with his cousins. What were their names? Luke, Simon and Barry? Something like that? Terry? Pete used to nick stuff from the local shops and then sell it to kids at school.'

Paige rolls her eyes: 'Can we just go?'

'He's not as scary as I remember.'

'Oh, you're the big man now, are you?'

'Not like that. It's just, if I ever thought of him, I'd think of this big kid towering over me – but now he's just the same as anyone.'

Paige scowls at me. 'He's *not* the same as anyone.'

'Well, no… he's got kids selling drugs for him and he's still bullying people beneath him.'

It was a stream of consciousness – but I only realise what I've said when Paige's eyes narrow. 'You think I'm beneath him?'

'I didn't mean it like that.'

Her chest rises and falls as she glares through me. 'I don't need saving,' she says firmly.

I open my mouth to reply but there's an instant realisation that there is no good response.

'I need to go back to my sister's,' I say instead. 'I can shower and change, then we can figure out what to do next.'

There's a moment in which it feels like Paige will say no. The way she said she didn't need saving made it sound like I wasn't the first to try… if that's even what I'm doing. I keep forgetting the girl who lived in the house next door isn't the same woman who's in front of me now. The same will be true of me to her.

*People change. Then they change again.*

'Did you ever find your keys?' I ask, an unsubtle change of subject.

The switch seems to jolt her back to the present as she hoists her bag from her shoulder and digs around. She holds up a small ring, on which three or four keys are looped.

'Like they fell into a black hole and then came back out,' she says. 'You ever have that?'

The tension has gone now and I remember the times we used to be like this. It wasn't only her mother with whom Paige could have a raging row. We would fight over the stupidest things; such as who got to sit on the biggest cushion at my house, or whether I was walking too quickly for her. There's an irony in that now, of course. She'd rage like a tornado from a quiet sky and then it would all be gone as quickly as it arrived.

It's only now that I remember all that. The sunshine sticks as the storms fade.

'I lost a shoe once,' I reply. 'Just the one. It wasn't in my cupboard, or anywhere in my apartment. I'd worn the pair the day before and it's not like I got home wearing only one. It *was* there – and then it wasn't.'

Paige acknowledges this with a solemn nod, before she buries her hands in her pockets once more. She whispers a 'sorry' that's so soft it's almost lost to the mist, the snow and the breeze. Maybe it was never there in the first place.

She sets off, walking more slowly now, and I slot in at her side as we head through the streets of Macklebury.

The snow continues to drift, though it isn't really accumulating on the ground. The pavement of the High Street has already become a slushy, soggy mess, while the powdery road has been sluiced by tyre marks.

It's a sodden slog – and Evie's house is empty when we arrive. I let myself in with the ancient key that I almost used on the first night I was back. The kitchen is as spotless as it was and I leave Paige there as I head upstairs to shower and change.

There's no sign Evie has been home at all. The bedroom doors are closed and everything is untouched, as if the house is up for sale and visitors are expected for viewings.

Evie was right when she said she'd hardly done anything with my old room. My parents hadn't, either. I'd been too tired to pay much attention before. The posters I used to have on the walls have all gone and so has the desk I used to have for the massive old computer and monitor. That was supposedly the thing on which I would do my homework. I ended up mostly playing games on it.

What does remain is the bed itself. It's a single that feels both short and narrow, while the bedding is unfamiliar and doesn't feel new. The shelves around the room are lined with various bits of clutter. Some of the books and VHS tapes are mine – but there are cookbooks and knitting patterns that would have been Mum's. It feels like Evie has taken everything she couldn't quite face throwing out – and stacked it in here.

Not that it really matters.

My suitcase is open on the floor and I grab some clean clothes and my wash stuff before heading into the bathroom.

By the time I get downstairs, the door from the kitchen to the living room is open and Paige has drifted from one to the other. I've not been in the main room since arriving home, although it's as meticulous as the other rooms Evie has worked on. All the old units that used to line the walls have gone – and so has the lifetime of tat that was once stored on them. All the ornaments, commemorative plates, spoons, coasters and other holiday-related nonsense have presumably been shipped off to the tip. In their place are a series of largely untouched, clean walls. The only exceptions are on a new floor-to-ceiling tower that's in the corner. Paige is in front of it, eyeing the framed photographs that have been arranged in tidy lines.

I slot in at her side and she doesn't turn.

'You were such a cute family,' she says softly.

The pictures look like they've been recoloured and reprinted. They're familiar as ones I've seen before and yet there's a vibrancy I don't remember.

Paige points towards the one that's front and centre. 'Where was that taken?' she asks.

The photo shows Mum, Dad, Evie and me on a beach, with a bright row of rainbow wooden chalets behind us. Evie's clutching a plastic spade, while I'm holding a bucket on my head. I'm pale, topless and thin, with ribs showing.

'Parkbury Sands,' I say. 'We used to go there every year when Evie and I were kids. One of Dad's friends had a caravan out there and we'd go for a week.'

'We went to Parkbury once,' Paige replies. 'Maybe the first summer we moved here. It might have just been for a weekend, though.'

'It was about an hour's drive and I used to think it was such a long way. Evie and I would be complaining after about fifteen minutes, wondering how much longer the journey would take. I used to think anything outside of Macklebury wasn't worth bothering with.'

'Funny that you're the one who left…'

I scan the other pictures. Almost all of them are portraits of Evie, me, Mum and Dad together. We're at a castle when I was ten or eleven, we're at the theatre when Evie was in a play, we're at university for my graduation, then at a different one for hers.

'What do you want to do?' I ask.

'I told you. Find out who actually killed Wilson.'

'How are we going to do that?'

'Let's find out what he's been up to – and then figure out who wanted to kill him.'

We're still facing the photos and my gaze slips to one where Evie is riding an elephant at the town's summer fair. It seems mad that this sort of thing was normal at one time. Where did the elephant come from? Who brought it to Macklebury? How did nobody think there might be a little cruelty involved in all that?

'Isn't that more of a job for the police?' I say.

'They think Richard did it. They're not going to be looking at anyone else.'

'But what can we *actually* do?'

Paige leans in and squints towards a photo of me standing next to a lighthouse when I'm seven or eight. I have no memory of the picture being taken, let alone where it might be. It has to be close, as we never travelled far.

'What do you remember about Wilson?' she asks.

'Not a lot. I didn't have much contact with him. The only ones who ever had much to do with the head of year were the kids who were always in trouble – or the ones who got good marks all the time. We were neither of those things.'

'Didn't he suspend you once?'

'I don't think so,' I reply.

'Maybe for one day. I remember something like that happening.'

'Not me. I was never really in trouble.'

That gets a snigger. 'Course you weren't.'

Paige cranes up to look at the highest picture on the unit. It's the only one that's been taken relatively recently and shows Evie from four or five years ago, at some sort of industry awards do, where she's clutching a glass trophy and a cheque. I still don't know exactly what her job is, though she must be doing well.

Paige's tone is playful: 'How does it feel to have a younger sister who has eclipsed your every achievement?'

'How does it feel to have a next-door neighbour who has eclipsed your every achievement?'

She snorts and then nudges me with her shoulder. 'You or her?'

'Both.'

Another laugh: 'You're such an arsehole.'

'You already said that once today.'

'Because you need reminding of the fact.' Paige rocks away from me and then turns to take in the rest of the room. 'Maybe it wasn't you who was suspended,' she adds, seamlessly changing subject. 'Maybe it was Richard?'

'Why would he have been suspended?'

Paige hrmms to herself but, now she's said it, there's something that does sound familiar.

'Richard was always the good kid, with good grades,' I say.

'Yeah but we dragged him down to our level.'

'Speak for yourself.'

'True. You're the one who went off to university and abandoned us.'

She laughs at her own words but the harshest jokes are always the ones rimmed with truth.

'Even if Rich was suspended,' I say, 'and even if it was Wilson who did it, why would that be a reason to kill him twenty-odd years later?'

Paige hrmms to herself a second time as she holds up her phone. 'Do you know the Wi-Fi password?'

I head through to the kitchen and pluck the printed business card with the details from the fridge. After that, Paige and I each use our phones as we get to work on googling Keith Wilson.

It doesn't take long for us to compile a short dossier on quite how boring our old head of year is. It is not exhaustive but he:

– Has retired to live at Parkbury Sands.

– Advertises as a private tutor.

– Takes photographs of trains and is part of the Macklebury and District train club. He is listed on their website as 'treasurer', although it is unclear what the train club actually does, other than, well, 'trains'.

– Was a somewhat frequent contributor on Warrington Wolves' Rugby League Club's fan forums, and organises minibus trips to visit at least two matches per season.

– Won the best marrow competition at last year's Macklebury and District garden festival.

Paige shows me a link about a 'Keith Wilson' who works as a dog breeder – but, when we look more closely at the details, we realise it's a different person.

I am about to click on a new link about last year's garden festival when Paige says she has to go to the toilet. As she says this, there must be something in my face that betrays my immediate thoughts of the powder on her top lip from this morning because she offers a sharp: 'What?'

'You're not going to…?' Paige's eyebrows rise and I know I'm in too deep as I add: 'It's just… It's my sister's house…'

She's calmer this time, which, if anything, makes her reply sting more. Even to me, it feels as if I'm attacking her… which I suppose I am.

'Who do you think I am?' she asks.

'I don't—'

Paige turns and heads through the house, then up the stairs. I almost call after her to say which door to use – except she's been here hundreds of times before. Thousands. Even if she hadn't, this is a mirror image of next door.

I wait for a door slam that doesn't come.

The truth is that I *don't* know who she is. I have been back for barely two days and wonder how much more we can argue like we are. Are the flashes of friendship worth the glimmers of darkness? Maybe they are? Maybe that's why I'm not only listening to her plan to investigate Wilson but actually going along with it.

When Paige returns a few minutes later, it's as if the moment from before never happened. She asks cheerily if I've found anything new and I twist my screen to show her the new photo I found of Wilson's best marrow win. The *Gazette* photographer clearly knew what he was doing because Wilson is clasping the giant green phallus with both hands and holding it up to his face, with his mouth wide open.

Paige's cheeks pop as the laughter explodes. 'If that photo doesn't accompany his obituary, then something's gone very wrong.'

'That's a low blow.'

Paige laughs again and it's hard not to join in.

I scroll down the page until I get to the comment section. I almost click away – except, under a relatively unassuming *Gazette* story about a vegetable competition, there's a single comment.

DISGUSTING HUMAN BEING! HE KNOWS WHAT HE DID!
                                    – Brenda Parkes, Parkbury Sands

'Do you think she's talking about the marrow?' Paige says.

'Have you ever heard of Brenda Parkes?' I reply.

Paige glances towards the window and the street beyond. The snow has stopped, although there's still a dusting across the grass on the far side of the road. The clouds have started to lift and there's the merest hint of blue in the sky.

'Do you fancy a bus ride to the seaside?' she asks.

'It's December.'

Paige shrugs. 'A beach is a beach.'

# THIRTEEN

We get off the bus next to the caravan park that's in the photographs of Evie, me, Mum and Dad. I pictured it as being a sprawling mass of metal boxes and well-trodden grass – but it's so much smaller than I remember. There's a newly painted sign at the front, advertising season-long pitches and favourable rates – but it's out of season and the whole area has a derelict feel about it. It certainly doesn't feel like the summer sunshine paradise that's been etched in my clearly false memories.

Paige and I head along the streets towards the centre of Parkbury Sands. As well as the quaint, run-down hotels advertising 'Colour TV' as if it's just come out, there is a giant bingo hall promising 'huge' prize jackpots of £20 – plus a boarded-up seafront caff saying they do, or did, 10p cups of tea.

A little on from that is the true centre. Most of the shops are closed for the season but the signs are still there, promoting four sticks of rock for a pound and 99 Flake Ice Creams for 99p.

We stand close to the pier, where a large sign says that it's closed until April, and stare out towards the ocean. In the summer, there would be an unquestioned charm – but the beach is muddy and empty, while the brown tide is raging somewhere near the horizon. It hasn't snowed in Parkbury Sands but the wind is vicious and biting, leaving me breathing into the collar of my coat, even though Paige seems unaffected.

'Beach is a beach, huh?' I say.

'Did you bring your trunks?'

'Should've brought a second coat to wear over this coat.'

'Don't you live in Canada?'

'Exactly! I don't think I've ever felt this cold.'

'I don't remember you being such a moaner.'

We turn back towards the town. It feels empty and abandoned.

'Do you remember where the Legion is?' I ask.

'Haven't you got your phone?'

'I can't feel my fingers.'

Paige sets off, crossing the empty road and heading along the side of a sweet shop that has a big 'CLOSED' sign across the windows. She keeps going until the next corner and then takes a right, then a quick left, before stopping in front of a low, long building that has a large poppy over the door.

As best we could find, there is only one Brenda Parkes who lives around here – and, according to her Facebook page, she is a member of, and frequent contributor to, the Parkbury Sands Royal British Legion page.

Immediately inside the door of the Legion is a small hall with a heater raging orange in the corner. Posters line the entire length, each advertising various events, past and future. A lot of it seems to involve tribute singers – with everyone from Cliff Richard to Take That featuring Lulu getting their own copycat versions.

Paige stops at the final poster, advertising a *Stars In Their Eyes* karaoke competition on Saturday.

'Fancy it?' she asks.

'Who could I sing as?'

'Bryan Adams? Now you're Canadian and all…'

'You know it's true.'

Paige ignores me and pushes through the double doors that lead into the bar area. We came here with a vague idea of asking around about Brenda, or perhaps leaving a phone number or message. Or perhaps we're here for something to do. For a reason to be friends again.

What we didn't expect was for Brenda to be sitting on a stool next to the bar. Brenda's long, platinum blonde hair is striking and she's wearing the same checked shirt from her Facebook photo.

Paige spots her right away and we exchange a glance to acknowledge that we both recognise the woman we're looking for. She's eating a plate of gravy-soaked chips and peas, while a pint of flat-looking ale idles at her side.

It's a weekday afternoon and the bar isn't exactly rocking, although there are more people here than I'd have guessed. Four guys in their twenties are crowding a pool table off in the corner, while another pair of blokes of similar age are feeding money to the fruity nearby. Five or six older people are slotted into a booth, talking loudly over one another – and there is one old boy playing darts on his own.

Brenda is alone, aside from the bloke behind the bar, who is cleaning glasses. Even from a distance, the way he's only half facing her makes it clear she's talking *at* him, not *with* him.

Paige and I head across to the bar and we order a pair of Diet Cokes, before going through the whole 'Is Pepsi okay?'-'Yes'-'Fine'-thing. Decades of advertising, billions of pounds, and nobody cares which is which.

The barman quickly takes the chance to get away from Brenda and disappears off to the other end of the bar to pour our drinks. Meanwhile, Paige has no qualms about inserting herself into someone else's existence. She leans across on her stool slightly, openly eyeing Brenda's food.

'That looks amazing,' she says.

Brenda stabs a fat, gravy-drenched chip with a fork and holds it up into the air. 'Best in the world,' she says. 'Two-fifty all-in. You can't get better than that.'

Paige sways backwards slightly on the seat. 'You're Brenda, aren't you?'

The woman's face darkens as her shoulders tense. 'You reporters?'

Paige snorts at this. 'Do I *look* like a reporter?'

Brenda doesn't soften and the chip she was holding remains in mid-air.

'Mr Wilson used to be our head of year,' Paige adds.

'So?'

'They're saying our friend killed him.'

Brenda puts the chip in her mouth and chews. She glances from Paige to me and back again before swallowing. 'Did he?'

'We very much doubt it.'

'Pity.'

The barman returns with our drinks and then scoots off through a door, out of sight and earshot.

'It's more of a pity if our friend ends up in prison for something he didn't do.'

Brenda nods along to this. 'True. Why do they think he did it?'

'Because he was in the area when it happened. Wrong time, wrong place. That sort of thing. We're not sure.'

'I had the police round this morning, asking questions about Keith and me. You know we were married, don'tcha?'

'That's why we're here.'

Paige replies so quickly that I wonder whether she actually *did* know they were married. I didn't. As far as I knew, all we had to go on was the comment Brenda had left on the news story. She doesn't seem like much of a woman in mourning.

'Who told you I'd be at the Legion?'

'No one. We stumbled across you on the Legion's Facebook page.'

Brenda nods along, though doesn't seem entirely won over. I think she likes being the centre of attention. 'What happened with Keith is none of my business,' she says. 'Don't know, don't *want* to know. Police had the cheek to ask where I was when it happened. Flippin' nerve of them.'

'Why did they think you might be involved?'

Brenda jabs the fork towards Paige, more in making her point than with any aggression. 'Because of the divorce. They always go after the close family – or *ex*-close family. Besides, it wasn't exactly amicable.' She half-turns as if finished – but I suspect she knows what she's doing as she adds a throwaway: 'Then there's the restraining order.'

Paige doesn't bite – at least not right away. She reaches for her drink and has a gulp before settling back on her stool.

Brenda's the one who can't take it any longer. She definitely likes being the centre of attention.

'He tried to tell the court I was some sort of danger,' she says.

'Why did he reckon that?' Paige asks.

'Cos he was an egomaniac. He had that narcissistic personality disorder thing. He thought everything was about him and, if it wasn't, he made sure it *became* about him.'

I almost smirk. Takes one to know one and all that.

Brenda jabs the fork back towards Paige. 'Don't you remember him from your school?'

'Definitely,' Paige says. 'Massive egotist.'

Brenda bangs the fork on the counter. 'Exactly.' She rams another chip into her mouth and is so keen to continue that she starts talking with her mouth full. 'Who taught you lot geography?'

Paige turns to pout her bottom lip towards me. 'It was a woman, wasn't it?' she says. 'What was her name?'

It takes a second or two for the name to appear to me: 'Ms Hill?'

Brenda snorts at this. '*Fiona* Hill. Absolute slag.'

'What did she do?' Paige asks.

'You should be asking "*Who* did she do?" – or, more to the point, who *didn't* she do?'

The delight with which Brenda speaks gives me the sense she's told the story around this bar more than once.

'My husband – my *ex*-husband – and Fiona Hill have a seventeen-year-old daughter together. They were having an affair for a good twenty years until I found out a few years back. Kicked him out on his arse. He came begging for me to take him back and, when I didn't, that's when he started getting all restraining order-*this* and let's sell the house-*that*.'

She pauses to push the nearly empty plate away.

'Anyway, Fiona Hill didn't want him, either – so he ended up living by himself. That's the type of guy he is.'

She downs the rest of her ale and then wallops the glass back onto the bar with a thud so forceful, I find myself wincing and expecting shards to fly.

'That what you wanted?' Brenda stands now, indicating towards Paige.

'I wouldn't say it's what we *wanted*.'

'Know this: if your mate *did* kill Keith then he had a very good reason.' She turns to go but then stops and twists back. 'You know she still teaches there, don't you?'

'Ms Hill?'

'Aye. *Fiona* Hill. Probably shagged her way round the entire school by now.'

With that, Brenda is done. She grabs her coat from the closest stool and strides off towards the toilets, slamming the door behind her.

# FOURTEEN

Paige and I sit in the Sands Chippy, sharing a large portion of chips with lots of vinegar.

'Bet you don't get chips like this in Canada,' Paige says.

'I don't think anywhere in the world does anything quite like seaside chips with a wooden fork.'

As if to emphasise the point, I smush the fork into a chip and gulp it down. 'Is Rogue Chippy still in town?' I ask.

'That place will never shut down. People travel in to visit. It's rated 4.95 on TripAdvisor. Technically, it's one of the best food establishments in the UK.'

'Is there even a "technically" about it?'

Paige points her wooden fork towards me. 'Good point. Think of all the pound coins we spent in there on large chips with a large sausage.'

'Bet it doesn't cost a pound any longer.'

Paige reaches for the table vinegar and empties another table-spoon or five onto the already waterboarded chips.

'Who'd have guessed Mr Wilson was such a dirty old dog,' she says.

'Do you really remember him being an egomaniac? I barely remember him at all.'

A shake of the head. 'Told her what she wanted to hear. I do remember Ms Hill though. Isn't she the one that everyone reckon shagged David Benson on that London trip?'

As Paige says it, there's something that makes me yearn for the immaturity and filthiness of those school rumours. I can picture

David Benson as the lad who would carry around a football with him every day. He and his mates had their own corner of the field where they would play every break time.

School was a non-stop merry-go-round of stories about who fancied whom, or – as we got older – who had got up to whatever act. Most of the time, we didn't even understand the exploits we were talking about.

'We never went to London with the school,' I say.

'No – but it's all anyone was talking about when they got back. Richard went and he was the one who told us. It probably wasn't true but I think Ms Hill and David Benson ended up in a room together for a while and everyone kept saying they'd done it.'

There's something wonderfully quaint about the way Paige says 'it' that makes me smile.

*It: Noun.*

*Definition: Childish word for sex.*

*Uses: 'I bet they're doing it', 'I bet they've done it', 'Have they done it yet?'*

Paige is still talking. 'She lives in that big house next to the church,' she adds. 'The one we used to walk past all the time. There was that dog that would sit at the front gate and bark at everyone.'

'How do you know she lives there?'

The idea of teachers existing outside of school still seems fantastical.

'Saw her coming out of it a few times. I think I probably knew she still worked at the school. Just one of those things that you absorb through osmosis.' Paige reaches for the vinegar again. 'What time's the next bus back?' she asks.

I check my watch. 'About ten minutes.'

She puts down the vinegar. 'Reckon we can get back before the school closes.'

'I thought they might have a snow day.'

Paige hrmms and then makes a decision. 'Only one way to find out…'

The bus back to Macklebury stops a short distance from the school, almost exactly at the spot where the shortcut from the railway arch emerges. Paige and I head along the street together, passing a large garage-like building with a scratched sandwich board reading 'Antiques World'. A man who is missing half an ear is standing near the open door, smoking a cigarette and, when we pass by, he says 'hi'. I presume he's talking to Paige – who ignores him – and when I twist to look at who's talking, there's something vaguely familiar about the man that I can't place.

Paige's speed means there is no time to waste as she hurries across the road and, in no time, we're resting on the wall that runs around the perimeter of our old school. Any snow that would have been on the car park at the front has melted away, leaving everything glistening and wet. I suppose there's also something to be said about the state of a teacher's pay, given the battered collection of hatchbacks that fill the tarmac.

Students in uniform soon start filing out of the large doors at the front – and I'm filled with another sense that things never really change. There are half a dozen boys bouncing a football between them as they head for the gates. There are groups of girls who walk so closely that they're almost conjoined, some goth kids, a boy who's juggling, a lad who's taken off his tie and is using it to try to lasso someone who's smaller… and so on. The same tropes and clichés that live forever. The only difference is the phone that's in most of their hands.

Nobody pays Paige and me any attention as we continue to wait. The sun is already on its way down, having hardly bothered for the day, and the temperature is falling. I zip my coat a little tighter and bury my hands in the sleeves. I'm beginning to wonder if this was a good idea when Paige nods towards a woman who is walking from the side of the building.

'That's her, isn't it?'

The woman is on the far side of the car park, carrying two bags over her shoulder. She stops to talk to a man in a suit, who's standing next to an open car boot.

'I've not seen her in almost twenty years,' I say.

Paige starts walking down some steps towards the car park. 'It's her,' she says decisively.

We cross the car park together and intercept Ms Hill close to a VW Golf in the corner of the car park. She has the back open and is unloading both bags inside when she turns to blink at the pair of us. I look to Paige but she is uncharacteristically silent.

'Harry,' I say, taking the lead and holding out my hand for our old teacher to shake. 'Harry Curtis.'

Her hand is cold and smooth as she shakes mine briefly and then quickly withdraws. The way she squints makes it fairly clear she has no idea who I am. I'm not sure I'd have recognised her if Paige hadn't pointed her out. She wears glasses now and her hair is greyer. When we were at school, she seemed like she wasn't that much older than us. Now I figure that must have been a misplaced guess because she must be well into her fifties.

'You used to teach me geography,' I say.

'How long ago was that?'

'About twenty years. I didn't know you still taught here but we were walking past and I spotted you. I figured I'd say hi.'

Ms Hill looks up to the wall that separates the car park from the pavement and gives a slight frown, as if to make clear she knows this is invented nonsense.

'I've been living in Toronto,' I say, speaking too quickly. 'When you taught me, we once did a project about the climate of North America and I remembered so much of it when I was deciding to move. I figured I'd say thanks for having such an influence on me…'

Ms Hill blinks and I feel sure she's about to call me out on the obvious arse-licking nonsense I've come out with but, instead, she touches her chest momentarily. 'That's really kind of you,' she says, seemingly meaning it. The generosity of spirit immediately fills me with guilt, although she's not done. 'Thank you so much for telling me. What brings you back here?'

I angle my head towards Paige at my side. 'Visiting friends ahead of Christmas. I got back here and then heard about Richard Whiteside and, well… I guess you've heard about that, too…?'

Ms Hill takes a half-step back towards her car and closes the boot with a *thunk*. 'About him and Keith… Mr Wilson. Yes.'

'I can't believe it. Richard and me were such good friends. *Are* good friends, I guess. Now this. I heard there was some sort of teachers' reunion at The Pines on Saturday when it happened. Were you there?'

She takes a step to the side, into the gap between her car and the next. 'Yes, um…' A glance sideways. 'Look, it's been very nice to see you again, Harry – but I've got to get home. It's been a long day with the kids and the police and—'

'The police?'

Ms Hill gives a smile that's anything but friendly. 'I don't think it's really—'

'Did you have his baby?'

Ms Hill and I both turn to stare at Paige, whose widened eyes make it look as if she's as shocked as I am that she actually asked the question.

Nobody speaks for a few seconds. It's like Paige has just unleashed a sentence containing the worst swear words while standing in the pulpit of a church.

'I don't think that's—'

Ms Hill doesn't finish her sentence because Paige talks over her. 'Someone killed him on Saturday night and it wasn't Richard.'

Ms Hill turns and opens the driver's side door of her car. 'I can't help you.'

She motions to get in but Paige is unrepentant and unrelenting. 'Other people are mad at him, aren't they? You know—'

'Stop!'

Our old teacher twists back towards us. 'I spoke to the police today,' she says. 'I don't have to talk to either of you – and you're trespassing on school property. You should both leave.'

'Did he cheat on you, too?' Paige asks. 'Like he did his wife.'

Ms Hill bites her lip and then raises her eyes past us, towards where a male teacher has appeared at our shoulders.

'Everything all right?' he asks.

Ms Hill looks between Paige and me and then opens her door wider. 'Yes,' she says. 'These two *former* students are just leaving.'

# FIFTEEN

'You've watched too many TV cop shows,' I say.

Paige is walking along the street as slowly as she has since I got back to Macklebury. It's almost dark, with the orange haze of street lights casting the gentlest of shadows as we head in the vague direction of the High Street.

'It's true, though,' she says. 'I bet he's a serial cheater. There's probably loads of people annoyed at him – jilted husbands and abandoned women. If he was having one affair for twenty-odd years, like Brenda reckons, I bet he was having more.'

'The police will know that, though. They've already talked to Brenda and Ms Hill.'

'But it feels good to be doing something, doesn't it?'

There's relish in Paige's voice. Genuine pleasure, perhaps – and I suddenly see it from her point of view. She's been fired from her job, separated from her husband and she's living in a small flat over a bookmaker's. Whatever money she has seems to go on pills, instead of food… and yet, out of nothing, suddenly the world is exciting.

If I'm honest, I feel it, too.

I wish it didn't involve one of my old friends being arrested for killing one of our old teachers – but it's hard not to have that buzz of one day being so drastically different to the last.

I feel it. I'm *relishing* it… and yet…

We stop at a red light and I look sideways at her. Paige returns it with one of her own. 'What?' she asks.

'Why are you so convinced Richard's innocent?' I ask.

'Aren't you?'

There's a hesitation that I don't plan. 'I guess... but I don't really know him any more. We've barely spoken in ten years or so. If he's anything like he was when we were kids, then I don't believe he killed anyone – but people change.'

'Not into murderers.'

'People change into all sorts of things we wouldn't expect.'

The light goes green and I start to walk. I'm halfway across the road when I realise Paige hasn't moved from the kerb. I turn to look back at her.

'You coming?'

'Was that about me?'

She has to shout to be heard and I end up heading back the way I came, so that Paige and I are standing on the same corner once more.

'Was *what* about you?' I ask.

'Saying that people change into all sorts.'

Her shoulders are tight, body clenched into a spring. 'Not really.'

'Is it, or isn't it?'

The cars start to flow again behind us, engines humming against the deadening day. 'I suppose drugs have never been a part of my life. I don't know how to handle you.'

Paige stares at me with confusion and hurt. 'You don't have to *handle* me.'

'I didn't mean it like that... I'm just saying that people change. When we were kids, I wouldn't have expected that you'd, um...'

'What?'

There is no good way to finish the sentence – not that I have to.

'It's none of your business,' Paige adds.

'It is if kids are handing you bags of pills on the street. If your dealer is getting out of a car to demand payment.'

Paige takes a step backwards. Two. She opens her mouth to say something but then closes it, spins, and walks away so quickly that she's almost at the next corner when it occurs to me that I could go after her.

I don't.

The fall-out came so quickly that it feels as if it was inevitable. I know someone could say I was being pious or judgemental – but the truth is as I told Paige. I'm not sure how to handle something that's so out of my comfort zone. It would be the same if she was a chronic alcoholic, or gambling addict.

Paige disappears around the corner and then I turn myself and cross the road, heading in the opposite direction.

There's an irony in that I live in a city where any number of awful things can happen day to day. There are stabbings and the odd shooting, car crashes, ODs, thefts, muggings – and everything else that happens when a huge number of people come together. I can put all that to one side and carry on with day-to-day life – and yet seeing Paige buying pills in a small community feels so much more personal. So much *worse*.

I'm walking in the general direction of Evie's house but paying little attention to where I'm going, which is why I end up surprised to find myself in front of Macklebury Parish Church. The dual steeples soar high above the rest of the town, with wide wings on either side, each dotted with grand stained-glass windows.

There was a time when I was in primary school that I used to sing in the choir here once or twice a week. There was a fundraising board that seemed permanently placed on the green at the front. I don't think there was ever a time in which the church wasn't gathering funds for a roof, or its windows, or something else.

There's no board now and, if anything, the church looks newer and in better condition than I ever remember it. The stonework is impeccably clean and the windows bright, even from the outside.

The gate is open and I head up the steps towards the church as memories continue to return.

We once had a primary school trip here, where our teacher had us go around the graveyard and find the oldest stone. I think we might have even done stone rubbings with crayons onto white paper that we then took back to school. It sounds invented but it would also be an odd thing for me to make up.

If nothing, I suppose it killed an hour or so for the teacher.

At the top of the steps, I head right and follow the slippery stone path around the side of the church. There are white lights on posts as I find my way across towards where my parents' graves sit side by side in a spot close to a hedge.

The stones are darkened by damp, with the merest hint of mossy green infecting the lettering. There are no flowers or trinkets on the patches of land, but there is standing water in a divot that sits between the two graves. Close to the hedge, the merest hint of snow remains from the morning's flurries.

I read the dates on my parents' gravestones and the brief messages inscribed below. None of it really means anything. Everyone's a loving parent or child at the end. We'll all be missed, and so on.

For some reason, I wonder whether it'll be me or Evie who goes first. Almost certainly me, of course. She's healthy and well. Will I be a 'loving brother'? Or perhaps there's still time to be a 'husband' and a 'father'…

One of the lights flickers and it shakes me back into the moment, away from the macabre nature of my thoughts.

I should head back to Evie's – or perhaps even message Paige to apologise. Except I don't. I keep following the path that rings the graveyard. I have no particular plan but perhaps it's the same fate that's been ushering me around that leads to a plot in the far corner that has a gravestone which is as bright white and clean as it likely was the day it was set.

Graham Boyes' name booms out to me through the silence.

That's the other reason I remember this church so vividly. At Graham's funeral, it felt as if the entire town had crammed itself inside. There were people standing along the sides and they were close to ten deep at the back.

The entire school went, with some of the younger ones having to settle for spots on the floor because of the lack of seats. Paige and I sat in the very back row, her on the aisle, me at her side, Richard next to me. I had to lean across her to get a view along the walkway as the man sitting in front of us was ridiculously tall with a perfectly annoying posture than made him sit even higher.

It's strange the details that are remembered against the ones that aren't.

In the time between the murder and the funeral, there was an enormous outpouring of grief, with flowers being left across a large section of the car park at the front of the school. The closest thing I can remember to how things felt was the time after Princess Diana died – and the country went bonkers with its books of condolence and non-stop anguish-a-thon. Macklebury was like that – but worse, because there was no escape to go anywhere else.

It was also worse because everyone knew I was one of the two kids who found Graham's body. I didn't want to talk about it but people would find ways to bring it up; to ask the question without explicitly asking it.

Even Mum and Dad. Even Evie.

Everyone except Richard – because he was there – and Paige, because she didn't need to hear it.

An overhead light blinks again and, for the second time, I realise that something morbid is setting in. I turn to leave, moving too quickly and almost slipping on the sodden stones.

There's a second reason I step back now. Somehow, as I drifted off to the past, a man has approached and is standing directly behind me, looking down towards Graham's grave.

'Hi,' he says. 'Fancy seeing you here.'

I don't recognise him at first. He's tall and fit, with angled cheekbones and a face that's slightly too thin.

It must be my blank look because he continues speaking. 'Martin,' he says. 'Graham's older brother.'

# SIXTEEN

I mumble something that I hope is 'hi' but I don't think it's enough to hide my surprise. I turn between Martin and his brother's grave.

'My parents are buried over there,' I say, pointing off towards their plots, trying to justify a reason for being here.

Martin doesn't turn. He has a beanie pulled down over the top of his ears and his chin is poking out from a scarf.

'I heard you moved abroad,' he says.

'Canada.'

'Cold there, isn't it? Colder than here.'

'Sometimes…'

Martin looks past me towards the gravestone. 'What are you doing on this side?'

I follow his stare, back towards the words.

*Loving son, cruelly taken*

'I'm not sure,' I reply. 'I was on my way back to my sister's and sort of found myself here.'

There's a long pause and I wonder if I've said the wrong thing. I'm not standing anywhere out of bounds but it's certainly odd for me to be here.

'I find myself here sometimes,' Martin says. 'I'll be driving through town, or walking, and then, without planning anything, I'll be standing here…'

His breath sails off into the night as he sighs and bows his head. I half think about walking away – but it feels as if we're tied into this moment at one another's side.

'Did you hear about Richard?' I ask.

'Yes…'

There's a hush that's so silent it's as if we're the only two people in the town. I shiver and try to push it away. It doesn't seem as if Martin feels uncomfortable at all.

'Mum and Dad have heard all the rumours,' he adds. 'That your mate killed his teacher, so if he's capable of that, then…'

I almost say that Mr Wilson *wasn't* our teacher but bite back the words just in time. It's one of those things that will become the truth, even though it isn't.

'It's brought it all back up,' Martin says. 'All these years later.'

'I don't know what to say.'

'You found Graham's body. You and *him*. You were both there. *He* was there.'

'We were kids.'

'You were sixteen.'

'It's still young.'

'People have killed at a younger age…'

There's something haunting about Martin's voice. Ghosts of decades past. I want to be able to say that Richard definitely couldn't have killed Graham but the words don't quite come.

Martin and I stand side by side for a while longer but I don't know where to look. I can't face the gravestone any more and instead find myself staring off into the darkness of the shadowed verge beyond.

'Who actually found the body?' Martin asks.

It takes me a moment to realise that he means Graham's body. That's he's talking about Richard and me. I'm standing in a graveyard and yet I'm back underneath the railway arch, walking with Richard, our schoolbags slung over our shoulders.

'It was never reported,' Martin says. 'I read back all the old reports and it wasn't there. They never named you, either. Everyone in town knew but I'd not realised how little made it into the papers. They always said that two of Graham's classmates found the body.'

'We weren't classmates,' I say. 'It didn't really matter but Graham was in our year, not our class. They got it wrong.'

He ignores this. 'But who actually found the body? You or Richard?'

I can't tell Martin the complete truth. Parts of what happened on that day are crystal clear. I remember the crooked shape of Graham's arm as it hung out of the bush. There was the reddy-black stain of blood underneath and the waxiness of his skin. I recognised him right away but it didn't even occur to me that he could be dead. It felt like death couldn't be an option.

'I don't remember,' I say – which *is* the truth. 'I wish I could give you an answer but I don't know who saw the body first.'

Martin doesn't reply, although his shoulders sink slightly. He lets out a long breath and so I continue.

'Is there something from your past, something big, but it's so big that it's almost as if you remember the memory of it, rather than the actual thing?'

Martin shuffles from one foot to the other. 'Like what?'

'I used to go on family holidays to this caravan park at Parkbury Sands. There are all these photos and I remember little snippets, like sitting on the wall over the beach and eating ice cream… except I don't think I actually *do* remember. It's because I've seen the photos and I'm thinking of that.'

Martin still doesn't reply. I turn to look at him but he's focused unmovingly at the gravestone.

'When we found Graham's body, it was huge,' I say. 'We talked to the police, to our teachers, to kids in the playground, to parents, to everyone. The papers never printed our names – but everyone in town knew who we were. *You* knew. People on the street would stare. They'd do that weird head-tilt thing and I'd sometimes see Mum or Dad whispering to their friends.'

'What are you saying?'

'That I'm not sure if I remember *actually* finding the body, or if I just remember having to tell people about it.'

There's a second in which I fear Martin will be angry. He looks sideways to me and then smiles thinly. 'The whole time around what happened is like that for me. It's like I watched myself at the funeral and I'm not sure if I actually remember the ceremony itself.'

'If I knew who actually found the body first, then I'd say. It might have been Richard but it might have been me.'

'Who decided to walk home that way?'

'That cut-through by the railway arch was the way we went most days. I doubt we'd have talked about it. We'd have walked on instinct because it was dry and the only reason to avoid that way was if it had rained. Everything would be squelchy on those days.'

Martin turns back to the gravestone and nods acceptingly.

'Richard was my friend before and after,' I say – and there's a relief that there's someone to tell this to, even if it's a relative stranger. 'Finding Graham was this huge thing that we went through and nobody else did. You can't just have a cup of tea and suddenly be over something. I used to dream about finding the body. Mum would have to remind me to eat because I wouldn't remember. It was only Richard I could talk to about it. In all that, it never felt as if he was hiding something.'

He doesn't sound convinced: 'People can lie.'

'True… but we were sixteen. Someone wanted to talk to me about what we found every day for weeks. Richard had it the same. How many teenagers do you know that would be able to lie *that* well for *that* long? I couldn't have done it.'

Martin doesn't reply at first. When he does, he sounds resigned. 'Mum and Dad don't know what to think. People on Facebook keep saying that Richard must've killed Graham – and they seem to believe everything they read on there. They called the police about it yesterday and officers were round last night.'

'What did the police have to say?'

'No idea. I went out because I didn't want anything to do with it.'

We stand together for another few moments. The overhead lights are casting a bluey glow across the gravestones and the silence is almost overwhelming. There isn't even a whisper of wind.

'The other thing is why,' I say.

'What do you mean?'

'*Why* would Richard kill Graham? Why would he kill anyone?'

I'm asking that question as much for now with the allegations about Mr Wilson as I am for eighteen years before, with Graham.

'People have reasons,' Martin says.

'We weren't friends with Graham – but we were hardly enemies. We knew each other from being in the same year. Say Richard *had* gone crazy, I could name thirty or forty people he'd have had an issue with before Graham.'

Martin shuffles again, taking it in. It feels comforting to have someone who's actually listening.

'He was bullied,' Martin says.

'Graham?'

'It wasn't a big, everyday physical thing… or I don't think it was. He was probably gay, though perhaps a bit young to know exactly what all that meant back then. He was literally a cliché at times. He'd be in his bedroom listening to a tape of showtunes. He preferred hanging around with the girls and could be really camp sometimes. Other kids would pick on him for that.'

This triggers a thought that I might have called Graham gay at some point – and not in a nice way. I can't remember. 'Gay' was definitely an insult when we were at school. Perhaps it still is? It feels as if the world has moved on… but that's easier to say when living in a big city with a gay village, rainbow crossings, and a pride parade every year.

'People have been killed for a lot less,' Martin adds, letting it hang in the air.

'Richard, me and our friend Paige spent almost all our time together then,' I reply. 'If the three of us weren't doing something together, then two of us would be.'

'Were you together all the time on the day Graham died?'

'No – but we weren't bullies. We weren't that bothered about other people. We were happy doing our own thing. People ignored us and we ignored them.'

'Paige…' Martin rolls her name around his mouth. 'Ollie's wife.'

'Right.'

'Are you still friends?'

'I suppose. I've been away but I've seen her since I got back.'

A pause and I can feel Martin weighing up what to say next. The moment lasts and lasts – and then it breaks.

'Do you know what she did to Ollie?'

Out of nowhere, snow starts to fall once more. The flakes are larger and wispier than the morning's and they swirl in the silent breeze.

I can't answer. I don't think I want to know… except that it's too late.

'She was sleeping around for money,' Martin says.

He lets that hang, too – and I still can't find the words.

'Ollie couldn't believe it,' he adds. 'He kicked her out. I don't know how he can face looking at her.'

I close my eyes for a moment and a snowflake lands on my nose before instantly dissolving. When I open my eyes again, Martin has shifted away a few paces, leaving me alone at his brother's grave.

'Weird group of friends,' he says. 'The whore and the murderer.'

'They're not—'

'Sometimes you have to pick sides in life. Are you really picking *that* side?'

'It's not like that.'

Martin shrugs and pushes his hands deeper into his pockets. He glances up towards the lights and the snow. 'Appreciate the talk,' he says – and then he turns and walks off into the night.

# SEVENTEEN

Macklebury High Street is quiet as I continue the roundabout walk towards Evie's. Snow is sticking on the grassy areas but dissolving on the pavements and roads. There are so many homeless people around tonight, all crammed into doorways and nooks, buried under sleeping bags, blankets and boxes. As I pass a man who has wedged himself into a space at the front of a bakery, he yells something I can't make out. It could've been at me – but it might simply have been at the world in general. I don't wait around to find out. I feel intimidated.

I shared chips with Paige at lunch but it's hard to avoid the allure of Rogue Chippy after we talked about it. It's one of the few places close to the High Street still open and I push through the steamed-up front door into the warm, welcoming embrace of fat, salt and vinegar.

Large chips and large sausage is up to the giddy heights of £1.90 now and I pay the young lad behind the counter before heading off to the window bench with my food. I use a sleeve to clear the condensation from the glass, though there's little to see on the gloomy streets of Macklebury after dark.

I'm like a child, having chip-shop chips twice in a day. Even compared to seaside chips from earlier, there's something special about Rogue's offerings. I'm already halfway through the meal when I realise that there probably isn't... that it's simply that these chips taste of childhood.

Paige, Richard and I would sit three in a row on this exact bench during our school lunch breaks. It wasn't every day – but it would be once a week or so. In my memory, it was sunny every time, although that can't have been true. I try to think of the things we might have talked about, although nothing comes to mind. Perhaps the sign of real friendship is that you can spend hours talking about absolutely nothing?

I check my phone and delete the spam emails, leaving nothing of note from Canada, as if nobody has noticed I've left. I consider sending something to Liane, letting her know I'm fine, except that I'm not sure what else to say, or if she's bothered. I put my phone away and eat a couple more chips, before taking it back out again.

I hardly ever use Facebook – but I am on it. Liane would complain because if our friends tried to organise social events on there, I would never go online to click and say that I was going.

When I log in, there are almost ninety notifications, all of which I ignore as I search for the Macklebury town page. I've heard plenty about the rumours regarding Richard – but haven't actually read any of them.

They're easy enough to find. People have linked to a handful of news reports, some of which list a few details I'm not sure I knew. Mr Wilson died from a single stab wound to the heart – but the police are still searching for the murder weapon. I guess that's why they looked through Richard's flat.

Apart from some posts today about the snow, almost everything on the town's page since the weekend is about the murder. I go through all of them, newest to oldest – and the first comment about Richard is all the way back as the third remark on the first article. It wasn't long after the killing itself, when few details were known – except someone wrote that they'd heard Richard had been arrested. The reply to that says: 'Isn't he the one that found that boy's body years back?' Two replies later and someone writes: 'I bet he did that one too' – and then the rumours begin to fly.

People say how they were always suspicious of the kid who found Graham's body. Only Richard is named – and I'm forgotten from that part of history, not that I particularly mind. Newer residents ask what people are talking about, which leads to someone outright saying that a teenager was killed by a classmate twenty years ago – and that 'it all got covered up'.

What Paige called 'rumours' are inventions and lies.

By the time I've finished reading, the rest of my chips are cold and I feel drained. It's incredible that people willingly put their names to comments and replies that are, at best, speculative and vindictive; or, at worst, wrong.

Someone says that Richard did their accounts but that he 'always seemed angry about something'. Someone else replies to say that they'd seen him drunk a few times and that they weren't surprised he was being linked to a murder. It's quite a leap from one of those things to the next. If drunkenness meant potential murderer, prison bars might as well be built around the whole of Britain.

It's amazing how many names I recognise through the comments. If it's not the full first and last name, then it's the last. Parents, siblings, children and grandchildren from generation after generation of families who live, live and live again in this town. There will be teachers who'll see entire family trees come through the same school.

Teachers, perhaps, like Mr Wilson, or Ms Hill.

It all makes grim reading. There's not a single person who comments on any of the links to say that people should step back and wait to see what happens, or who speaks up for Richard. It's no wonder there seems to be a general sense around town that Richard is guilty of two murders, even though he hasn't been found guilty of one.

I keep scrolling, unable to look away, until I stumble across a comment from someone who says her best friend was engaged to Richard. It ends by saying 'she can tell some stories' and then tags someone named 'Joanne Gilchrist'. There are no replies after that – certainly not from Joanne.

This is the first I've heard of Richard being engaged. He never mentioned anything in the messages we've shared these past few years – and Paige hasn't said anything either.

Joanne Gilchrist is another of those names I recognise. She was a girl in our year at school, a little like Graham in the sense that she wasn't part of our circle of friends but that we would have recognised and known one another. She once got sent home from school because she was wearing a denim jacket. At the time, I would have shrugged that off as normal and it's only now that it seems such a power-trip thing to have happened.

I click on Joanne's name, which takes me through to a page where there is a photo of a pink-faced woman with short, sweaty blonde hair. She's grinning as she shows off a medal while wearing a T-shirt about a 10k that has a number pinned to the front. Other than that, there is little more information except that she lives in Macklebury and works in a shop called The Wine Store.

I wonder if I can really be called Richard's friend. He's been engaged and separated, all while I've known nothing about it. That's more on me than Richard, as I've made so little effort to maintain the relationship.

I'm thinking of that when I realise the allure of the chips have worn off. They've congealed into a cold mass of mushy potato and I fold the paper around the container, then dump it in the nearest bin, before leaving.

The snow has stopped again, although the lack of people on the streets has left a gentle, largely untouched, dusting of white across the pavement. I leave the High Street and head into the darker reaches of the town. It dawns on me that I've been outside for the best part of two days. Life used to be like this in the summer holidays; when Richard, Paige and myself would somehow manage to spend entire days doing very little other than being away from our respective houses.

I follow a darkened street towards a hazy glow at the end. A gentle melody clings in the air and I am suddenly at the side of a recreation centre that's attached to a playground. There's a plaque above the door, saying it was funded by the National Lottery and opened by Princess Anne twelve years ago. A Christmas tree sits between the centre and playground, with a collection of bulbs winding their way up to a bright, white star on the top.

I head inside, drawn to the warmth, where there's a carol service happening. A mix of adults and children are on a stage clasping instruments and there's a choir off to the side. The school-style plastic seats are packed with people – and I slot in at the back of the hall, standing and wedging myself into an alcove that's half covered by a floor-to-ceiling curtain.

There's a girl on stage who steps up to the microphone by herself. She can't be any older than thirteen and is wearing a smart skirt and top that's identical to all the other women on the stage. The music builds and suddenly she's singing 'O Holy Night' with such perfection that the hairs stand up on my arms.

It's been too easy to sneer at early closing times, or the small-town attitudes of the Facebook comments – but, as I stand and watch, I'm filled with a sense of community for what is probably the first time since I got back.

There are *real* people in this town. Real people with real lives who are scared because someone was murdered in their midst. I'm not sure I blame them for wanting to find a bad guy on whom all this can be pinned.

It's just a shame that person seems to be Richard.

I watch the girl complete her solo and join in with the rapturous applause. She smiles widely and bows, then nods towards her parents, who are sitting a few rows back. The man I assume to be her father is clapping with his hands above his head.

I feel like an imposter. Someone posing as a local who simply isn't.

I shouldn't be here.

The cold hits me hard as I head back out the way I came. Needles of ice stab at my cheeks and my teeth begin to chatter almost instantly. I walk more quickly this time, heading away from the recreation centre and towards Evie's house. My hands are in my pockets, my chin tucked into my jacket – and I suppose it's the fact that I'm not really looking where I'm going that almost makes me miss what's in front of me.

The Macklebury Wine Store sits on a corner where I'm fairly sure there used to be a pub. There's a dimly lit sign over the door but it's the sandwich board on the street that I nearly fall over in my hurry to get out of the cold. Something about it seems familiar but in a way I can't quite process. Lots of things feel the same but different.

I carry on past to where there's a shop called Vape World on the opposite corner of the street. Two men are standing outside, leaning on a wall and defying the temperature as they send plumes of fruity-smelling guff into the air. I'm past them when I stop and turn back. It doesn't take long for me to make up my mind, which is when I re-cross the road and head into The Wine Store.

# EIGHTEEN

The bell over the door jangles as I head inside and the woman behind the counter looks up from her phone to see who's there.

Joanne's hair is longer than it was in her Facebook photo – but it's undeniably her. Now she's here in front of me, I can picture her arguing with Mr Wilson about her denim jacket and how it was unfair that she was going to be sent home for breaching the school's uniform policy.

Of everyone I've run into since returning, Joanne is the person who seems to have changed the least. Her freckles give her youth and it's almost as if the past twenty years haven't happened. She blinks at me, holding the stare for a fraction longer than feels normal, probably trying to place who I am.

'Hi,' she says, although it's more of a general greeting to anyone who might have come into the shop. I'm so used to living in North America that I'm expecting a five-minute speech about what's on special this week and then some questions about whether I need help and how my day is going.

The simple act of going into a shop can be thoroughly exhausting – but Joanne offers none of this and I'm so taken that I accidentally mumble a confused-sounding 'oh' before I'm aware of what I'm doing.

She doesn't seem to notice and so I mooch around the store, picking up a few bottles, examining the labels, and then returning them – as if I have a plan. After a loop of the store, I end up back at the front with a bottle of Johnnie Walker, which I place on the counter.

Joanne asks if I want anything else and then scans the barcode, before I pay with my card. She's handing me the bag when I stop and squint towards her.

'Joanne, isn't it?' I say, trying to sound casual.

Her eyes narrow and I can sense her searching for a name.

'Harry,' I add. 'Harry Curtis. We were in the same year at school.'

She begins to nod along. 'Right, yeah… I remember you.'

'I've been living in Canada,' I say, holding up the bottle. 'I'm back for Christmas.'

'Welcome home,' she says, with the gentlest of smiles.

'I was expecting to be back for a wedding,' I say, forcing enthusiasm that isn't really me. 'I was waiting on an invite…'

It's a gamble, a naughty one, and – for a moment – it feels as if Joanne is about to tell me to get lost. Her brow furrows as she presses her lips together.

'I forgot you and Rich used to be friends,' she says in a far more kindly tone than I deserve. 'I didn't realise you were still in contact.'

'Not regularly but here and there. We message more than we talk.' I nod at her phone. 'It's so much easier nowadays than when we were kids.'

She glances to her phone and then shifts it to the side of the counter.

'What happened to you two?' I say, still forcing the cheeriness.

Joanne eyes me with suspicion for which it's hard to blame her. I know I'm pushing my luck – but that outright turns to crushing guilt as she slumps backwards onto a stool.

'Have you heard what happened to him these past few days?' she says.

'Couldn't miss it.'

'I can't believe it. They're saying he killed our old year head – and then people are talking about Graham from back in the day. It's ridiculous. That's not who he is.'

'I was with him,' I say. 'Back when we found Graham. We found him together.'

Joanne breathes in through her nose, watching me as if the memory is returning. 'I don't know what to make of it all.'

'Me either.'

She sighs loudly and glances away towards the door, which is closed. 'Did Rich tell you we'd broken up?'

I shake my head and she frowns a tiny amount before continuing. 'If you're friends, I don't want to say bad things about him.'

'How much worse can they be compared to what's happening now?'

'True…' She stares past me towards the empty shop. 'I guess he was just angry all the time after he fell out with his dad. He'd say he didn't care that they hadn't spoken for a year – but it was all front. The longer it went on, the worse he got.'

I'm speechless for a moment. In the time I've spent with Paige, Oliver and Richard's family, there was no explicit mention of any fall-out between Richard and his dad – let alone not speaking for an entire year.

'Why did they fall out?' I ask.

Joanne shakes her head. 'I was wondering if you knew. It might have been easier to put in a message to someone you don't really see.'

'I didn't know anything like that. The last time we messaged back and forth was when they announced the World Cup would be partly held in Canada. We were thinking about looking into tickets and I said he could stay with me.'

Joanne reaches for an e-cigarette that's on the counter. She picks it up and starts to roll it between her fingers.

'He never told me why they fell out. You know what he and his dad are like. They're so similar to the point that they both became accountants. They were both too proud to make it up. Rich never used to work late – but he'd suddenly be at his office all hours. I thought he might be having an affair – but I went down there a few times and he'd be inside, sitting at a desk in front of a computer with all the lights off. It affected him so badly.'

'That must have been a big argument with him and his dad…?'

Joanne gazes towards the e-cigarette and then her eyes flick towards the door.

'If I ever asked, Rich would either go silent or start yelling. It wasn't worth it in the end. I talked to his mum about it but I don't think she knew why they'd fallen out, either. If she did, then she didn't want to tell me. Rich and I were living together at the time but I moved back to my mum's for a while. I thought the time apart might bring us back but…' She tails off and then adds: 'He didn't even text. He just let me go.'

She slumps a little lower on the stool, her head dipped to her chest.

'I'm really sorry,' I say – meaning it as much for this deception as anything else.

'It's not your fault, is it? You've come back for Christmas and, suddenly, all this is going on.' She stops for a breath and then adds: 'Have you seen him since you got back?'

'Briefly. I was in court this morning – but he was only there a few minutes.'

'How did he look?'

'Tired but otherwise good. His mum said he was looking well.'

'Did his dad go to court?'

I shake my head – and it's only now that it makes sense why he wasn't there. Or it makes sense to some degree. It must have been quite the falling out if he wasn't even in court to see his son, who's on a murder charge.

'The police came to Mum's house earlier,' Joanne says.

'For you?'

A nod. 'They asked why Rich and I had broken up. They seemed to think we'd had some sort of huge fight. They asked if he'd ever been violent.'

She looks up and locks eyes.

'He hasn't,' she says. 'Ever. Even when he was angry about his dad.'

'Did the police believe that?'

'I have no idea. They asked about Wilson and whether Rich had something against him.'

'What did you say?'

'The truth – that we were together for close to three years and that Rich hadn't mentioned Wilson in all that time. He was nobody to us. An ex-teacher that neither of us had given a second thought to.' She nods at me. 'Did he ever mention Wilson to you?'

'I don't think we've had a conversation about any teachers since the day we left school.'

Joanne thumps the counter. 'Exactly! That's why I don't understand any of this.'

I'm not sure what to say. Everyone seems as bemused as the next person.

'Do you remember when Wilson sent me home for wearing a leather jacket?'

I look up to Joanne who's pointing towards a leather jacket that's hanging from a hook behind the counter.

'I thought it was denim?' I say.

'It's that exact one.' She's still pointing towards the leather jacket. 'It was vintage then and it's even more so now. Not that he wanted to listen. I'd completely forgotten about that until I heard Wilson was dead. Funny the things you remember, isn't it?'

It's not really a question but it seems to snap Joanne back into the shop and the present. She pushes herself off the stool until she's standing and then points past me towards the rest of the shop. 'Was there anything else, or…?'

I hold up the bottle in the bag. 'Just this.'

A sad smile fills Joanne's face as I take a step towards the door. I have an urge to tell her everything will be okay – except I have no way of knowing that, nor why I'd want to say it.

I'm at the door when Joanne calls after me. When I turn, she has her phone in her hand once more.

'Merry Christmas,' she says.

'Same to you.'

I turn and head out, letting the door swing closed behind me as I wonder quite what went on between Richard and his dad.

# NINETEEN

I am at the end of the path leading to Evie's house when my phone starts to buzz. When I fish it from my pocket, there's a WhatsApp audio call coming from Oliver, which is immediately strange as I never gave him my number.

When I answer, Oliver says my name as if he's unsure whether he has the right person, before he explains that it's 'Rich's brother'. It's as if I might have forgotten who he is. I ask if there's news about Richard but Oliver brushes this off with a swift 'no'.

He continues without giving me a chance to say anything more: 'I was wondering if you had more time to think about when the two of you found Graham,' he says.

It's abrupt and unexpected. I've thought of little else except Richard and me finding Graham – and yet I remember no more than I did yesterday.

'I've not come up with anything,' I reply. 'But I did hear Richard had a big fall out with his dad. I wondered if that has anything to do with all this…?'

There's a silence that lasts so long I have to check the screen to make sure the call hasn't dropped.

'Who told you that?' Oliver says eventually.

'I heard it around…'

There's another pause, which I choose to break this time.

'Have you heard anything more about Richard getting bail?'

'No…' There's a pause and then it's as if Oliver remembers why he called. 'I was also wondering if the police have spoken to you yet?'

'Should they have? I only landed in the country after Wilson was already dead.'

'They've been talking to lots of people over the past few days – about Wilson *and* Graham. They're bound to come to you sooner or later.'

'Do they even know I'm back?'

'Probably.'

'But it's something that happened twenty years ago. I told them everything I knew then. I don't know what they'd expect me to remember now that I didn't right after it happened.'

'I agree with you. I'm just saying that you might want to prepare yourself.'

The hand holding my phone is starting to stiffen in the winter's night and the needles are back poking at my face.

'Is there anything else?' I ask.

Oliver clears his throat far too loudly for someone who's holding a phone. 'There's one other thing,' he says. 'There's a chance we might be able to visit Rich in prison tomorrow. Do you fancy it?'

It takes me a couple of seconds to realise what he's asking.

'Aren't visitors limited?' I ask. 'Surely your mum or someone who's family should go? I've not seen him in years.'

'Dad won't go – and Mum had a few minutes with him today. I was thinking the two of you might be able to talk about things from a different angle than any of us.'

'Talk about what things?'

'Graham. Wilson. Have you seen what people are saying online? Everyone thinks Rich is some sort of serial killer.'

'That doesn't mean the police do.'

'Did you see what that officer said on the court steps earlier? He could have ruled it out – but he didn't. If the police are going to come at Rich about what happened to Graham then who better to refresh his memory than the person who was there with him?'

Oliver makes it sound obvious… as if Richard and I are used to cosy chats about the darkest moment of our lives. We didn't have them at the time, let alone in these years since. I want to say no but it feels like an honest request that might be coming from Richard's mother as much as it is his brother.

As if sensing the reluctance, Oliver keeps talking. 'Have a think about it overnight,' he says. 'I can message you in the morning.'

'Okay.'

'Great. We'll talk then.'

The line goes dead and it takes me a few seconds to process everything before I re-pocket my phone. I try to work my mind around Oliver's logic. For now, Richard has been charged with a murder that happened while I was out of the country. I'm not sure why his family are so focused on something else that – for now – he hasn't been charged with. The only thing I can come up with is that Richard's solicitor might have tipped them off to something I don't yet know.

With that on my mind, I hurry to Evie's front door and fumble through my keys until I find the right one.

It's warm inside the house, sending memories surging of the way Mum would always win the battle of the thermostat when it came to our childhood. Dad would preach prudence and energy costs – but Mum would say she didn't want to be cold and that was that. It was common for me to wear shorts inside during the winter, even when it was below freezing outside.

I move through the house into the living room, where Evie is sitting on the sofa, with a laptop on her knee. She's wearing glasses that I didn't know she needed and her fingers are poised over the keyboard.

'I was starting to think you'd moved out as quickly as you moved in.' There's a definite edge to her words.

I offer her the bag I got at The Wine Store and she puts down the laptop to take it.

'Christmas present,' I say.

She reaches in and pulls out the bottle of Johnnie Walker. 'I don't drink whisky,' she says, before placing it on the sofa at her side. 'But I will take it for the secret Santa at work.' A beat. 'I've not got you anything – and it's not Christmas for two weeks yet.'

'You don't need to get me anything.'

'That's handy, because I wasn't planning on it.' She says this with a smile. A truth.

I sit on one of the armchairs and Evie peers over her glasses towards me, before resuming typing. It takes me a minute or two to realise why things feel odd. There is no distraction of music or TV in the background and no sound from the road outside. A city has a constant buzz that simply isn't present here.

I get out my phone and load the CTV and Global websites to scan through the news from Toronto. When I first moved there, I found it fascinating to read about the things that people would obsess about in a different place. Every other day, there would be something about a crash on the Gardiner or 401 highways. Problems around things like Airbnb and Uber would get a daily airing and the weather was a constant topic of interest.

As I scan today's headlines, it seems as if little has changed and I realise I take in almost nothing as I read. Instead, I drift back to here and the articles about Mr Wilson's killing.

There has been another post on the Macklebury Facebook page, with a link to a piece about his teaching career. I don't bother to read that but I do register the comments underneath – almost none of which contains any positivity. Someone again names Richard as the singular boy who found Graham's body, while the next person wants to know if the police are looking into that, too.

The other thing I notice is that there isn't a single positive comment about Wilson himself. I can't be certain but I would guess that, when a teacher dies, there would be a selection of students who would leave kindly RIP messages.

Not here.

Nobody says anything negative about Wilson – but there is no praise or well-wishes, either.

I stop reading as there's a loud bump from the adjoining wall that connects to Paige's old house. Evie's fingers stop typing as she looks across towards the unseen source of the noise. She says nothing, then, twenty seconds later, there is another *whump* that's louder than the first.

'Does that happen often?' I ask.

'There's always some sort of noise from next door. You'll find out if you stay here for any length of time.'

Evie resumes the clicking of her keyboard and it's hard to tell if that was a dig about me not being around, or Paige's mother for being noisy. It's possibly both.

*Click-click-click-click.*

'What are you working on?'

I try to sound interested and Evie glances up to me, even though her fingers continue to type. 'Work,' she says, before turning her attention back to the screen.

I wait, wondering if there might be more, except that there isn't. We're brother and sister but blood is the only thing that links us. We might as well be strangers.

'I'm going to read in bed,' I say.

Evie's stare doesn't leave her screen: 'Have a good night.'

Upstairs, and my room is untouched. My suitcase is still open on the floor, with my clothes starting to spread as I create clean and dirty piles.

I sit on the bed and google 'Oxy', which leads me to OxyContin and oxycodone. When Paige told me this is what she was buying, I only had a vague idea of it being some kind of painkiller – and, more importantly, what it could do.

The searches leave me with little doubt.

It's a strong painkiller which, in pill form, releases over time. Addicts get around this by crushing the pills and snorting the powder, which gives what's described as a 'euphoric high'.

I suppose that explains the powder around Paige's nose – plus the way she can sometimes feel as if she's directing everything, while, at other times, it's as if her body is in the room but *she* isn't.

The link says that it's easy to get addicted to Oxy – and that a lot of people first get the pills through legitimate means but then get hooked. That leaves me wondering if this is what happened with Paige. She did talk about a prescription from a doctor, although I can't work out if that was some sort of cover story.

There's another *thump* from the adjoining wall that's a lot quieter this time and more the sort of general sound that might bleed between adjoined houses.

Paige's bedroom was on the other side of the wall that my bed is against. All these years on, there feels something a little creepy about that, even though it wasn't something we manufactured and even though neither of us thought too much of it at the time.

In the evenings, we would sometimes tap on the wall to one another. It wasn't quite a system of Morse code, or even any specific message, more something to let the other know that someone was there. Sometimes, I would hear Paige and her mother raging at one another and then there would be a loud smash. I would spend hours up here, gently tapping the wall and hoping to hear a sound back so that I'd know she was safe.

I stare at the wall, *touch* it with my palm, and it all feels so close that I could be fourteen again. Before Graham's body, before Paige started seeing Oliver.

Before, before, before…

I lie back on the bed and close my eyes, listening to the sounds of the house. Evie's hammering fingers echo up the stairs but, aside from that, there's the wonderfully familiar clink of the heating pipes in the walls around me.

In the past, jet lag has hit hard and this has to be the only time where I've landed in a place and been able to function right away. Paige has to be a big part of that because, from the time she met me on the street, we were off on a mission.

Then I remember the 'euphoric high' from her pills and it's hard to see the past few days as anything other than me being a part of her highs.

I open my eyes and look at the time on my phone, which shows a little after half past eight. It's not particularly late but it does feel good to rest. To close my eyes again…

The curtains are open and the light of the moon soaks through, leaving everything in my room a hazy blue. I'm in the same clothes from earlier and, when I check my phone, it's twenty-five past midnight.

I try to remember which lights were on when I decided I could get away with simply resting my eyes. At the moment, the only one shining is the lamp at the side of the bed, though the light is facing directly down to create a spotlight on the carpet. I thought the main light might have been on but, if it was, then it's off now.

My head is groggy and everything feels sluggish as I pull myself around into a sitting position and start to pull at my top in order to get it off. I slept in my clothes at Paige's flat the night before and don't fancy a repeat tonight.

I have one arm out when there's a bang on the wall. I stop to listen – frozen in position and straining to hear. When Paige lived next door, bumps in the night could be followed by her turning up at my door the following morning with bruises on her arms or legs. Perhaps even a black eye. It never meant anything good.

There's silence now.

Stillness.

And then, suddenly, there is a much louder second bump, which is immediately followed by a shrill, howling scream.

# TWENTY

I pull my clothes back on properly and then head onto the landing. A small night light is connected to the plug socket at the top of the stairs, which casts a gentle white glow across the carpet.

Evie's bedroom door is closed, which isn't a surprise considering the time. I wait for a moment, listening to see if she's going to react to the scream from next door.

Silence.

Evie has always been a heavy sleeper.

I edge quietly down the stairs and, when I get to the bottom, type a nine into my phone as I consider calling the police. There was only one scream – but is that enough by itself? In the old days, there would be more noise than that on a near nightly basis.

I exit out of the call and instead use the phone's flashlight to find my shoes on the rack in the hall. I unfasten the front door and then latch it so I can't be locked out, before stepping out onto the frosty path.

It's as cold as I can ever remember Macklebury being. The mist hangs low and I can feel my bones rattling as I keep walking until I'm halfway towards the pavement. When I turn back, the curtains are wide and there are lights on inside Paige's mother's home. I look both ways along the road and it's the only house where there are any signs of someone being up. A dusting of frost coats the road and the pavements and the bare bushes and trees are again white.

Evie's house has gravel on either side of the path – and I crunch onto it, heading towards the neighbouring house. Although the curtains are open and the lights on, I can't actually see anyone inside.

There's a low wire fence that separates the two properties, although it's more of a symbolic border considering it only comes up to my ankles. I have a foot raised, about to step over it, when there's a second scream.

I freeze, listening…

This one is more muffled than the previous. It sounds as if it's coming from upstairs, possibly towards the back of Paige's mum's house – but it's difficult to know. I spin around, expecting more lights to go on around the street – but there's nothing.

With a quick hop, I'm over the fence and at the front door to Paige's old house. I try the handle just in case – but it's locked – and there is silence once more. I head to the front window and peer into the living room – but there's nobody in sight.

I take out my phone, ready to call the police. I almost do it, except, this time, I call someone else.


Paige hurries along the same street in the same thin jacket she's been wearing since I saw her on the High Street. She's taken barely fifteen minutes to get here and, in the meantime, I've gone inside to get my full winter coat – which is offering little protection against the icy night.

'Have you heard anything since you called me?' Paige asks, as she reaches me.

'No. I've been waiting here. I thought about calling the police.'

She gives me a stare that's colder than the weather. 'You didn't, did you?'

'No.'

I follow Paige along the path leading to her mother's house and she fishes in her pocket for a key, before opening the front door and heading in. I trail behind as she calls a hesitant 'Mum...?' into the silent void.

The house is cold, with a chill creeping through the hall that seems to have no regard for layers. There's a radiator near the door but, when I touch it, it's icier than outside. Even after closing the front door, I can see my breath.

When I turn, Paige is already on the third step, as if this isn't the first time she's had to do this. She hurries upstairs as I try to keep pace. The house is a mirror of Evie's – except it's more of an evil twin. Evie's is pristine and modern, while this is barren and dirty. There is carpet on the stairs but it's patchy, with the floorboards showing through. That matches the ripped wallpaper and scratched skirting boards that line the route upwards. There are empty shelves loosely attached to the walls – but the layer of dust is so thick that it visibly bounces to match the vibrations of us moving. The air is hard to breathe, like the cloud that puffs up when emptying a vacuum.

Paige heads into the bedroom that was once hers, the one that shares a wall with mine. In another universe it could be my room, except that it couldn't be more different. There are bare floorboards and paint-scratched walls. The only piece of furniture, if it can be called that, is a double mattress on the floor. It's even colder here and, when I look towards the window, it's wide open.

A single sheet is splayed across the mattress, with a pair of bare, hairy legs poking out the side. Paige crouches next to the makeshift bed and nudges aside the sheet to reveal a woman that, at first, I don't recognise – even though it can only be one person.

Her mother is nothing like the last time I last saw her. She is missing clumps of hair from her head, which leaves her with thinning grey strands covering bald patches. It's as if she's shrunk, with her entire body shrivelling into itself. She's bony and angular, with eyes that have sunken into her skull. She barely looks like a real person, more a CGI villain in a fantasy movie. I'm not a particularly strong man – but she's so emaciated that I suspect I could pick her up one-handed.

Paige pulls her mother into a sitting position and then slaps her hard across the face. A crack reverberates around the desolate room, bouncing from the floorboards and making it sound like it happens twice. Her mum starts to fall sideways but Paige holds onto her, keeping her upright.

'Wake up, Mum,' Paige snaps.

Her mother's eyelids flutter but her eyes roll back into her head. Paige slaps her again, harder this time. I wince at the sound and the swiftness of the violence.

The whites of the woman's eyes roll forward, leaving her staring unfocused towards her daughter. This is barely any consolation to Paige, who pushes her mum back onto the bed and hauls herself up. 'God's sake, Mum. How many times?'

She turns and takes in the room, which is scattered with Rizla papers, at least four lighters, and little else.

'We have to get her in the bath,' Paige says – although it takes me a moment to process the 'we' part of her sentence.

The two of us end up each hooking an arm under Paige's mother and hauling her up. Even though she's a bag of bones and surely can't weigh very much, I didn't realise how heavy a *dead* weight can be. She slumps towards the ground, eyes closed, offering no help at all as we drag her out of the room, along the hall, and into the filthy bathroom.

In the house next door, Evie has ripped out the bath and replaced it with a modern shower and wet-room drainage. Here, the original bath is still in place. It has to be fifty years old minimum, and the ceramic surface is stained with a black-grey mould that clings to the surface like a spider's web. I try to avoid gagging, although Paige seems unaffected. She asks me to open a window and, for once, the blast of cold is welcomed as it offers a brief respite from the bleakness of the bathroom.

I turn my back as Paige starts undressing her mother and then, as I hear the water hit the bottom of the bath, I leave the room and close the door. That alone is nothing like enough to drown the soundtrack of Paige swearing as she tries to bathe her mum.

It feels a long, long way from my cosy apartment close to a city centre. I'd welcome the roar of middle-of-the-night sirens compared to this.

As the volume of Paige's frustration grows, I head back along the hall and into the bedroom. The ceiling is mottled with black and brown patches and, despite the open window, the smell of tobacco cloys. A single light bulb dangles from a cord attached to the ceiling, though there is no shade.

As I go around the room, tidying the Rizla papers into a pile, I find two small baggies filled with a green-black powder. It looks like marijuana but doesn't smell much like anything. The zip ties are open on the bags and I seal them, more through convention than anything else, and then spin as the door creaks and Paige appears behind me. Her jacket is off and her sleeves rolled up, plus there's a large wet patch across her middle.

'I've left Mum on the toilet,' she says.

'Aren't you cold? You're soaking.'

Paige glances down at herself but then dismisses it with a shake of the head. She reaches for the baggies, eyes the contents, and then stuffs both into her pockets.

'What is it?' I ask.

'They call it Super-K around here. Synthetic weed. It's not grown; someone in a lab makes it.'

'Isn't weed supposed to mellow you out?'

'Not this stuff. It's much stronger than anything organic. Some people hallucinate or get paranoid. They scream at nothing. Some just sleep, or drift lifelessly around, like a zombie. Almost all the homeless people you see around town are on it.'

I picture the people I've seen in doorways since getting back. The ones moaning to themselves, or shouting at the invisible.

'Where does it come from?' I ask.

Paige looks up and then quickly turns away. I know the answer without her needing to say.

'Pete…?'

She doesn't reply.

'I gave him money,' I add.

The weight of handing over the cash on the street suddenly starts to hit as Paige replies with a dismissive: 'I told you not to.'

I want to ask her what I've contributed to, except there's no chance because Paige's mum starts to call for her from the bathroom.

I'm dreading what might await us inside – but Paige's mother is dressed and semi-coherent as we follow her cries into the bathroom and help her back to the mattress. We gently lay her down and, as her head sinks into the almost flat surface, her eyes suddenly focus onto me.

'Francis…?' she says.

'No, Mum,' Paige replies for me. 'It's not.'

Paige rocks her mother onto her side and the pair of us step back and watch for a few moments. As best I can tell, her mum falls instantly to sleep.

It's only when we're out of the room, with the door closed, that Paige tells me Francis is her dad.

'He died when I was seven,' she adds. 'That was before we moved here.'

She would have definitely told me that before but there's a matter-of-fact tone now that makes it all sound so routine.

Paige leads me downstairs, into a grubby kitchen that matches the rest of the house. She turns on the tap and drinks from her cupped palms, before turning it off again.

'I wouldn't risk the mugs in this house,' she says, as if that explains it.

'What are you going to do with the baggies?'

Paige hesitates for a moment, although I quickly realise it's because she's trying to find something with which to dry her hands. She can't see anything – and neither can I, so she ends up shaking them over the sink. For a moment, I think she's going to use this as an excuse not to answer but then she does.

'Mum has cancer,' she says, taking them out of her pocket. 'She's refusing all treatment and they gave her six months to live about nine months back, so what the hell?'

She lays both bags on the draining board and steps away.

'What's it going to do?' she adds. 'Kill her?'

There's grit and fire in Paige's voice. Borderline rage.

'Sometimes it feels like half the town is on this stuff,' she says. 'Super-K?'

'That or something like it.'

I wait a second and then risk it. 'Are you?'

Paige won't catch my eye and there's a gap before her quiet reply comes. 'No.' She looks up now, facing me. 'Thanks for the call. Sometimes I wonder if she might… choke on her own vomit, I suppose. That sort of thing. I keep thinking I'll come in one day and that will be that.'

It doesn't feel as if there's anything to say to that and so I keep quiet.

'What are you doing tomorrow?' Paige asks.

The change of subject, and the earliest of hours, leaves me momentarily perplexed until I remember.

'I might be visiting Richard in prison.'

Her eyebrows shoot up: 'Really?'

'Oliver called me. I don't know how he got my number or details but he said he thought I might be better visiting to see if Richard and I can jog one another's memories about Graham.'

'Why would they want you to do that?'

'I'm not sure. I wonder if the solicitor has tipped them off to say that he expects Richard to be charged? I don't think I want to do it – but I don't think I can say no.'

Paige starts to bite one of her nails and she stands with her mouth open, listening as if she's heard something above. A few seconds pass until her attention returns to the room.

'Did you know Richard fell out with his dad?' I ask.

'Has he?'

'That's what Joanne told me.'

'*Joanne?* Where did you run into her?'

'The wine place where she works.'

Paige takes a second to process this, probably wondering how all the pieces came together. We've never spoken about Joanne or Richard's apparent engagement. I wonder whether she knew and, if so, if she's kept it quiet for a reason. Perhaps she thought I knew and we've talked around it without realising?

'Why did Richard fall out with his dad?' Paige asks.

'Joanne didn't know. She did say it made Richard so angry and resentful that he ended up burying himself in work and they broke up.'

'I wondered what happened with them. I didn't want to ask Richard because it was fairly obvious he didn't want to talk about it.'

'I also ran into Martin this evening.'

This gets more of a reaction, as if a cloud has passed across Paige's face.

'What did you talk to him about?'

She speaks slowly, hesitantly, expecting the worst. I think of him telling me that Paige was sleeping around for money. I've told myself it must have been a bitter lie because I don't think I can let myself believe anything else. Sometimes it's better not to know. Better not to ask.

'Nothing,' I say, figuring it's for the best.

Paige's eyes narrow but she doesn't question this.

'We said "hi",' I add, 'and then we went on our way.'

# TWENTY-ONE

Evie is already in the kitchen when I get down the next morning. She's dressed for work and sitting at the breakfast bar, with her juice and a small yoghurt pot in front of her. The kitchen smells of coffee and Evie nods across to the counter, where a French press is two-thirds empty. Or, as Liane would point out to me, one-third full.

'Were you up in the night?' she says. 'I thought—' Evie stops herself as Paige trails in behind me and stops in the doorway.

'It's not like that,' I say.

Evie watches Paige for a second and then turns to me. 'I'm not Mum and Dad, telling you what you can and can't do under their roof.'

'Paige came over because I heard her mum screaming through the wall from next door. We went across to check on her.'

A smile was beginning to tease across Evie's lips but this isn't what she expected. She turns back to Paige. 'Everything okay?'

'As much as ever.'

'Every time I see her, she tells me how much longer she's lived than the doctors reckoned.'

'She takes pride in outliving the timeframes. I think she wants them to tell her five years, just to make a competition of it.'

Nobody laughs and Evie picks up her mug, before draining the coffee. She places that into the dishwasher, then washes out the yoghurt pot, before dropping that in the recycling.

'I have to get to work,' she says, largely talking to Paige. 'I hope everything works out with your mum. I've told her she can knock on the door any time she wants.'

'I don't think she wants anyone's help – whether it's a doctor's, or mine.'

Evie had started to leave the kitchen but she stops, seemingly considers saying something, but then decides against it and continues through to the hall. There's a rustle of a coat, a clink of some keys, the thump of the door – and then she's gone.

'I don't think your sister likes me,' Paige says.

'You're half right – I don't think she particularly likes anyone.'

'Did you bully her too much as a kid?'

'If anything, she bullied me. Thing is, Evie's always been into her work. She was talking about breaking into a man's world and glass ceilings before I understood what she meant.'

'She must have time for things other than work…?'

'You know her as well as I do. You've probably talked to her more in the past few years than me.'

I want to change the subject and end up searching through the cupboards until I find the cereal. There are no boxes; with everything tipped into plastic keep-tight tubs, each with an individual measuring scoop inside.

'Do you want breakfast?' I ask.

'I don't eat in the mornings.'

I keep hunting until I find the bread. It's in what I thought was an anonymous wooden block – but what turns out to be a bread bin with no handle.

It's not pre-sliced but there is a serrated knife next to the loaf, so I cut myself two slices and then go hunting for a toaster, which I find unplugged and buried in a cupboard, next to a rice cooker.

'Evie won't like that,' Paige says, as she points to the crumbs on the counter.

I brush everything up with my hands and dump it into the sink, then sit and wait. It's hard to know where this overexuberant cleanliness and tidying comes from. My sister and I grew up in the same house – *this* house – and yet we couldn't be more different in our outlook to things being in places.

There's an impish smile on Paige's face. 'The knife wasn't there,' she says.

I move it from the counter back to the bread bin, only for Paige to point out that there are now crumbs on the floor. I give her a glare but she laughs as I fuss around for a dustpan. By the time all that's done, the toast pops – although I then struggle to find a plate. I'm about to start eating when Paige reminds me that the toaster was in the cupboard, not on the side.

The buzzing of my phone is a welcome relief, except for when I see Oliver's name on the screen. I show it to Paige and then press to answer.

'You still on for the visit?' Oliver speaks with little hint of a greeting – and no acknowledgement that, technically, I hadn't agreed. I don't get a chance to point that out, because he quickly adds: 'I'm leaving in fifteen minutes. If you message me an address, I'll grab you on the way round.'

I already knew there was no option but I somehow feel more penned in than I did before.

'See you soon,' I say – and then I hang up.

# TWENTY-TWO

The visiting area of the prison is not what I'd expected, although – with that – I guess that's because I've watched far too many US TV shows. There is no glass divider, with a telephone to talk from side to side – and no surly guard standing nearby with a baton at the ready.

Instead, it is more of a school canteen – but without the annoying, screaming children. It's a wide, echoing hall that's filled with tables and chairs that are bolted to the floor. It could probably fit fifty or sixty people in total, except, for now, there is only one.

Me.

I thought Oliver and I would be seeing Richard together but that was apparently never the plan. Not for Oliver, anyway. He turned himself into my chauffeur without me realising until we got to the prison. He ushered me onwards, saying only one visitor was allowed. There was no time to question who, what or why.

There are vending machines on the other side of the room and I cross to them and scan the contents, more to re-familiarise myself with British junk food as opposed to anything else. In the time I'd been away, I've forgotten about Flamin' Hot Monster Munch, not to mention Cheesy Wotsits and Roast Beef and Mustard Brannigans. There are small packets of Jaffa Cakes, Double Deckers, Topics, Boosts, and Wispas.

I have no idea why I ever left the UK.

There's a clunk and then a heavy door swings open and a guard appears who's wearing a white shirt and dark tie. There is a bunch of keys attached to his waist that rattle around like a loose screw in a jam jar.

'Can you sit?' he asks – although it's more of an order than a question.

I cross back to the table where I was before and take a seat. The guard reopens the door, says something to whoever's outside, and then two more people appear.

The first is another guard, who could be a non-identical twin of the first guy.

The second is Richard.

There's still no orange jumpsuit; instead, he's wearing something drab and grey that's at least a size too big. He looks both ways, taking in the almost empty room, and then homes in on me as the guard leads him across. I stand and offer my hand to shake but there's a moment of ungainliness as the guard has to undo Richard's cuffs to release his wrists.

I half expect to be told 'no' by the guard – but there's little objection as we shake hands. Richard leans in and we end up transitioning into an awkward double-pat-release, something I don't believe we had ever done as teenagers.

Richard slots into his chair, with me opposite, and the two guards drift away to the wall near the vending machines. The two of us spend a second or three looking at one another. He seemed trim and fit in his suit at court but here, face to face, he is a lot thinner. It feels more as if it's from a lack of food than exercise. His hair is so short at the sides that it's almost aggressive.

'Been a while,' he says.

'Are you surprised to see me?'

'Not really. My solicitor had me fill out a visitors' form yesterday and he had me put you on it.'

That's news to me and I'm unsure how to reply at first. It feels like Richard's brother, and possibly his parents, seem to know something I don't. By the time Oliver had called to ask if I wanted to come here, I was already on a list. When he sent me in by myself, it had already been decided for me.

'Oliver asked me to come,' I say. 'Something to do with… well, you know… *Graham*.'

I find myself whispering the name, although none of this seems to come as a surprise to Richard. He bats away a yawn, then a second, and then blinks away the accompanying tears.

'I saw you in court,' he says. 'How come you're back?'

'I heard what was happening and wanted to show some support.'

'You flew halfway round the world to be in court?'

A shrug. 'More or less…'

It's Richard who's short of words now. He rocks back gently in his chair and sucks in his cheeks. 'With Graham, it's just…' He glances away and then finds a spot on the floor, at which he stares. 'The police were asking me about Wilson and then, out of nothing, they brought up when we found Graham's body.'

I don't answer, largely because of the way he skipped over the 'Wilson' bit, as if being accused of *that* murder is something that happens every day.

'I don't think I spoke for about thirty seconds,' Richard continues. 'It's so crazy. It was so long ago.' He pauses, then adds: 'I didn't kill Graham. I promise. It wasn't me… I didn't kill Wilson, either. All of it is wrong. I keep trying to tell people but no one is listening.'

I let all that sit. He's spoken quickly, as if he's been waiting to get it all out. I suspect it isn't the sort of thing he'd say to his mum, for fear of worrying her too much.

'How have you been?' I ask.

Richard fights away another yawn. 'It's hard to sleep. I'm in a cell by myself but the bed is really hard and the pillow is so old, it's practically a U-shape. They never fully turn off the lights and I suppose it's just…' He tails off and yawns again. 'My solicitor says I should be in court tomorrow or the day after. He reckons I should get bail.'

'Did he actually say that?'

Richard's gaze slides sideways, betraying himself. 'Sort of…' He looks across towards the guards and the vending machines. 'Did they let you bring in any money?'

I stand, which attracts the attention of both guards, who focus their attention on me as I reach into my back pocket and remove a handful of coins.

'What would you like?'

'Chocolate – and something fizzy. Full fat, full sugar: the works.'

I cross to the machines and feed in a few pound coins, which pays for two Pepsis, a Snickers and a Dairy Milk. I hold them up to show the guards and then cross back to the table, on which I place the lot.

'All for you,' I say.

Richard smiles for the first time since he walked into the room. 'I never ate this stuff when I was outside. Now I'm in here, it's all I want.'

He pops the tab on one of the cans and then tears the top from the Dairy Milk before scoffing the first two squares.

'Do you remember when we used to get packets of McCoy's in the pub?' Richard asks. 'One of each flavour and then open them up across the table. Feast for a king.'

He has more of the chocolate and then gulps some of the drink.

'What happened?' I ask.

'With the crisps?'

I say nothing and watch as Richard shuffles uncomfortably. 'Me and Wilson argued at The Pines,' he adds.

'What about?'

Richard sighs loudly and finds his spot on the floor once more. 'It's so stupid. I was in the hotel and we sort of set eyes on one another. He'd been drinking and so had I. He said that he always knew I'd never make anything of myself.'

'Why'd he say that?'

'The drink, I guess.'

'But you were doing fine, with the accounting and everything, weren't you? Why would he even think that? Why would he *remember* you?'

There's a long pause, then a gulp.

'I did some accounting work for him a year or so ago. He found me online and I didn't realise who it was at first.'

'That still doesn't explain it.'

Richard has another drink from the can, taking up time. 'I made a mistake with his invoice. It was nothing malicious, more a typo than anything else. He paid but then spotted the error a few days later. He came to my office, shouting and demanding the money back. He was saying I was a thief and that he'd call the police. Then he was going on about how he'd leave reviews everywhere to make sure nobody ever hired me again.'

'Did you give him back the money?'

'Of course! It took a couple of days because these things do. Literally forty-eight hours – but, in that time, he left fifteen or sixteen messages on my phone and sent almost seventy messages. Anyway, I'd not seen him since then until we were at the hotel. I'd been drinking, he'd been drinking, I said some things, he said some things – and that was about it.'

'I heard you threw a punch…?'

Richard absent-mindedly flexes his fist. 'I didn't connect – and none of that means I killed him.' He thumps the table at the last part, sending a metallic rumble around the room. The guards look across towards us but neither of them move.

'Paige says Wilson suspended you when we were at school.'

Richard was reaching for the can but his hand freezes in mid-air. 'Did she?'

'She thought it might have been for a day or two.'

He frowns a little. Surprised by either the memory or the mention of Paige. 'I told the police about it. I told them about the accounts stuff as well. I'm surprised Paige remembered the suspension, though.'

'I don't remember any of it.'

'There was a fight with Pete Baker. I don't even remember why but I think he said something and I reacted. We rolled around on the field for about ten seconds – but Wilson saw it and suspended the pair of us for two days.'

Richard finishes off the can and then squeezes the sides, before putting it back on the table.

'Do you remember Pete and his three cousins?' he adds. 'I still see them around town now and then.'

It's hard to know whether Richard's asking if I *actually* remember Pete and his cousins – or if he's hinting at Pete's current business activities. There's something speculative about the way he asked.

I decide to ignore it.

'We found out something about Wilson,' I say instead. 'He was having an affair with our old geography teacher for twenty years or so. They've got a seventeen-year-old daughter. His wife kicked him out and I think he ended up on his own.'

Richard is open-mouthed for a moment and then he snorts. 'Do the police know that?'

'I'd guess so. It wasn't hard for us to find out.'

'There it is then. I bet he's got a long line of people who have it in for him. I'll make sure my solicitor knows.'

'But why were you at the hotel? I heard there was a teachers' reunion going on.'

Richard turns away again, picking up the rest of the Dairy Milk as he does. 'Just in the area.'

'You were seen waiting outside after they'd thrown you out for fighting.'

He spins back, eyes focused with suspicion: 'Who told you that?'

'Someone who works there. The staff saw you. I think that's why you were arrested.'

Richard fills his mouth with the remainder of the chocolate and chews slowly and deliberately. When he's finished, he reaches for the second Pepsi can. 'I wasn't waiting for Wilson.'

'Does that mean you were waiting for someone else?'

Richard cracks open the second can and sips. I watch him breathe in and out, and can see in the steel of his stare that I'm not going to get a reply.

Between Paige, me and him, Richard was always the most stubborn. He was the person who did the one thing he said he always would: follow in his father's footsteps by becoming an accountant. Not that there's anything wrong with that but it feels so small now. It's a goal with so little ambition, but it wasn't like that then. Wanting to be like his father was a lofty desire. I fell into university and whatever came after that. Paige did her thing. So did Evie. It was only Richard who did what he said he was going to do.

'My solicitor says there's no evidence,' Richard says. He sounds more confident now. Excited, even. 'The only reason I'm being held is because the argument was witnessed in the hotel. I'm the one who told the police about the accounting mix-up. I told Oliver the other day that they'd probably raid my flat again to get the files. None of that is proof, though. My solicitor said it was a single stab wound to his heart – but they can't have any physical evidence because I wasn't there. He reckons they don't even have the weapon. When he saw me earlier, he said that it was one of the weakest cases he's ever heard of. He thought the only reason I'm still here is because of the Graham thing from years ago.'

As Richard focuses back on me, I realise this is why I'm here. Richard and his solicitor – which, by proxy, means his family – are convinced the Wilson charge will go away. The wild card is if the police really do think Richard might have had something to do with Graham's death. No wonder that's been their focus. No wonder I was sent in alone.

'Have the police spoken to you yet?' he asks.

'No. I didn't think I was on their radar as being back.'

'You're bound to be. You were in court.'

I can feel the puzzle pieces sliding into place. Oliver told Paige about the court date, knowing she would tell me – and that we'd likely go. That's why neither Oliver nor his mother complained about us sitting with them in the public gallery. They wanted us to be there. Or, more to the point, they wanted *me* to be.

Richard's right: the police will definitely know I'm back.

It feels as if I've been used – except I can't figure out what for.

'Can you believe it?' I say.

'What?'

'That, after all this time, Graham is still a part of our lives. We've never escaped him. Imagine how different it would have been if we'd walked home the other way, or if we'd not been paying attention…'

For the first time since he was brought through, Richard falters. He puts the can back on the table and presses forward, arching his back. He stands and stretches, acknowledging the guards as he does so.

When he sits, the eye contact is gone again. 'I still think of Graham's body most days. Not *every* day… not any longer. But I'll be doing something unrelated and it'll pop into my head. It's always the colour of dried blood on the ground. I always thought blood was red but that was black.'

I close my eyes and can still see the colour. Not red and perhaps not black. Something different that I've never again seen.

'I remember the blood, too,' I say. 'But it's also his face. That waxy skin, like it was him but… not him.'

We take deep breaths together and there's something within me that feels relieved to be saying this. These are words that only Richard and I can fully understand.

Richard sinks, resting his elbows on the table and his head in his hands. 'How could they think I did it?' he says. 'We were sixteen and it's not like I was some massive overdeveloped kid with muscles and a beard.'

'I guess if you hit someone in the back of the head with a rock, you don't have to be big…'

Richard looks up to me and his eyes are red. It's only his look of betrayal that makes me realise what I've said.

'I didn't mean it like that,' I add quickly. 'I was talking hypothetically. The blunt object they always talked about, remember…?'

Richard pushes himself up and rests against the back of the seat once more. I think he's given me the benefit of the doubt.

'My solicitor says there's nothing in the whole Graham thing. I've not been charged with anything and he thinks it's all speculation based upon the circumstances. They didn't have evidence then – and it was eighteen years ago, so they can hardly have it now. And, besides, I *want* them to find evidence. I didn't do it, so it wouldn't point to me.'

'What I don't understand is when they think it might have happened with you and Graham.'

'I guess either before school, or that I snuck out, or something. I have no idea. I do remember walking on my own that morning – but it only stands out because we were together later on. They've not asked about that yet but it'll all be in the files.'

Richard stops for a drink and then opens the Snickers.

'Do you actually remember finding the body?' he asks.

I open my mouth to answer and then stop as I realise the specifics of what he's said. 'You mean when *we* found it.'

'No, *you* found it. You called me over. Don't you remember?'

We stare at one another and I wait for the inevitable follow-up to say this is a weird joke – except that it doesn't come.

He's serious.

'I can't remember who found the body,' I say.

'It was definitely you. You were walking a little ahead because I'd stopped to tie my lace just before we got to the arch and was in the process of catching up. You stopped and called me – and then we were side by side looking down at the blood.'

I want to say that it isn't true, that it's not how I remember things, but Richard speaks so earnestly that I start to wonder whether it *is* true.

Perhaps I *was* ahead…?

Perhaps Richard *had* stopped to tie his lace…?

Can it really be true? It's not that my version disputes his, it's that I don't remember. It's plausible that what he says is correct.

'Why have you fallen out with your dad?'

The question is an abrupt turn and leaves Richard craning his neck back and blinking with surprise. 'What?'

'I heard you haven't spoken in a while. He wasn't in court and he didn't come today.'

Richard holds the Snickers to his mouth, using what's left to hide the lower half of his face behind. 'It's between me and him.'

'Does it have any effect on this?'

His eyes dart away and back so quickly that I almost miss it. 'No.'

It's a firm reply but that swiftness of eye movement leaves me wondering if it's the truth.

I don't get a chance to say anything because one of the guards on the far side guffaws a deliberate cough and then shouts a louder 'two minutes' to make his point.

Richard quickly glugs the can and then pulls the final third of the chocolate out of its wrapper.

'How did you hear about me being arrested all the way over in Canada?' he asks.

'Paige called me.'

'*Paige?* I thought you were going to say it was Oliver, or my solicitor.'

'It was Sunday morning my time when she called. I think she'd seen something on Facebook.'

Richard motions to put the Snickers in his mouth but stops midway. 'She's not back with Oliver, is she?'

'No – although I didn't know they'd broken up until I got here.'

'What has she told you about the break-up?'

A chill whispers its way along my spine. 'Nothing.'

'She can't get back with him.'

'I don't think your mum would allow that anyway.'

Richard drops the chocolate and grips the table, leaning in and lowering his voice. 'Will you keep an eye on her while you're in town?'

'We've been hanging around with each other a fair bit.'

'Good… it's just… they *can't* get back together.' Richard's eyes are wide and pleading.

'I don't think she—'

'I'm serious. They *can't* get back together.'

Richard thumps the table this time as he repeats the point, before glancing behind towards where one of the guards is checking his watch.

'There's something else,' Richard says quickly. 'Do you remember the thing that was never revealed about Graham? It was only us and the police who knew. I don't even think his family did.'

'Of course I remember.'

'Have you *ever* told anyone?'

'No. You?'

Richard shakes his head. 'I wonder if they'll try to use it against me if things come to it. I couldn't stop thinking about it last night.'

'Have you told your solicitor?'

Another shake: 'No one. Not ever. They told us not to.'

Footsteps break the moment as I glance over Richard's shoulder to see the guards approaching.

Richard quickly pops the remaining bit of chocolate into his mouth and starts to chew. He gets it down in record time and then offers his wrists to the guards for cuffing.

'Remember what I said about Paige. Keep an eye out for her.' He pauses and then adds a quick: 'Thanks for coming.'

I stand and watch as one guard takes Richard back towards the door adjacent to the vending machine, while the other leads me in the opposite direction.

The walk back out of the prison involves a series of clinks and clangs, plus a lot of echoing footsteps – except I focus on none of that because I realise the newest oddity about everything Richard said.

If his brother was the wronged party in the break-up, like everyone seems to think, why would Richard want me to keep an eye on Paige instead of Oliver?

# TWENTY-THREE

Oliver reaches for the air-conditioning dial of his car and cranks it up to maximum heat as he pulls out of the prison's visitors' area. In seconds, the windscreen is clear of mist and so he turns it down again. He drives without a satnav or map, heading onto a country lane and taking what I presume to be the turn towards Macklebury. Until now, I had never been out to this area of the county.

'Have you ever been in a prison before?' Oliver asks.

'No.'

'Me neither. I still haven't. Mum has done the other visits.'

Oliver slows for a bend and, perhaps worryingly, takes the racer's line through the centre as he turns. I assume he could see there was nothing on the other side, because I certainly couldn't.

'How's Rich?' he asks.

'He seems in decent spirits. Better than I thought. It sounds like his solicitor knows what he's doing.'

'Did he say much about everything?'

'Mainly that he didn't do it and that he was in the wrong place at the wrong time. I doubt it was anything his solicitor wouldn't have already shared with you.'

I let that sit with a passive-aggressive flourish that hopefully tells Oliver that I now have a decent idea of how and why I ended up here.

It's all country lanes around the prison, with high hedges lining the roads and spindly, barren trees still coated with dustings of white. Frost or snow lines the shadowed verges and I suspect it will hang around until the new year, with temperatures unlikely to climb above zero.

Oliver drives on for a short distance, taking a couple of sharp bends on the correct side of the white line and then settling in as the road widens out. We've not seen another vehicle since leaving the prison.

'Did you talk about Graham?' he asks.

'A little.'

I wait, not wanting to give too much. Oliver seemingly doesn't want to prod me too hard for information, so he takes another bend before slowing for a junction and then accelerating through it.

'What did you talk about?'

'Richard said that he remembers me finding the body first. He said he'd stopped to tie his lace and that I was a little further ahead.'

'Is that right?'

'I don't remember. It could be.'

Oliver drums his fingers on the steering wheel and then shifts gear for the next bend as we pass a sign saying that Macklebury is eighteen miles away. On these roads, it's probably another forty minutes minimum.

'Richard seems to trust his solicitor,' I say.

'Not much else he can do…'

Whatever I've said seems to have left Oliver content because he goes quiet for the next bit of the journey.

For perhaps the first time since I landed, I begin to feel genuinely tired. The gentle heat from the vents in front of me mixed with the familiarity of the surroundings has my eyelids drooping as I rest my head on the window.

The combination of being alongside Richard's brother and the dreamy, muddled state of my jet-lagged thoughts has me drifting through time again. Oliver is sixteen or seventeen months older than me and a tiny bit more than that compared to Richard. He was in the year above us at school but, despite a relatively small age gap, he always felt so much older. It was probably because of the way he and Martin looked down on us, both literally and figuratively.

There was that time when wrestling was huge – and it felt like our entire year was into it. Oliver and Martin would say it was fake, even though we already knew. They would say that comics were for babies and that, if we wanted to be grown up, we should play football and rugby like they did. I remember the pair of them carrying around copies of *FHM* or *Loaded*. They would talk about finding 'real women', not the girls at school. They would bring up graphic terms they'd read in the magazines and ask if Richard and I knew what they meant. We didn't – which they found hilarious.

Once, when the three of us were in the park together, Martin came across with Oliver and asked Paige who she fancied the most out of Richard and me. I think we were thirteen – and Martin was far more blunt with his choice of words.

The three of us looked at the floor, embarrassed, as the two bigger boys ran off laughing to themselves.

The difference between them and us wasn't even necessarily the fact they *were* older, it was that we *felt* inferior. Martin played rugby for the county and Oliver had won the 800m and 1,500m at our inter-schools championships. It felt like they were bigger, stronger, smarter, and generally *better* than we were.

At least that was the case for Richard and me.

And, perhaps, all of that was why, when we were a bit older, it was such a surprise when Richard told me Paige was going out with his older brother. I thought it was a joke – but Richard insisted Paige had been around his house on the Sunday night and that she'd spent her time in Oliver's room.

I suppose things were never quite the same after that.

My eyes are closed when Oliver next speaks. I might have dropped off because we're away from the country lanes and onto a wider A-road. There are cars on the other side of the road and the windscreen wipers are leisurely flicking back and forth to clear the spray.

'Are you and Paige…?'

Oliver is focused on the road and I jolt away from the window into a more rigid sitting position. 'Huh?'

'You and her. Are you…?'

'Of course not.'

'But she called you to come home – and you instantly came. You've been more or less inseparable ever since.'

I haven't forgotten that I'm talking to Paige's husband. Separated or not, it feels dangerous.

'It's not like that,' I say. 'We've been friends a long time. She didn't call and ask me to come back for her, it was about Richard.'

Oliver doesn't reply. He reaches to move the heating dial and then I feel him glancing towards his mirror. I know what's coming.

'Has she told you anything about me?' he asks. 'About the break-up?'

'No – and I haven't asked. I figured it was none of my business.'

There's more of a silence now. It feels pointed and deliberate. Martin told me Paige was sleeping around for money; Richard said I need to keep an eye on her and make sure she and Oliver don't reconcile. Then, by her own admission, she was fired for theft and is hooked on painkillers. There's a lot going on.

We're at the Welcome To Macklebury sign when Oliver asks where I want to be dropped off. I tell him my sister's house, which is where I was picked up, and he continues driving without reply.

The snow has almost entirely cleared now, with only a few shovelled mounds on the edges of the pavements, plus a powdering on some of the grassy areas.

Oliver has no issue with navigating the town, even though he lives on one side, with Evie's house on the other. He takes the turn for the street and is starting to slow when I reach for my seat belt.

That's when I spot the parked police car directly outside the house.

# TWENTY-FOUR

Oliver pulls in behind the police car and leaves the engine idling.

'I guess it's your moment,' he says.

I get out of the car and hesitate as I pass the police, before walking along the path towards Evie's front door. I have the key in my hand when there's a clunk of a car door and, as I look back, a man in a suit strides towards me. He's smart, with shiny shoes and gelled, curly hair. There's something rugged about him; more a look in his eyes perhaps. A sense that he doesn't suffer fools.

'Detective Constable Henderson,' he says, offering his hand towards me. 'Are you Harry Curtis?'

The handshake is unavoidable and his grip is firm.

'That's me,' I reply.

He digs into his pocket and pulls out an ID card that shows his photo. I don't pay too much attention, although it seems official. If it's fake, then he's done well to get the car as well.

'We heard you lived in Canada but might be back in the area…'

It's not really a question, so I say nothing and let him hang for a second before he continues.

'Have you got a minute?' he asks.

'Depends what for.'

I put the key in the lock and open the door, then take a step into the house.

'I'm sure you've heard about Richard Whiteside and we were wondering if we could ask you some questions about what happened with Graham Boyes.'

He glances back to the police car, where I see the face of another officer in the passenger seat.

'That was eighteen years ago.'

'We know.'

'I talked to the police a lot then. There were at least three separate interviews. There were tapes and transcripts. Don't you have those?'

'We do.'

'That's my clearest memory of what happened. I don't know why you think I'd remember something now that I didn't then.'

Henderson smiles to me in the way a mother might smile at a child who thinks he's getting his own way. 'I guess you never know what might come up. It shouldn't take up much of your time.' He looks up towards the clearly empty house. 'Unless you've got something else on…?'

I consider saying that I have a very important bit of suitcase tidying to do but there seems little point in antagonising the police.

Henderson seems to take the silence as consent. 'Is there somewhere we can go?' he asks.

The driver's side of the police car opens and a woman emerges and starts walking along the path towards us. As she does, Oliver pulls away and disappears around the bend.

'Detective Sergeant Allen,' she says as she offers her hand, which I end up shaking. 'Are we going in?' she adds, nodding past me towards the house. 'It's freezing out here.'

'It's not my house,' I say. 'It's my sister's.'

'Is she in?'

'She's at work.'

Allen pouts her lips and raises both eyebrows, making a silent point with which it's hard to argue considering I unlocked the front door and was about to go inside anyway.

'I suppose we could go to the station,' Henderson says airily. 'I think interview suite two is free today.' He turns back to me. 'Whatever's more convenient. It shouldn't take long either way…'

Like asking if I want a kick in the balls or a punch.

I hold the door wider and both officers head past me and wait at the bottom of the stairs. I lead them through to the kitchen, where any chat will be less intimate away from the family photos in the living room.

Even though Allen is the senior officer, it's Henderson who does much of the talking. He explains that the case of Graham's death has never been formally closed and that, with one of the two people who found the body having been arrested for a separate incident, they're 're-examining all angles'.

'That sounds suspiciously vague,' I reply, which gets no reaction from either officer.

Henderson runs through a lot of things I already know, largely relating to times, dates and places. After that, and without any build-up, he goes direct.

'I was wondering if you know who found the body out of you and Richard?' he asks.

'I can't remember.'

'I gather the body was under a bush – but do you know if you were in front of Richard, or at his side, or if he was the one leading…?'

'I don't remember that either. Sorry…' I turn between the officers. 'What did I say at the time?'

They glance to one another and a silent conversation happens in under a second.

Allen answers this time: 'It's not mentioned in any of the statements,' she says. 'As best we can tell, the question was never asked.'

'We were only kids. I think we were interviewed together at first, then separately.'

'Do you remember if either of you stopped to do something like tie a lace…?'

Henderson asks this matter-of-factly but it's clear he must have taken this line directly from Richard. I wonder if they know I visited him this morning. I could back him up, give some degree of credibility and say that he's right, except that I can't.

'I don't remember that.'

There's another momentary glance between the officers. I wonder if this came up at the time. Whether Richard told the police back then that he was tying his lace when I first found the body – or if it's only now.

'I know you were asked this back then,' Henderson says, 'but do you remember any sort of blunt object being in the vicinity?'

'Blunt, as in…?'

'A large rock that could've been used as a weapon… something like that.'

'You're asking me questions that, if I knew the answer, I'd have told you eighteen years ago. If I didn't see a rock then, I'm not sure how you expect me to remember it now.'

I try not to let out too much frustration but it's difficult to smother.

'I blocked out a lot of this,' I add. 'I was young and used to have nightmares. This isn't the type of thing I've spent years hanging on to.'

Without noticing, I realise I'm gripping the counter of the breakfast bar so hard that my knuckles are white. I wonder if there's some sort of trigger around 'blunt object'. It's such a nonsense term, although I do understand why the police didn't want to say the murder weapon was a 'rock', in case it wasn't. We had a school assembly not long after Graham's death, where our form tutors asked if we had any questions or concerns. A girl put up her hand to ask what a blunt object was and, from the way nobody took the piss, it became fairly obvious that nobody really knew.

'Did you and Richard walk to school that morning?' Henderson asks.

'You know I didn't…' I want them to move on but, when a silence persists, I figure I might as well go along with it. 'I had a dentist appointment that morning,' I say. 'I went to that and got to school late. We only walked home together.'

'Was there something *specific* you remember about Graham's body?'

I eye both officers, wondering what they're really asking. The word 'specific' feels so deliberate.

'Have you read the file?' I ask.

'We have.'

'So you've seen the photos?'

'Of course.'

I have to take a breath. I've not spoken about this to anyone since we found the body. The police at the time asked me not to tell my parents or friends – and I kept to that. Perhaps that's why I had nightmares, or why it feels as if this has never quite gone away?

'Graham's top was pulled up,' I say. 'There was a mark on his side. I didn't realise what it was at first.'

I breathe deeply again. The words feel like a betrayal.

'Have you seen this in the file?' I add.

It feels as if they know what I'm asking. It's Allen who replies with a gentle: 'We have.'

'There was a bite mark,' I say. 'A *human* bite. You never released that. It wasn't in any of the papers or on any of the news reports. Someone explained that, even though I'd seen it, even though there were photos and everything else, that you weren't going to release the information. I didn't understand but you said it was because, aside from Richard and me, only the killer would know about the bite.'

They both nod and, out of nothing, there's a lump in my throat. I try to swallow it but my eyes feel watery and I have to turn away to settle myself.

'I've never told anyone that,' I say. 'Not a single person. This is the first time I've said it out loud in eighteen years.'

Allen leans across the breakfast bar and touches my hand. 'You've done so well, Harry,' she says.

It could be patronising but it isn't – and the reassuring tone puts that lump right back in my throat. I tell them that I need the toilet although, in reality, it's probably more of a mumble. With the kitchen door closed, I hurry upstairs and spend a few minutes sitting on the toilet and breathing. There's an irrationality over feeling so deeply about this but it's not something I can explain.

When I get back downstairs after six or seven minutes, both officers are sitting exactly where they were – but something has changed. It's hard to pinpoint but it might be the way they're sitting. There's something more relaxed. Something freer.

'You'd be able to check the bite mark, wouldn't you?' I say. 'If you arrested someone, you could take a cast of their teeth and compare…?'

'Maybe,' Henderson says, as if this question might have been expected. 'But jaws keep growing into the late teens, so there's no assurance. Even a partial match could be disputed, depending on the age of the perpetrator.'

I was thinking this could be what gets any thoughts of charges against Richard dismissed – but the opposite could be true. It could have no effect at all.

Allen speaks next. 'Are you going to be around for a while?' she asks.

'I'm not sure.'

'Do you have a date that you're returning to Canada?'

'Not yet.'

'Is there a number we can reach you on in case we need to check something?'

I give them my Canadian details and we debate what numbers need to be put at the beginning in order for it to work. With that, Allen hands me a card and says I can call if there's anything I think of that might help. I tell them I'll do that and then both officers stand and again shake my hand. I follow them out to the car, offering cheery assurances that they weren't imposing and the like. I watch their car pull away and a part of me needs to see it leave. I can't help but think of how my mum would have been horrified with a marked police car being parked outside the house. She'd have worried what the neighbours would have thought and then instantly gone on a door-to-door charm offensive to insist that everything was in order.

When the police are completely out of sight, I turn back to the house, except I'm distracted by a flicker of movement. I look across and up, towards the upstairs room of Paige's old house, where her mum is standing and watching everything that has just happened.

# TWENTY-FIVE

The talk with Paige from the night before has given me new context as I walk through the centre of Macklebury. Before, I'd see a homeless person in a doorway but now I understand what she was saying about the effect of Super-K on the community. There's a man who's screaming at the sky, while standing in the freezing cold wearing little more than jeans and a vest. That's the exception as there are many more in the zombie state she described. Men and women sitting in doorways and alleys, slumped against walls and staring lifelessly ahead. I start counting and get to twenty before I've reached the end of the High Street. It might not be a huge number in comparison to a city but, for Macklebury, it's massive.

When I reach the kebab shop, I stop to ring the bell that's next to the door which leads up to Paige's flat. I've already pressed it four times when I realise the wires hanging out the back have been cut and that it isn't connected to anything.

I'm about to call her when the door shoots open and narrowly misses catching me in the face. I step backwards quickly – and so does the man who was on his way out.

Pete's eyes narrow as he takes me in. He uses up most of the width of the doorway and doesn't appear to have much of a neck. Since we were teenagers, as best I can tell, he's only grown outwards, instead of up. It takes him a second to place me but, when he does, he puffs himself up a little taller.

'What were you doing in there?' I ask, surprising myself.

'What's it got to do with you?'

It's as we stand more or less nose to nose that something strange washes across me. I don't do confrontation and never have. I've grown out of any competitiveness I might have once had but a combination of emotion from finally talking about the bite on Graham's body, plus a frustration at walking past the street zombies which are arguably Pete's fault, emboldens me in a way that hasn't happened in a long time.

If it ever has.

It's as if I'm watching myself as I grab Pete by the collar of his shirt and slam him back into the wall. My forearm is pressed against his collarbone and everything's happened so quickly that he's left staring at me with wide eyes. He tries to push back and there's a moment in which we both realise that he's no stronger than I am. It could be momentum but, if anything, I have the upper hand.

Except I am then struck by a crucial realisation of, 'Now what?'

Pete pushes me away and I let him. His shirt is ruffled as he yanks it back straight.

'Just leave her alone,' I say, relieved that my voice remains firm.

He snorts a short laugh and that charming help-an-old-lady-across-a-road smile reappears. 'What makes you think it was my choice to come here?' He looks sideways towards an invisible sidekick. 'Did you ever think that she doesn't *want* to be left alone?'

I stumble over something that doesn't come out right and Pete laughs again.

'Are you really picking this fight? *You?*'

He nods over my shoulder and I almost fall for it before I stop myself from turning away and missing a sucker-punch.

Except it wasn't a trick.

'Everything okay?'

A deep voice sounds from behind and I quickly take my attention from Pete to see a man who looks similar to him – albeit taller and leaner. The sort of bloke who'd stand outside a nightclub in a suit and let in all the women, while simultaneously shaking a head at a lad in black trainers.

A moment later and two more men appear, both of whom look like slightly comparable versions of one another. Between the four of them, there's a tall one, a fat one, one with a beard and one who's missing half an ear. Similar but different: all likely bad news.

Pete and his three cousins: the gang of bullies who preyed on our year at school.

I also recognise all the newcomers for a different reason. The one who is missing half an ear is the man who was standing outside the antiques place near the school who said 'hi' to Paige. The other two were outside the vape shop when I changed my mind and decided to go to The Wine Store and look for Joanne.

Before I know it, the dynamic has flipped and I have my back to the wall next to Paige's door. Pete and his three cousins stand around me, offering no escape.

I've only been beaten up once in my life – and I would have been eleven or twelve at the time. It was in the summer holidays and I'd been out playing. On my way home in the evening, I'd been crossing a field where there are now a few dozen houses. Some bigger boys had jumped out of the hedge and given me a bit of a kicking for no particular reason. It wasn't a robbery, it was simply one of those things. At home, I told Mum I'd fallen out of a tree I was climbing. I never saw those boys before or after and a part of me started to think I might have dreamed it. The fear I felt as those boys appeared as if from nowhere is what lets me know it happened – because it's precisely what I feel as I realise I'm trapped.

Pete stares at me with a curious half-smile, as if he doesn't quite know what to make of things.

'Harry, right?' he says.

'Yeah.'

'I think you should probably mind your own business.'

I don't reply but I suspect my heavy breathing and wild eyes probably tells a story.

The group motion to move back as one but then Pete lunges towards me with his head. I flinch away – except that was what Pete wanted. He was never going to make contact, which is borne out as he laughs another time.

'See ya around,' he says – and then he and his cousins turn and walk away.

# TWENTY-SIX

My heart is thumping so loudly that it is as if I can hear it. I can certainly *feel* it rampaging against my chest. None of the four men look back as they stride along the street side by side, taking up the entire width.

At school, Pete never much bothered with people like me. It's why I was slightly surprised to hear Richard say he'd been suspended for fighting with Pete. Pete and his cousins would save the bulk of their tormenting for the smaller kids with no athletic ability. Richard had a big brother, with big mates like Martin, and Pete wouldn't have wanted to risk embarrassment by picking on the wrong person. I had a degree of protection because I was with Richard so often.

None of that meant that I wasn't fearful of them each time I had to pass a table where they were sitting, or if I saw them outside school.

I turn back towards Paige's door and realise that Pete left it open a fraction when he went. I head in and close it behind me and then go up the stairs. The smell and the darkness provide a noxious combination as I move along the corridor towards Paige's door. I'm already jumpy but there's a squeak that I instantly feel certain is a rat.

When I knock, I say a silent prayer that Paige will answer quickly. There is nothing pleasant about this small row of flats.

She doesn't answer quickly.

There's a wait of perhaps thirty seconds until her muffled voice comes from beyond the door, asking who it is.

I tell her it's Harry and then there's the sound of a chain unlatching before the door swings inwards. She waves me in and then rechains the door behind, before she presses herself against it. Her eyelids flutter and her pupils are dots.

'Oh—' she says, before another blink. 'How was prison?'

'I had a run-in downstairs,' I say, ignoring the question.

'Who with?'

'One of your apparent friends.'

Paige and I stare at each other and there's such an invisible hostility that it's as if this is her unknown twin and not the girl who grew up next door to me.

We feel like such strangers.

'Are you going to lecture me, or…?' The accusatory edge to Paige's voice is unmistakable.

'I don't understand what's happened, Paige. With your mum last night, you seemed so angry about the town and the Super-K. About her. About this. And then we're here again today and Pete is in your flat. He said you invited him round.'

'There's no way he said that.'

'Close enough.'

She clamps her lips together and breathes through her nose. Her eyes never leave me and the pupils are so small and searing that I can almost feel them drilling through my skull.

It only lasts a moment and then her shoulders slump.

'Can't we just be friends?'

It's as much of a sigh as it is a question. Her sadness is almost too much to take. It's not simply a question, it's as if she's a starving woman asking for food.

Sadness is the wrong word. It's desperation.

'I don't understand what's going on,' I reply.

'Do you need to? You don't live here. How *could* you understand?'

She almost shouts that final line and we continue staring at each other for another second or two before she releases herself.

She crosses the room and sits on the sofa, curling her legs beneath her and picking up her mug from the table.

'The kettle's just boiled,' Paige says. 'There are still the teabags you bought the other night.'

There's a decision to make. I either accept Paige and everything this is, or I don't. She asked if we could 'just be friends' – and I could say no.

I could.

There are planes I could be on. I'm a permanent resident of another country and have no need to be here.

I could simply go, except…

I find myself making a cup of tea I hadn't planned to have and then taking a spot on the armchair opposite Paige.

'I don't think I've had a single cup of tea in Canada,' I tell her.

'What do you drink?'

'Coffee in the mornings. Fizzy water or Sprite, something like that, later in the day. Liane and I used to share a bottle of wine more or less every evening.'

'You're not a wine person, are you?'

'I think I'm a large chips and jumbo sausage person.'

A laugh. 'I don't know how you live without tea.' Paige cradles the mug and sips from the top. 'Sometimes, when I'm in all day, I must have ten or twelve cups.'

'That's a lot of caffeine.'

She smiles a little. 'How was prison?'

I tell her about the building and everything Richard said about how confident his solicitor is. I don't say that it feels like we were both manipulated to get me into court, where the police would realise I was back – or that something felt off with Richard insisting I found Graham's body.

'Richard says everything with Wilson is a misunderstanding,' I add. 'Something to do with a mix-up around an invoice for accountancy work. That's why they were arguing in the hotel. He says he's told the police everything.'

'But the chef at the hotel said staff saw Richard waiting outside *after* he'd been thrown out.'

'I said that but he wouldn't talk about it. Everything was a bit cryptic. I mentioned something about Wilson and Richard said "I wasn't waiting for Wilson" – which implies he was waiting for someone else.'

'Who?'

'That's what he wouldn't say.'

'Wouldn't he *want* to tell the police?'

'Maybe he has? Maybe it's just me and his family he was uneasy about telling?'

Paige has another sip of her tea as she muses on that. I don't tell her that I wasn't convinced by that part of Richard's story. He was also evasive about the reasons for him being at the hotel in the first place.

'Did you talk about Graham?'

'A bit – and then the police were waiting for me outside Evie's when I got back.'

Paige shows no surprise at this. I'm seemingly the only person who thinks it's not normal.

'Did they interview you?' she asks.

'I suppose. It was fairly informal and there wasn't a lot I could tell them. They were asking about things from eighteen years ago and I said that my statements from the time would give the best memory of what happened.'

Paige has more of her tea, a bigger gulp this time, and then she uncurls her legs and puts the mug back on the table. 'Hmmm…'

'Why's everyone so interested in Graham again? A man died a few days ago – but people seem more interested in a death from nearly twenty years back.'

I'm unsure if I expect an answer, though another smile creeps onto Paige's face. It's more in bemusement than amusement. As if I'm a man asking where my glasses are, despite them being on my head.

'Don't you remember?' she asks.

'Remember what?'

'How big Graham's death was? People talked about it all the time. Adults, kids, teachers, parents. *Everyone.* There was that memorial on the school car park where everyone left flowers and soft toys. It took over half the space and it was there for weeks, until everything rotted away. There were posters all over town saying "RIP" or "justice".'

'But that was then.'

'Except the killer was never found and it's hung over the town ever since. It's a myth that's passed down from generation to generation – except it's actually true. They held memorial services for at least ten years. Young kids here know about Graham, even though they weren't alive. They *saw* those services and went to them. Parents will use it as a reason not to let their children out on their own, or to stay out late. They'll talk about this kid at school who was found in a bush. People will look at their neighbours and wonder if that's the person who killed a boy and got away with it.'

'I get that but—'

'You *don't* get it. You have to be here to understand. It's not like there's a murder every week, or even every year. There was Graham when we were kids and now there's Wilson. Locals *want* it to be Richard who killed both because then they can tell themselves that everything's fine.' She stops and sighs sadly, before adding: '*You* went away – but this never did.'

It's probably the most fervent I've ever heard Paige sound. There's fire but compassion, too. Everything she says is logical and understandable. She's right that I shouldn't judge a place by what I think it should be – and, by extension, perhaps that means I shouldn't judge her either.

'What now?' Paige adds.

'What do you mean?'

'We're supposed to be trying to prove Richard didn't kill anyone.'

'It sounds like his solicitor thinks he'll be fine anyway.'

'But we could still find something to guarantee it.'

Paige is animated now and the words 'euphoric high' come spilling back into my mind.

'What do you suggest?'

Paige literally leaps from her seat and bounds to the kitchen. She grabs her bag from the counter and starts fumbling inside until she pulls out her keys.

'If we want to do something for Richard, why don't we just go to his flat?'

# TWENTY-SEVEN

Paige strides back across the room and picks up her jacket from the back of the sofa. She slips an arm inside and then leaves it hanging half-on, half-off.

'Let's go,' she says.

'You haven't finished your tea – and I just made mine.'

'You also said you don't drink it. Let's go now.'

'What are you hoping to find?' I ask, curious as to what's changed.

She wrestles with her coat to get the other arm inside. 'We won't know that until we get there.'

Paige spins in a circle, momentarily confused, and then says she needs to get her stuff. She heads into the bedroom and closes the door, leaving me temporarily breathless at the speed of everything. If nothing else, it sounds as if she is on her way to Richard's flat and I figure I might as well go with it.

I stand, ready to put my own coat back on, but then the bedroom door bursts open and Paige is there with a white carrier bag in her hand. Without a word, she disappears into the toilet with that and the bag she was already carrying.

I watch and wait, trying not to judge and forcing myself to remain quiet.

*Euphoric high…*

By the time the bathroom door springs open, Paige is back down to her original bag, which is the one she's carried with her most of the time since I got back. She hoists it high onto her shoulder. 'You ready?'

'I guess.'

She bounds to the table and picks up her mug of tea before downing whatever's left, then she turns and leads the way out of her apartment, down the stairs, and onto the street.

We don't talk a lot as we walk. Paige's pace is as relentless as ever and she navigates the streets of Macklebury with a fluid, unremitting ease. In some ways, there's a distinct beauty to it. She'll keep an eye on traffic and then cross roads at the perfect moment so that she doesn't need to break stride. Once across, she'll slip through alleys, or cut diagonally across small areas of frosted grass. Everything for maximum speed.

By the time we get to the river and the solemn Christmas tree on the towpath, the chill has once again set in. I have buried my chin in the collar of my jacket in a failing attempt to stop my face from freezing – but Paige seems unaffected.

For the first time, I realise how often Paige seemed to be outside when we were kids. In the summer, it wasn't an oddity – but she'd always be the person asking if I wanted to go out and do something, even when it was cold. There were a few times when I might have been off to the supermarket with Mum for something to do – and we'd see Paige sitting by herself on a bench, or a wall. Mum would say mumsy things, like that Paige would catch her death and so on – but Paige would always reply to say she was fine.

Mum must have known the sorts of thing that were going on in next-door's house. For me, there was a normality to the raging arguments, or hearing Paige slam the front door as she left at eleven in the evening. I thought that's what neighbours were like because it was more or less the only thing I'd known.

But my parents would have realised it wasn't normal.

Perhaps that's why having Paige over for food or to do 'home-work' was never an issue for them?

Paige works her way along a low row of apartments. When I left Macklebury, this area was a floodplain for the river. I'm not sure what changed that allowed them to send the water elsewhere when it rains – but it's now a couple of hundred luxury flats. They're modern but boring: all identical cream-brick low rises with red-tiled roofs. Each block is named something like 'Willow' or 'Acorn'. They're either trees, or Disney princesses. It's hard to know at my age.

Paige leads me through an archway, up some stairs and along a covered walkway until we get to door number thirty-two.

The key slips straight into the lock but, as we head into Richard's flat, it is immediately clear that someone's been in before us. The door opens directly into an open-plan kitchen, with a living room beyond, but it's like walking into the before shot at the beginning of some TV show about cleaning. The carpet corners have been pulled up in the living room and there are cushions scattered on the floor. A lamp is on its side and the sofa is inexplicably upside down. In the kitchen, there's nothing obviously amiss – except that the toaster, blender and kettle are all in the middle of the counter, instead of pushed against the wall like it's clear they should be. The oven and microwave doors also both hang open, revealing empty interiors.

Paige closes the door behind us and then steps past me and turns in a circle to take in the mess.

'It must have been the police,' I say.

'Do they usually make a mess?'

'I don't know. It might depend on what they were looking for.'

We move into the living room together and telepathically share the same idea as we shift the sofa back into the correct place.

The living room is partly a home office, with two black filing cabinets in the corner, both of which have the drawers unlocked and open. They sit next to a computer desk, where a monitor and keyboard are on top, alongside a rectangular, dustless spot where the main box would have been before the police presumably took it.

'I think Richard used to have an office in town,' Paige says. 'I guess he moved everything here at some point.'

I nudge the top drawer further open and flip through the blue cardboard wallets, each of which has a name written in the top corner. I don't bother to open them. They certainly look like accounting files.

'Where do you want to start?' I ask. I am still not certain what we're doing here, let alone what we might be looking for.

'Do you want to look around this room?' she says. 'I'll do the bedroom and bathroom.'

I tell her that's fine and she unzips her jacket, before disappearing through a door at the other end of the room.

I suspect the reason Paige offered me this room is that she didn't fancy going through the filing cabinet. I don't either – so I leave that and sit on the spinning office chair before I open the top drawer of the computer desk.

Inside, there are two old cabled computer mice, a good dozen intertwined cables, an international plug adapter, two empty phone boxes, some coins, a manual for a Bluetooth speaker and a dozen or so black biros.

It's such a *man*-drawer.

The next one down has a couple of decks of cards, plus some printouts of poker tips that have handwritten scribbles on the side and across the top. I have something similar back in Canada, from when I was invited to a poker night and had no idea what I was doing. I scan through the dozen or so pages but it's only the top one that has been scrawled on. I turn the page upside down, wondering if I'm reading it the wrong way – except I'm not. As best I can tell, it's a string of unrelated numbers and letters, with '!! PAY ATTENTION !!' written underneath.

I put the pages back in the drawer but then take them back out again and take a photo of the writing. The letters and numbers could be a password, although I'm not sure for what.

There is little else in the drawers, so I go around the rest of the living room. There are a couple more drawers built into the unit underneath the TV but they are filled with envelopes, printer paper, ink cartridges and other office-like stuff.

Past that is a bookshelf that is largely empty, except for a pair of IKEA catalogues and two pot plants. I fill a cup with water from the kitchen and then empty some into both plants.

With that done, I'm left with little option other than to tackle the filing cabinet. The first of the blue cardboard folders is marked with 'Adams, P' in the top corner. Directly behind is 'Ball, D'. It quickly becomes clear from the gaps that the police have likely taken some of the folders themselves. I skip straight to the bottom drawer, looking for 'Wilson' and wondering if there might be some clarity about the billing problem that Richard says caused their public argument.

There are no Ws.

I presume the police have taken the particular files, likely because Richard told them the same thing he told me.

I scan through the other drawers of the first cabinet, not searching for anything more specific than names I might know. There are a few – but it's mainly familiar last names in the same way I recognised the ones on the town's Facebook page. I don't bother looking through the folders themselves, figuring it's none of my business. Nothing jumps out as odd.

The second cabinet is fuller than the first, which I guess means the police had less interest. This one contains folders relating to businesses as opposed to individuals. Everything is still in alphabetical order but there are far fewer industry clients than individuals, although most of the businesses have two or three fat folders dedicated to them instead of one.

It's all a bit… *boring* – and I don't get any sense that what Paige and I could be looking for is in here. That's especially the case as the police have been here already.

I flip through the four drawers of identical-looking folders and have already stepped away, ready to give up, when my brain kicks into gear.

In the bottom drawer, there is a set of folders marked 'Antiques World', which, as far as I can tell, is the only one that's out of alphabetical order.

It's also right next to 'Vape World'.

I take out both folders and open the one relating to antiques, which is bulging with pages of largely identical receipts printed on crisp A4 pages. Inside the one for Vape World, there are more receipts that are equally neat and have been created using an identical template. Aside from the different addresses in the top corner, there's almost nothing different about them.

The antiques file is particularly interesting in the sense that I never realised how much money could be in the business. On one day last year, an oak table was sold for £22,000 and, the next day, a writing bureau went for £16,000.

The owner's signature scrawl on the bottom is captioned 'Simon Baker'.

I swap to the vape shop's receipts, where a slightly different squiggle is identified as 'Terry Baker'.

I return the receipts to the folders and the folders to the drawer and then close it.

Richard was doing accounts for two businesses owned by the cousins of Pete Baker. There's nothing particularly outlandish in that. He's a local accountant and it's natural a local business might have someone nearby process their receipts. Richard probably set them up with similar software, which is why the receipts are so similar. It's probably fine…

*Probably.*

'Harry…?'

Paige's voice drifts through from the other side of the apartment. I follow it through to where she's standing in the bathroom.

There's a shower, sink and toilet and not much room for anything else – which includes more than one person. Paige is in front of the toilet, with the lid of the cistern upside down at her feet.

'Why's it on the floor?' I ask.

She shakes her head and she's pale and emotionless.

'What's happened?'

Paige turns and looks towards the lid-less cistern. I slide around her, which is difficult as there's little room and she doesn't move. Inside, and underneath the float, submerged in a plastic bag, is something small and round.

'What is it?' I ask.

'I put it back,' Paige replies. As she scratches her nose with one hand, I notice that the other is wet, and so is the lower part of her sleeve.

'Why?'

'You had to see for yourself.'

I reach into the water and pull out the bag. Whatever's inside is solid and heavier than expected for something that fits in my palm. Water drips from the bag onto the floor and the toilet seat.

A creeping sense of inevitability sends shivers along my arms. I know what's inside without looking.

Paige doesn't move, doesn't look. She stares straight ahead, towards the tiled wall.

I unfurl the bag, which sends more flecks of water onto the wall and the floor. When I reach inside, my hand wraps around something hard and unforgiving.

I drop the bag and leave myself holding the perfectly palm-sized rock. When I flip it over, a dark red pigment is stained into the very fabric of the stone.

When I turn to Paige, she is open-mouthed. I'm not sure she moves her lips but the words are there, quiet and haunting.

'A blunt object…'

# TWENTY-EIGHT

I put down the rock on the floor and then sit on the shuttered toilet seat and stare at it. Paige is standing next to me and doing the same. The reddy-purply tinge is as clear as can be against the light grey of the stone.

Time passes.

Neither of us speak. I struggle to comprehend what to say, or what to think. The only words rattling around my mind are 'blunt object'. I have the sense of being at the top of a roller-coaster track just as the train begins to fall. There is less than a second of feeling weightless and then the ground comes thrashing upwards faster and faster until…

'What do we do?' she says quietly.

Paige has barely moved since I came into the bathroom. She's pressed with her back against the wall, neck craned slightly forward as we both continue to stare at the rock. The surface is smooth, perhaps more like a large pebble. When it was in my hand, it fitted perfectly into my palm.

'Why were you looking in the cistern?'

Paige shuffles her weight from one foot to the other. 'You wouldn't understand.'

'I don't think you get to say that now.'

She sighs and then crouches so that she's resting on the tips of her toes. 'I keep things in the back of my toilet,' she says. 'As long as the bag is sealed properly, everything inside is safe. Nobody would ever think to look. Well, *almost* nobody…'

'The police have already been here, though. Why wouldn't they have found it?'

'I guess they didn't look.'

It's an obvious, almost sarcastic, reply – but Paige has a point. It's not as if the floorboards have been torn up, or that holes have been punched through walls. Even to my untrained eye, it doesn't look like there was any sort of forensic search. In fact, given the accounting folders that are missing, it's more likely the police knew what they were after and happened to move a few things around at the same time.

'We should call the police.'

It doesn't sound like me who's speaking. My voice is husky, like a forty-a-day man.

Neither of us move.

'The police asked me about this earlier,' I add after a while.

'What did they want to know?'

'Whether I'd seen a blunt object in the vicinity of where we found Graham. It was strange wording.'

'Trigger words,' Paige says. 'You hear "blunt object" and you think Graham. It happens with me. There was something on TV a while back and one of the characters said it. In that instant, I was back sitting on the floor when we had that assembly.'

'When that girl asked what a blunt object was?'

'Her name was Karen. She was in the year below us. I always remember thinking that it was a silly question and then immediately thinking that I didn't know for sure either.'

We continue staring at the rock, where a bubble has formed on the top as the water dribbles down to the bag below.

'Did you notice the bag?' Paige says.

'What do you mean?'

'It's from Green's.'

I hunch over a little further, staring at the lettering that's visible on the part of the bag that isn't obscured by the rock. There's a clear G-R-E printed in capital black letters. Vague memories of carrying home magazines from Green's Newsagent in this exact type of bag start to form.

'It's a juice bar now,' she adds.

'I saw. When did it shut down?'

Paige edges around the stone and leans against the sink. 'At least ten years back. Probably more.'

'Do you think…?' I stop myself because the thought is unfinished and rough. I can't process what's happening. 'Where do you think it's been kept all this time?'

'It's a rock,' Paige speaks as if she's telling me that two and two is four.

'I know.'

'What I mean is, it could have been kept on a driveway or in a garden. People have those rockery things. There's gravel at the front of your sister's house. A rock has to be the easiest thing to hide – because you put it with other rocks.'

It sounds so simple – but it's also true. If the murder weapon used to kill Graham was *this* stone, then it could have been left in plain sight all these years. No wonder it was never found.

'We should call the police.'

I sound firmer this time. Stronger and more decisive. Except still neither of us move. We continue to stare at the Green's bag and the rock.

'If it was hidden with other rocks, why put it in a bag and bring it inside?'

I'm thinking out loud, trying to come up with reasons this isn't true.

'Because people move?' Paige pauses and then adds: 'I'm only guessing.'

'But why not just leave it with other rocks? Or throw it in a river?'

Paige doesn't reply instantly.

I can feel the weight of my phone in my pocket. The shape of it against my leg and the way it makes my trousers bulge. I should take it out and call the number Detective Sergeant Allen gave me. Her card's in my wallet. I could do it now. Right now. I definitely should.

'Do you listen to podcasts?'

I can feel Paige watching me now, her gaze drawn away from the rock.

'Not really,' I reply.

'There are thousands about serial killers. Literally thousands. It's like every other person you've ever met now has their own true-crime podcast. It never ends. You subscribe to one and then all the recommendations you get are for others that are nearly identical. Like those Amazon recommendations. You buy a pillowcase and then it thinks you need a thousand.'

'I'm not sure what you mean.'

'I listen to a couple of podcasts and it comes up quite a lot that people hold onto mementoes. There was this guy who would cut bits of hair from his victims and keep them in a jewellery box under the floorboards of his house. Someone else stole underwear from the women he killed. I guess, for some people, you want something to help you remember the moment by. You could hide this quite easily – in plain sight, or not – but you wouldn't want to leave it behind somewhere.'

'Do you think we should call the police?'

Paige doesn't reply – not that I take the phone from my pocket either.

'If it was… *Richard*…' I whisper his name. 'If it was him. Why would he do it?'

'Why do people do anything?'

'But the three of us were good friends. We did more or less everything together and didn't much care for people outside our group. It's not like we hated people but someone like Graham wasn't even on our radar. He was just there.'

I look up from the rock for the first time in a long time and Paige is watching me carefully. Her pupils are wider now and she's steady. Still.

'Maybe that was just you,' she says.

Paige continues to look at me and I have to turn away. I wonder if that's true. Paige and Oliver got together despite the fact that I didn't know they'd ever spoken properly. Perhaps a lot of things passed me by in those days? Perhaps Richard wasn't the person, or the friend, I thought he was.

I remember those middle teenage years of being the three of us versus the world – but then I can't remember any rainy days in among the long summers and that wonderful snow day. I remember getting my exam results but I don't know how it came to be that Richard and I went back to do A-levels, while Paige started work in cleaning glasses in a pub. The night that the three of us stayed up to watch *WrestleMania* is etched in my mind – but the hundreds of nights where I went to sleep uneventfully are gone.

'We could just… put it back?'

Paige sounds as haunted as she did when I first got into the bathroom.

I try to make eye contact, to see if she's serious, but she is staring at the rock again. I follow her gaze towards the stone once more.

Towards the blunt object.

I've spent so long looking at it that it feels like I know every curve of its surface.

The upturned cistern lid is still on the floor, next to the bag. Could that really be an option? Could I put the rock back where I found it – and where Paige found it before me – and then slot the lid into place? Could I fly home tonight or tomorrow and never have to think about it again? The police had their chance to find it – and they blew it. Why should this have to be on me?

On us?

'What about Graham?'

It's my voice but it's not. The forty-a-day rasp is back.

Paige doesn't reply.

'He deserves justice,' I add. 'His family do.'

Paige pushes herself away from the sink and steps across to the open door. 'I can't make the decision.'

'Maybe it's just a random rock?'

They're my words but I don't believe them.

'Maybe…'

Paige doesn't believe it, either.

'Maybe it was here before Richard moved in?'

'Maybe…'

Paige continues standing and I continue sitting. Time passes and then, finally, I take out my phone.

# TWENTY-NINE

An officer in a white paper uniform leaves Richard's bathroom with the rock in a large see-through bag. Moments later, a second one follows with the Green's Newsagent bag in a separate transparent packet. Detective Sergeant Allen is in the area between the living room and the kitchen, watching everything be carried away. Not long after, a third officer leaves, this time carrying the toilet's float in another bag.

Once all three have gone, Allen turns back towards me and Paige, who are sitting on Richard's sofa. DC Henderson has been standing over us for a good fifteen minutes with little to say, although quite the imposing manner. We've already talked him through what we found and where we found it as Allen listened on while wearing an apparently permanent frown.

Henderson looks across to his senior officer but she only has eyes for us.

'I suppose the final thing is to ask why you're here,' she says.

Paige shuffles deeper into the seat and then reaches for her bag. 'I have a key,' she replies. 'I know Richard's due in court in the next few days and figured we should come over and check the place in case he gets released. I didn't think it would be much fun if he got home and found the place a mess.'

Both officers look between us with half-frowns. I can't quite believe that Paige has lied to the police so boldly. It would be bad enough but she has to know that *I* know it's a lie. In telling it in front of me, I'm part of it as well.

The irony is that we came here to look for something that could help Richard and, instead, we've done the opposite.

Allen lets the lie settle, which makes me think that she probably suspects.

She's very measured when she next speaks: 'I understand that you came here to tidy up the place. It's very kind of you both. Friends do stick together, after all. What I *don't* understand is why tidying up a flat involves looking in a toilet cistern.'

I look to Paige as I realise I've snapped around to face her far too quickly. Even *I* seem suspicious of the motives and I'm supposed to be the calm one.

Paige seems undaunted. 'I went to use the toilet but it wasn't flushing. I took off the lid and saw the bag inside. I took it out because I wondered if that's why the toilet wasn't flushing.'

'Was it the reason?'

'I don't know. I gave the chain a tug and it flushed. I've not tried it since.'

It sounds… *plausible*. Perhaps that's what happened?

Except I don't remember the toilet ever making a flushing sound.

Allen's eyes flicker to me. 'Is that what happened?'

'I wasn't in there with her.'

'Where were you?'

'In here.'

'Doing what?'

'Watering the plants.'

I get such a thrill from being able to answer the questions truthfully that I have to stop myself from seeming too excited. Henderson turns to look at the plants on the shelf and I almost beg him to go touch the soil to verify the story.

He doesn't.

'Did you already search in here?' It's my question this time. I sound a lot bolder than I feel – and it only leads to a death stare from both officers. Neither of them answer, although I already know they have. It's not based on anything other than their hostile body language but I also get the sense that they both know the inside of the cistern wasn't checked. It's the sort of thing that I imagine could get someone disciplined.

'This flat is off limits.' Allen speaks in a tone that someone might use with a dog who has pooped inside. 'Regardless of whether you have a key, it is *off* limits. I'll get tape put across the door and any violations will be seen as trespassing.'

I stay quiet but Paige is bolder than me.

'What if Richard gets bail?'

Neither officer replies to that but Allen does stand up straighter and take half a step away from the sofa, which gives us room to leave.

'Before you go,' she says, 'is there anything else either of you would like to say? This might be your last chance.'

Paige tenses and I wait, wondering if she has something to say. I sense her breathing and feel sure… but she remains silent.

'Either of you…?'

Paige is defiant: 'I still don't think he did it.'

'That who didn't do what?'

'I don't think Richard did anything.'

'What are you basing that on?'

'Because I know who he is.'

Allen offers a narrow, unamused smile as she takes another step back, leaving a larger gap on one side of the living room that leads directly to the front door. She doesn't say it but the implication is clear.

Paige picks up her bag from the arm of the sofa and stands, with me following her lead. She heads out of the apartment onto the walkway and then the stairs. I keep close, not realising how cold it is until we get all the way outside.

I lost track of time in the apartment but it's now imposingly, clawingly dark. A marked police van and separate car are parked at the front of the building, although there's nobody anywhere near either. There are lights on in the surrounding windows, and faces too. I can sense people squinting into the darkness, trying to figure out if Paige and I are either important, or in trouble.

Paige keeps striding until we get to the towpath, where the night is being eaten away at by the desolation-inducing Christmas tree lights as they blink on and off.

'Are you coming back to mine?'

Paige's voice makes it sound less like a question and more like a request. Before I can start a reply, she quickly adds that there's some vodka left from the other night. I'm not in the mood for drinking but it feels as if we each might need a friend.

Macklebury High Street is quiet. The chill of the air hits me harder than usual and I can feel the cold filling my lungs to the point that even breathing stings. I'd be happier to move at Paige's usual speed but she's slower tonight and she comes to a stop as we get to the juice bar that was once Green's Newsagent.

The bar is closed for the day, with steam on the windows and the lights off. Paige presses herself against the door and tries to peer through the darkness.

'I know I said that a rock could be hidden with other rocks,' she says, 'but maybe it was kept in that bag the whole time.'

There's no time to process this because she moves away from the door and looks up towards the sign, before turning back to the street.

'Did you really nick a porno mag from here?'

'Why would I make it up?'

'I thought to cheer me up, or something.'

'If I wanted to cheer someone up, I would invent something that didn't include me, stealing, and pornography.'

That gets the smallest of smiles. 'Do you remember Mr Green?'

'Not really.'

'I think his wife died when we were about twelve or thirteen. The shop was closed over a weekend but then he reopened the next week as if nothing had happened. People at school were daring other kids to come in and ask him about it. I don't think anyone did.'

'You've got such a good memory. I don't remember any of that.'

'It's easier when you see the same things every day.'

We stand in the doorway for a moment and could be teenagers again. We would be heading out of Green's on our way to school, with a couple of Freddos each. It might have been a shop that sold newspapers and magazines – but our biggest outlay at that age was the junk food we bought from Mr Green.

After that, we would meet Richard halfway along the street and then continue on to the railway arch, before popping out at the school.

From the way Paige hovers for a second, I wonder if she feels it, too.

She quickly snaps out of it and then we walk together further along the High Street until we reach the kebab shop. Paige unlocks the adjacent door and we head upstairs and into her flat.

It's cold inside, much more so than the times I've been here previously. Paige goes directly into the kitchen and fishes under the sink, where she pulls out a half-full bottle of vodka. She rinses two mugs under the tap and then pours liquid into both, before we move across to the living-room area.

'You cold?'

Paige nods to where I realise I have my arms crossed. 'I suppose.'

She stands and heads over to the thermostat next to the front door. She twiddles the dial before returning to the sofa. We make small talk about central heating, of all things, which inevitably fizzles out. Now we're together in Paige's flat, it all suddenly feels awkward.

Our friend, the person we spent hours with day after day during our teenage years, could be a double murderer.

It doesn't seem real and yet, in the moment, it's hard to see too many other explanations.

I tell Paige I need the toilet and then head into her bathroom and lock the door. It's functional, though basic – and there's no window. The dusty extractor fan doesn't give the impression that it can shift much more air than a person could by windmilling their arms. It's probably that which has led to the brown spots of mouldy damp across the ceiling and in between the tiles that surround the shower. There's crusty scale across the surface of the sink and rips in the thin linoleum floor. It's all a bit grim.

I lift the lid of the cistern as quietly as I can and peer into the water beneath. I expect the worst, some sort of mini pharmacy, but there's nothing that shouldn't be there. There's a loud, unintended clunk as I accidentally drop the heavy lid back into place. The walls are thin in Paige's apartment and, if she's paying any sort of attention from the living room, there's no doubt she must have heard it.

A couple of minutes pass where I wait, before I flush the toilet and let the taps run. I half expect Paige to be waiting for me outside the door when I leave, full of an accusatory stare. She isn't though. She's standing by the kitchen counter, keys in her hand.

'I have to pop out for five or ten minutes,' she says.

'Are you—?'

'I won't be long.'

Paige is out the door before I can get another word in and I hear her footsteps echoing along the corridor before there's a faint bump of the downstairs door slamming.

I move across to the window and crane my neck around a nearly impossible angle to watch her hurrying past the kebab shop and along the High Street.

I'm alone in Paige's flat and there's a part of me that wants to go hunting around to see what I can find. I think there's something natural in that I would guess everyone has an urge to poke around given the opportunity. There's more than that when it comes to Paige, though.

She's an addict with no job who is separated from her husband – and, despite all the time we've spent in one another's company the past few days, it's impossible to escape the sense that there's far more going on than I can quite figure out.

But going through her things is still a betrayal of trust.

I move away from the window and pick up the mug of vodka from the table. Just a sip, while both simultaneously trying to talk myself into – and out of – going into her bedroom to look around. I tell myself it is natural curiosity, one friend looking out for another, except I know it wouldn't be.

The vodka tickles my throat and clears my nose. It's a cheap own-brand supermarket version that's as smooth as sandpaper. The bottle sits on the kitchen counter, perhaps now a third full – and it's as I'm looking at it that I realise Paige's phone is sitting on the counter right next to it.

The screen is cracked but lit up and when I cross the room and look properly, the messages app is open. 'P' sent Paige a message six minutes ago that simply read: 'Outside now'.

Is that Pete? He seems the most likely person, considering he's her supplier.

I return to the window but there's no sign of Paige outside. Then I'm back in the living-room area. Sitting. Standing. At the window. Looking.

Back in the kitchen, I pick up Paige's phone once more and scroll up to see the previous messages between her and P. They certainly prefer brevity in their conversations. Paige's messages to P are only ever a single number, with '2' as the lowest and '8' as the highest. P then replies to say 'outside now' or 'pub now'.

There are forty or fifty messages between them that follow the same pattern over and over. The most recent is Paige texting '2' and the reply coming back with 'Outside now'.

I can guess at what's going on – but there's no evidence of anything being amiss in their entire cache of communication.

I put the phone back down where I found it, with the most recent message displayed exactly how it was. After that, I check the window again – although there's still no sign of anyone being outside. I sit back in the chair, have another sip of vodka, regret it, and then stand and cross to the kitchen once more.

It seems very unlikely that Paige left her phone here on purpose. She was ready to leave but waiting for me to come out of the bathroom. I had inadvertently slowed down her hurry and, in doing so, she'd forgotten her phone.

After picking up the phone again, I instantly put it back down. Then pick it up. The devil on my shoulder has won and I swipe backwards to the other messages. I'm in there under 'H' but there's 'Mum' and 'Ollie' too. I click onto his name and read the most recent message from yesterday.

*WTF you doin with him?*

Paige didn't reply and I assume Oliver is messaging about me.

I swipe back and continue looking at the other people who've messaged her. There is one from British Gas about an overdue bill, another from 'Twat' saying that she can't keep paying her rent late.

I keep scrolling, almost going too far before I realise the name blazing back at me. The name that shouldn't be there. That *can't* be there.

Mr Wilson.

# THIRTY

The world has frozen over. Chills flitter across the back of my neck and along my arms. I have to force myself to press the name 'Mr Wilson' because a large part of me doesn't want to know.

The messages should be loading but a second passes, then another. I tap the cracked screen again but nothing happens.

Paige's phone has frozen.

Another second passes. Two. Five. Something is very wrong but then, as quickly as it died, the device returns to life as the screen flashes white before finally showing the messages.

I realise I've been holding my breath – and let out a long, low gasp.

The most recent message from Paige reads:

*I'll be there!*

The one before is from 'Mr Wilson':

*Tuesday at 6?*

The thread continues in much the same fashion. Wilson will suggest a day and time and Paige will either say she'll be there, or she'll offer an alternative. Once they've established agreement, Paige's replies are full of enthusiasm: 'Sure!', 'OK!', 'Great!', 'Fab!', 'Can't wait!'.

I start scrolling up but there's a vibration of something slamming from somewhere nearby. I quickly swipe backwards and then return to the original thread with 'P', before I put the phone back on the counter and dive back towards the armchair.

Two seconds later and the door opens. A pink-cheeked, slightly out of breath, Paige appears with her keys in her hand. She instantly looks towards the kitchen and mutters 'There it is,' before snatching the phone from the counter. She bounces onto the sofa and plucks her mug from the table before having a large gulp.

We sit silently for a few seconds as she cradles the mug, with which she offers a half-hearted toast. 'I guess it doesn't much feel like a celebration, does it?' she says.

'No…'

I have a mouthful of my own drink and, in the moment, enjoy the acrid burning sensation.

Paige fiddles with her phone and, perhaps for the first time since I got back, I watch her. *Really* watch her. I've been swept up in so many other things and seeing her as an old friend, not as whoever she is now.

Paige and I have talked about Mr Wilson many times since I got back. We even went on an adventure of sorts, out to the seaside to talk to his ex-wife. Yet at no stage did she ever mention that she knew him as an adult.

I remember saying to her that I'd not thought about Mr Wilson in fifteen years or more – and I try to recall if she ever repeated that back to me. Perhaps she didn't? Perhaps she let me do the talking and went with it? I suppose she might not have lied – except that this degree of omission feels so much like an outright untruth.

Then there's Mr Wilson himself.

It's hard not to think of an old teacher as Mr *This* or Mrs *That*. I never knew *Keith* Wilson as anything other than through his head of year role. He would have always been a grown-up compared to me. I understand why Paige would have stored his number in her phone under 'Mr Wilson' – but what I cannot figure out is why she had his number at all.

Or, perhaps, I *can* figure it but don't want to admit it to myself.

Martin told me while we were standing next to his brother's grave the reason why Paige and Oliver had split but I didn't want to accept it.

*She was sleeping around for money.*

I suppose the money she gives to Pete for the Oxy has to come from somewhere. The money for her late rent, too.

Paige keeps tapping her phone screen and I continue watching her, desperately wanting to ask her outright but knowing I can't. That I won't.

And that's when the creeping, worming thought slithers into my mind.

Moments before we left to go to Richard's apartment, Paige disappeared into her room and came out with a white carrier bag, which she could have put in her own bag. I only saw it briefly and wasn't paying too much attention. She took that all the way across town to Richard's place.

And then a very similar-looking bag appeared in the cistern of Richard's toilet – into which she just happened to be looking. She told me it was because she kept things hidden in the same place here – but she told the police she was trying to fix the flush.

I try to push the thought away.

There are innocent explanations…

It was Paige who suggested putting the rock back where it was found. *I* made the decision to call the police – and then actually did it.

'You okay?'

I realise I've not been looking at Paige for a while. I've been staring at the wall instead and I snap back into the room to see she is now watching me.

I hold up the mug. 'I think I need a night off the booze.'

'You were staring at the wall for so long that I thought there was something there.'

She turns to look at the spot where I was staring – but there's a blank patch of mottled cream paint.

'Why did you have to nip out?'

Paige barely reacts. 'I had to pick something up from a mate.'

'I didn't see you come in with anything.'

Paige snorts this off as a joke. 'You're worse than Mum.'

I wait, not laughing, not letting it be the joke she wants it to be. We stare at one another and then Paige's frown deepens before she digs into her pocket and pulls out a small baggie. She tosses it onto the table between us, where it slides so that it's closer to me. There are two greeny-white pills inside the bag.

Paige cradles her knees up to her chest and hugs them as she angles herself away. 'Happy?'

'That's the opposite of what I am.'

'I told you that I don't need saving.'

'But you thought Richard needed saving. It's the only reason I'm here.'

Paige breathes in and holds her knees tighter. Her eyes burn. 'I didn't *have* anybody else.'

I have to turn away. Her controlled, pained rage is so intense that I can feel it gripping me.

Paige isn't done.

'I was eleven when we moved in next door to you. I had friends at my old school but that was because we'd all grown up together. Then Mum got moved by the council and they put us in a different town on the other side of the county. It was two weeks before school started and I was terrified about not knowing anyone. I didn't have *anyone* – but then I saw you on that first day, in your front garden when it used to be grass. You were wearing a pink and black Bret Hart T-shirt and I *knew* we'd be friends.'

My memory is awful but I feel the moment as if it has just happened.

'You were so small,' I reply. 'My sister was younger than you but taller. I didn't know you were my age at first but you were carrying this huge box into your house effortlessly and I remember thinking that you must be really strong. Then you said hello and I suppose I kind of… *knew*.'

Her stare flashes past me towards the crooked shelf close to the window. I've not paid it much attention before but I now realise there are eight or nine scuffed paperbacks resting against an empty bottle. I know what they are without looking. They're the Lovecraft paperbacks that we got from the Oxfam in town and then shared back and forth. They were battered then but no worse off now.

Not battered. *Loved*.

'We were always into weird stuff,' she says. 'Or *weirder* than the other kids. We read Ninja Turtle comics and collected Lovecrafts. We stayed up and watched wrestling through the night. I didn't know any girls who were into that stuff – but *you* were.'

Those days feel so close and yet so achingly distant.

'There was that year,' Paige says, 'only the one, when it was just us. We ended up in the same form room and all the same classes. We hadn't planned any of that, it just happened. We didn't care that the other kids thought we were weird because it didn't matter. We'd be together all day at school and then come home and spend the evenings doing homework or generally messing around. When it was the holidays, we could spend whole days outside and, even now, I can't quite remember how we wasted so many hours.'

I try to think but it's blank for me, too. I can barely go ten minutes nowadays without checking my phone but, back then, we had none of that. We'd still somehow create our own form of time travel by using up all those hours without ever achieving anything.

Paige is on a roll now. 'The next year, a new kid started at school and they wanted you to look after him and show him around. I used to sit next to you in class but they moved me so Richard had that seat. I was jealous at first but then we became a trio. It just sort of… happened. I felt sorry for him to begin with. He wasn't into the same things we were but went along with everything because he didn't know anybody else. We'd talk about The Rock or Stone Cold, or we'd go on about Providence, Rhode Island because of Lovecraft.'

'I didn't even know what Rhode Island was back then,' I say. 'I pictured it as an *actual* island on its own at the edge of the US. I only really knew of New York, so I thought it was just floating there.'

Paige smiles the merest amount: 'It was some mythical place where all these weird and wonderful stories came from.' She stops. Breathes. 'Have you ever been?'

'No.'

I almost ask whether she has, except I already know that she's hardly left the *county*, let alone the country.

Paige unfurls her legs, stretches, and picks up her mug, before finishing whatever was left inside. She crosses to the kitchen and refills it, then settles back on the sofa. I eye the two pills in the baggie on the table.

'I spoiled it,' Paige says quietly.

'Spoiled what?'

'When Oliver looked at me like a girl and I decided I actually liked it.'

I don't reply at first. I can't.

'You, me and Richard were never going to be friends like that forever,' I reply eventually. 'School finished. Life moved on.'

A shrug. 'You only went to uni because there wasn't much left for you here.'

There's truth to that. Macklebury is many things but it's hardly a thriving hub of industry. As well as working in the local shops and restaurants, there is a steady trade for estate agents, financial advisors, insurance brokers and accountants, plus the administration staff associated with all those things. Then there is the medical centre and the schools, which offer the sort of work that would be needed in any town.

People can get by and live happy, comfortable lives here. There is nothing wrong with that… but those with ambition almost all leave.

It's why I left.

And then I realise that might not be what Paige means at all. She's talking about her and Oliver.

'Do you think I left because you were with Oliver?'

Paige has another drink from her mug, then stands and heads to the shelf by the window. She takes down one of the books and opens the cover, before passing it to me. Our names are written on the title page in blue biro. Her swirly, neat handwriting is something I've not seen in years but now feels unmistakable. Mine is far more untidy and somehow feels less familiar. I can't remember the last time I had to write something down. It almost feels archaic now when there's a notes app on a phone.

I check the cover and it's *The Case of Charles Dexter Ward*.

'It's the US edition,' Paige says. 'Do you remember how excited we were when we found it on the market? The guy who ran the book stall said he'd bought it as part of a job lot and then put it to one side for us.'

'He always wore a flat cap and wax jacket. He was Irish and thought you were called Niamh. We went along with it.'

Paige lets out a small laugh: 'That's him. Do you remember how much we paid?'

'It was supposed to be three quid. We didn't have it all at the time but he let us take the book and said he trusted us to come back with the rest of the money the next week. When we went back, he'd forgotten about the money and said it was fine.'

I hand her back the book and Paige puts it on her shelf.

'I've sold almost everything I've ever owned,' she says. 'But I kept the books.'

Paige sits again and we both stare at the two pills. It feels as if a long time passes in which that's all we do. This isn't what I thought life would be like when I got on a plane in Toronto.

'I have money,' I say. 'Not loads but enough. If you want help, or… *rehab?*'

I whisper the final word and, after a few seconds, with Paige's lack of response, wonder whether she's heard. I almost say it again except that I can't.

She's twice told me she doesn't need saving – and here I am trying to do precisely that.

We don't speak for a while. Perhaps there is nothing left to say? I want to ask her about the rock and Richard's apartment but I can't do that either. Something feels broken and perhaps the reason is because I was never meant to come back.

I feel my phone buzzing through my pocket and fish it out, before realising that I have a missed call and a series of WhatsApp messages from Oliver. He says that Richard has a Crown Court bail hearing in the morning and asks if I want to come.

The court itself is in the nearest city to Macklebury, a good forty-five minutes away if the roads are clear.

I start to reply and then stop.

*WTF you doin with him?*

I can only assume he meant me with that message to Paige. It feels aggressive and yet…

His wife, no matter what might have happened between them, is spending much of her time with a man who used to be her friend decades before. I twice told Oliver nothing was happening between us but he has no reason to believe me.

The fact he's willing to drive me out to visit Richard in prison, and then again to see him in court, perhaps says more about his feelings for his brother than I give him credit for.

I stand and tell Paige that I'm going to go to the Crown Court in the morning.

'I should probably leave,' I add. 'I'm getting picked up at eight and could do with some sleep. We can maybe catch up tomorrow…?'

Paige doesn't respond until I get to the door. I have my fingers around the latch when she calls my name.

'I called you because I'm selfish,' she says.

'What do you mean?'

'I was hurting and I wanted you to see what you left behind. I still felt like that little girl looking for the boy next door in his pink and black T-shirt.'

The lump in my throat has returned. It's bigger than it's ever been and I can barely swallow.

'I felt like I knew you then,' she adds. 'And I suppose I wanted to know if you would still come to me.'

Paige isn't looking at me. She has the mug in her hand and is staring into the bottom.

I wait but there's no follow-up and I couldn't speak, even if I wanted to.

With that, I unlatch the door and step through it, then close it behind me.

# THIRTY-ONE

The ground is crunchy as I step onto Macklebury High Street. I'm unsure if it's frost or snow – but it's fresh and unspoiled by footprints as I immediately put a dent in it. I head past a row of closed shops and continue on until I reach the Co-Op supermarket. Aside from the takeaways, it is more or less the only place open in Macklebury after darkness.

I go in and there's a young woman behind the counter who is scanning items with a steady *beep-beep-beep*. She's in her early twenties and I can picture her as someone like Paige who went to the High School and then fell into a job that she'll do as long as she can. Or, in Paige's case, until she's fired for theft.

I mooch around the aisles until I'm in the seasonal section. The shelves are piled floor to ceiling with chocolate selection packs, tins of biscuits, mince pies, Christmas cakes and Christmas puddings. The display reminds me of when I was seven or eight, and Dad came home the weekend before Christmas with at least a dozen battered boxes of mince pies that he'd got from a mate of a mate. He stacked them next to the tree and refused to let them be opened until Christmas Day itself. It was the same with the chocolate, nuts, fruit, cake, and everything else my parents had amassed for the festive period. On the twenty-fourth, we'd have to *look* at everything; from the twenty-fifth onwards, we could scoff whatever we wanted until the point that Evie and I would almost make ourselves sick.

It was a long time until I figured out that 'mate of a mate' or 'off the back of a lorry' meant that someone at his work had either nicked a bunch, or knew someone who had.

I pick up a box of Cadbury's Roses from the shelf and head to the front of the shop where I get in line behind a woman who has cleaned out the display of two-for-one Jaffa Cakes. I wait my turn, pay, and am on my way out of the shop when I spot Ms Hill on her way in. The last time I saw her was in the school car park when things got very awkward, very quickly because Paige asked her outright about the love child she'd had with Mr Wilson.

I don't fancy another conversation, or even the awkwardness of being seen, so it's through embarrassment that I find myself hiding behind a giant display of chocolate oranges. My old geography teacher plucks a basket from the stack and turns towards the fruit and veg, before she twists to talk to the young woman who's trailing behind.

It's only when the girl calls the older woman 'Mum' that I realise she must be the daughter that Ms Hill and Mr Wilson had together. She has blonde hair with pinky-red streaks and is severely underdressed for the temperature, with no coat, a sleeveless top, and both arms decorated with braided, colourful bracelets that snake up and around her forearms.

I wait until they're past – but then step out from behind the chocolate oranges at what turns out to be precisely the moment that Ms Hill turns to ask her daughter something. She spots me and does a double take, perhaps wondering if I'm some sort of stalker.

I consider apologising for the awkwardness of the other day – or, more to the point, the accosting in the car park – but the fierceness of her stare offers too great a warning for me to attempt to say anything. I head towards the exit, where I stop and risk a look back towards the produce aisle, where neither woman has moved. Mother and daughter stare at me, with a mix of combined curiosity and anger. They have a dead lover and a dead father to grieve.

There's little else to do, so I turn, duck my head, and then hurry off along the crisped path in the direction of Evie's house.

# THIRTY-TWO

Evie's morning routine is nailed down seemingly to the minute. It's not only that she gets up at the same time, which would not be unusual, it's that she has spent an identical amount of time in the bathroom every morning since I've been here.

That makes it sound as if I'm waiting outside with a stopwatch but the truth is less sinister and more down to age-related bladder issues. A close eye on a clock after waking up becomes a necessity.

My sister also seems to have the same breakfast of a small yoghurt and juice every day. The wild card is that the juice could be any colour from the rainbow – and today's is a bruise-coloured bluey-purple.

She barely looks up as I enter the kitchen. 'On your own today?'

I ignore the implication. 'I didn't hear anything from next door last night. Did you?'

Evie doesn't reply. When we were younger, we could go back and forth with passive-aggressive digs for hours at a time. *Days* sometimes. We were crueller to each other then. She had spots and I must have brought them up every day for close to three years. She'd tell me I was going to fail my exams and end up working in a McDonald's. I'm almost certain she told me that on the morning of my first GCSE. I had braces for about a year and, every time she saw me, she'd jump back and say I was terrifying to her and all her friends.

'Are you staying for Christmas?' she asks.

'I'm not sure.'

'I've got plans with some friends. We do a pot-luck thing every year. I hosted last time and it's someone else's turn now. I won't be around on the day itself. I'll be gone at some point on Christmas Eve and won't get back until late Boxing Day. If you want to do something here, or have someone over, then you're welcome.'

The 'someone' sounds suspiciously like a dig but I let it go and reply with a simple 'thank you' instead.

Evie scoops the last spoonful of yoghurt from the pot and then washes it in the sink before placing it in the recycle box. She returns to the breakfast bar and alternates between her coffee and juice.

'Is Liane visiting for Christmas, or is the separation official?'

'I wouldn't have said "official", but…'

My sister looks up from her coffee. 'You're here and she's there.'

'Exactly.'

'What about Paige?'

'What about her?'

Evie raises her eyebrows and it's impossible not to see Mum in her asking a question without asking it.

'There's nothing going on,' I add.

'I hear things.'

'About Paige and me?'

'About her.'

We stare at each other but it only lasts a second until Evie scoops up her mug and finishes the coffee. She rinses that, too – and then places it carefully in the dishwasher.

'What have you heard?'

'Things.'

'What does that mean?'

Evie stands over me. With her heels and the fact that I'm on a stool, she's a good foot taller.

'I don't gossip – but I'm just saying maybe she isn't the little girl you used to sit in the garden reading books with.'

'We all change, though…?'

'Some people more than others.'

My sister touches my shoulder momentarily before pulling her hand away. It could be the first physical contact we've had since I got back. We were never a touchy-feely family. Love was implied, never spoken of, and certainly never expressed with anything more than a hand on the shoulder.

Evie picks up her bottle of juice and steps around me until she's half in the hall. 'I have to go to work,' she says. 'Are you going to be in later?'

'I think so.'

'I'll see you then.'

She offers a narrow smile and then turns to grab her coat and keys before heading outside. With the door open, cold air momentarily blasts through the house until she closes it once more.

With Evie gone, I check my phone again. I had no messages from Paige overnight and didn't send any to her. I keep thinking of the object she put in her bag before we went to Richard's. It could be nothing, or it could be everything. I don't know what rumours Evie might have heard but they're likely the ones I've heard. Either that Paige is an addict, or that she was sleeping with people for money. Both could be true.

She's *not* the girl I knew.

But then I'm not the boy *she* knew, either.

*People change. Then they change again.*

I had definitely heard that somewhere before she said it the other day. It could be a famous saying, or quote, though it feels like something more familiar.

There's a beep of a horn from outside and I take the hint, hurrying to the front door and waving to Oliver to let him know that

*I* know he's waiting. I put on my shoes and grab my jacket – and then I'm outside and in his car.

I am reaching for my seat belt when I notice he's wearing a suit.

'Should I change?' I ask.

Oliver looks across to my jeans. 'You'll be fine.'

He sets off and neither of us speak until he's on the same A-roads that we took out to the prison.

'How were the police yesterday?' he asks.

There's a moment where I think he's talking about Richard's flat. Then I almost correct him to say that Henderson and Allen had been waiting outside Evie's house longer ago than that – but then I realise that it *was* yesterday he drove me to the prison and back to Evie's. So much has happened that one day has blurred into the next.

'Fine,' I say. 'It was all over with quickly.'

'What did they ask about?'

'Mainly when Richard and I found Graham. I said they'd get better answers from looking at my old statements.'

It feels like there's going to be a follow-up question but Oliver remains quiet.

'Have you heard anything from Richard's solicitor?' I ask.

The question hangs unanswered for a few seconds as Oliver navigates a bend and mutters something to himself. I wonder if he knows that we found a blood-stained rock in Richard's apartment, or that the police now have it.

'Nothing important.'

I glance sideways, wondering if there might be a visual clue that Oliver could know. If he does, then there's nothing in his face to give it away.

Given I'm trapped in a car with him until we get to court, it doesn't feel like the best time to tell him.

'Are your parents going today?' I ask.

'Just Mum. She's driving herself. Something about having time to clear her head and driving being therapeutic. I did offer to take her…'

Presumably, his father isn't even an option.

The rest of the journey is punctuated by a series of phone calls or messages that Oliver doesn't acknowledge. He knows the way to court and skirts around the side into a small car park off a side street. His mother is waiting for us a little inside the courthouse doors. There are people hanging around but, given we're away from Macklebury, it's nothing like as claustrophobic as it was when Richard made his previous appearance.

Mrs Whiteside – *Veronica* – spends a good few minutes asking how I am and how I've been keeping since she last saw me. She talks about the jet lag she had when she and her husband visited Cuba the year before and how she feels like she lost a week of her holiday. She speaks quickly and nervously, wanting to avoid any particular thoughts about what's about to happen. She soon moves on to talking about a new country pub that opened last summer, which she says I absolutely have to visit.

She only stops when the doors to the court open, which gives us an invitation to head inside.

This court is far grander than the one at the magistrates' back in Macklebury, with vast arched ceilings and elaborate carvings etched into the curved stone. The smell of dust and wood is almost overpowering, as if history itself is embedded into the architecture.

An usher leads Oliver, his mother and me across to the public gallery, where we sit a level or two above the rest of the court and watch as others start to file in. The room is bigger than the one at the magistrates' – but it's emptier, too. There are seats in the public area that are unfilled, while the lack of journalists in the press area makes whatever's happening today feel like more of an afterthought than something as important as determining whether Richard should be released.

Everyone goes through the ritual of standing for the judge and then Richard's name is announced, before he is brought up to the dock. He is in the same suit as the last time he was in court and looks up to the public gallery, where he acknowledges us with a nod. He whispers something to the guard at his side and then scratches his hip feverishly, before taking a deep breath.

The Crown call no witnesses as the lawyer runs through the reasons why she thinks Richard should be kept in prison until a full trial.

Even to my incredibly untrained ear, it feels spurious. She goes over information I've already heard or found out – that Mr Wilson and Richard had an argument in a hotel relating to a disputed accountancy bill. That led to a drunk Richard being thrown out of the hotel. He was witnessed waiting outside the gates and then, not too long later, Wilson's body was found a short distance away.

There are other details about how Wilson used to be Richard's head of year and that involved needing to discipline him on various occasions – although the fact this was two decades before is not mentioned.

She concludes by saying that Richard being an accountant means that he could be adept at hiding money, which could be used to leave the country.

The tenuous nature of everything is addressed immediately when Richard's solicitor gets his turn. He says that Richard admits to being drunk on the night of the killing but adds that Keith Wilson was as well. It was two drunk men saying silly drunken things to one another. Not a one-way tirade and not a murderous vendetta.

He points out that Wilson was Richard's head of year two decades before and that there are no documented feuds between the pair. If anything, the opposite is true because Wilson hired Richard to do accounting work for him in the recent past.

The idea of Richard hoarding money to escape the country is 'plainly ridiculous' – and then he points out that, by omission, the Crown aren't trying to claim that Richard is a danger to the public.

After that, he says that Richard has a respected job as a local accountant, with no criminal record and no history of violence. The only thing he's guilty of is being drunk, arguing with a former client, and being in the wrong place at the wrong time. As best he can tell, there is no physical evidence linking him to the scene, no murder weapon, and no witnesses who saw anything other than Richard being outside the hotel a little before the killing.

The suggestion is that Richard could be bailed to his parents' home, with appropriate tagging and conditions. He would also happily surrender his passport.

The lawyer concludes by saying that, if what was put forward by the other side is enough to deprive a man of his liberty for months on end, then 'everyone in this courtroom is in danger'.

There is a whiff of middle-classishness about it – that a white-collar worker could *never* be guilty of such a senseless killing – but it's also hard for me to disagree with the sentiment. It was all such a whirlwind demolition of the Crown's case that I feel exhausted having watched it.

The judge says he will retire to consider his verdict – and then everyone's on their feet once more as he leaves the court. Richard is quickly shuffled away through the door behind the dock.

I spend the next thirty or forty minutes mooching around the courthouse waiting to be called back. Oliver sits with his mum in a side room but it wasn't the right place for me to invade. The grand hall itself is an endless bustle of people hurrying from one end to the other, while stopping to check listings boards outside each individual court. Men and women in suits tear around while balancing improbable mounds of files under their arms – and there's a general sense that nobody quite knows what's going on.

I end up sitting on the bench closest to the court, wondering what I'll do if Richard is bailed. I came back to help and, though it's debateable that I've actually done that, it doesn't feel as if there is much else I can do here.

There are connections from Paige to Wilson that I'm not sure I want to think about. Perhaps connections from Richard to Graham. The one constant is that it doesn't have to have anything to do with me. I could book a flight and head back to Canada to have Christmas there.

Those thoughts disappear as an usher appears to start beckoning people back into the court.

The pantomime continues as Richard is brought in, everyone stands, the judge returns, and then everyone sits.

With an outside eye, it's all ridiculous – although, mercifully, the judge does not spend much time messing around once he's back. He tells Richard that he's 'minded to grant bail'.

At this, Richard's mother gasps and leans forward in her seat. She holds her head and stage-whispers a 'thank you' as Oliver places a hand on his mum's back.

Richard himself takes an enormous breath and lets his head rock backwards as he stares up towards the ceiling. One of the two guards reaches towards him with a sharp lunge and I don't realise immediately that it's because Richard's knees have gone. The guard ends up supporting him as the judge continues reading.

The conditions seem relatively standard. Richard has to live at his parents' house and be indoors from eight at night until six the following morning. He'll be tagged and has to report to the police station every fourteen days.

His solicitor hastily agrees to this and then calls up to the public gallery to say that we can all meet outside the court.

It's taken less than five minutes – but suddenly it's over. Oliver, his mother and I drift through the door to wait outside the court. Oliver says he'll call his dad to let him know, and then he disappears out through the main doors, leaving me standing awkwardly around his mum. Around *Veronica*, as she insists I call her.

'It's such a relief,' she says to me with a quivering voice.

'It really is,' I reply, not knowing what else I could say.

'Hopefully, with him outside, the rest of it can be sorted.'

I nod along, wanting to be anywhere but here.

Luckily, Oliver returns after a minute or so. He says his dad is going to make up the spare room in preparation, although a silent, darkened look is exchanged with his mother which makes me think about the fall-out Richard had with his father. It must have been serious for them not to talk to one another and, essentially, lead to the breakdown of Richard's relationship with Joanne. None of that was mentioned in court, presumably because it might have led to bail being denied as Richard wouldn't have a viable place to live.

It's not long before Veronica lets out an excited squeal. I turn to follow her stare, as Richard walks through the main hall of the court, with his solicitor at his side.

It was only yesterday that I visited him in prison and he understandably seems more at ease now. He's standing taller, unburdened by having to return to prison. When he gets to his mum, he pulls her in for a hug and she squeezes his middle tightly until he eventually has to extricate himself from the pincer grip. He shakes hands and pats the back of his brother and then does the same to me.

'I can't tell you how grateful I am that you're here,' he says.

I tell him that it's no bother – and then we all turn to head towards the exit.

I realise what's about to happen about three seconds before it actually does.

Detective Sergeant Allen and Detective Constable Henderson are sitting on a pair of chairs close to the main doors. They're smartly dressed, in uncrumpled suits, ready for business. As we get closer to the exit, the pair of them stand as one. Nobody else seems to notice them, certainly not Richard, who is beaming as he gets closer to the doors. Light floods through the glass of the windows, a precious glimpse of freedom, but he's not going to reach it.

Before he gets to the doors, the two detectives swoop forward and block the way.

It's Henderson who does the talking. 'Richard Whiteside?' he asks, obviously knowing the answer.

Richard stammers a clumsy 'yes…' – and then Henderson goes in for the kill.

'I'm arresting you in connection with the murder of Graham Boyes. You do not have to say anything. But it may harm your defence…'

# THIRTY-THREE

'The police must have found something new...'

It's either the fourth or fifth time that Oliver says this since we got into his car.

I don't reply in any way other than a non-committal 'I guess...' as if I'm mulling over the prospect. I don't know what else to say. The truth of telling him I know exactly what they found doesn't feel like an option. The *other* truth – that it was Oliver's wife who *actually* found that rock feels even less appealing. The idea that she might have planted it is the worst revelation of all.

I console myself by repeating silently that the police know what Paige found and where she found it. They're too smart to take everything at face value and will surely be doing their own due diligence to ensure that she couldn't possibly have left it there herself. I tell myself that because I can't quite face having to choose between my two old friends. Either Richard *did* have something to do with Graham's death all those years ago – or Paige knows something. I can't see an alternative. There's betrayal whatever happens.

I keep all of that to myself, instead allowing Oliver to talk himself in circles. It will come out eventually that Paige and I were at Richard's flat when the rock was found. I'm a coward but I hope I am long gone by then.

We're away from the court and back on the road towards Macklebury. Hot air is blasting from the vents and freezing rain has been falling ever since we dashed to the car.

'The police must have stumbled across something,' Oliver repeats. 'It's been almost twenty years. I wonder what it is…?'

I don't answer and Oliver falls quiet. There's no radio or music, with the only sound being the gusts from the vents.

'Why *did* Richard fall out with your dad?' I ask. 'I can't understand why he's not been around.'

It's a dangerous question but I know I won't be alone with Oliver in a car much longer. It feels as if I might as well get it out.

'Did the police ask you about it?'

'No – but people around town seem to know, so there's every chance they do.'

'Does that mean *you've* been asking around?'

There's something underlying and sinister in the question and I watch Oliver's fingers grip the steering wheel tighter.

I choose the words carefully: 'It's not like that,' I say. 'It's hard to keep anything private in Macklebury. People know I'm Richard's friend and they like to gossip because he's in trouble.'

Oliver's fingers loosen on the wheel, though I don't risk turning fully sideways to take him in.

There's no reply at first and I assume the rest of the journey will continue in silence, until he unexpectedly answers.

'I don't know exactly,' he says. 'Something to do with money. I don't know how well you remember him but Dad's an old-school man's man. He's set in his ways and spends his evenings at the golf club, or the Conservative club. When he's had a drink, he goes on about snowflakes, woke culture and political correctness. He hates gays and protestors and foreigners and socialists and… you get the picture.'

Oliver spits the words with a barely disguised fury as he pauses for breath.

'He's never caught up to the twenty-first century and he's been getting worse over the past three or four years. Anyway, you know he's an accountant – and then Rich ended up doing the same thing. There was a point where I figured Rich wanted to follow in Dad's footsteps and take over the business but it didn't quite work out like that. Rich didn't want to work *with* Dad; he set up by himself. There was this uneasy co-existence for years, where they were both doing the same job, in the same town, but finding a way to not step on each other's toes.'

Oliver slows for a set of traffic lights and then drops the car into neutral as an old woman hobbles her way across the junction while laden with a pair of heavy-looking shopping bags.

'What happened then?' I ask.

'Rich didn't want to talk about things – and Dad simply wouldn't, so I only know any of this because of Mum. I'm not saying she's wrong but there's a pretty good chance Rich told her one thing, Dad told her another, and I'm getting something in between. All that and we're not a family to talk about feelings in the first place. That's why I'm saying I don't know *exactly* what happened.'

'What did you hear?'

Oliver doesn't reply right away. He puts the car back into gear and edges forward until we're moving again. 'It's family business really, but…' He tails off and then seemingly decides that I should hear it anyway. 'Rich took a contract or three from Dad. I don't know the exact details but they were from some local businesses. Rich lowered his rates, so they went with him. Mum said that there'd been a few cross words, with Dad telling Rich it isn't a race to the bottom but I wasn't there for that. Either way, I guess things were never quite the same.'

'They must have worked something out if Richard was going to be bailed to your parents' house…?'

'That was more Mum than Dad. She'd spent the last few months trying to get me to be a go-between, despite the fact that neither of them wanted to talk about it, least of all to me. She couldn't get through to them, so I don't know why she thought I could.

They're too similar. Too stubborn. I guess Dad figured having Rich out of prison was more important than whatever's going on between them.'

'Not important enough to go to court, though…'

As soon as I've said it, I realise how blunt it sounds out loud. I wouldn't be surprised if it was too much for Oliver to hear about his father but it doesn't appear to faze him.

He continues to drive and then, before I know it, we're passing the town's welcome sign once more. It's only then that I realise the biggest curiosity in everything Oliver has been saying. He talked about the police having to have found something new on Richard but he never once said that he didn't think his brother was capable of killing. He's not said that in relation to either Wilson or Graham, even though others have. We're not too close but if anyone told me Evie was accused of killing someone, my first reaction would be that there had to be a mistake. That's what it was when I heard about Richard.

'I'll message you if there's news.'

I realise Oliver is slowing as he speaks. We're close to our old school, where Paige and I accosted Ms Hill in the car park what now feels like weeks ago.

'I've got a few errands to run,' he adds, as an explanation for why we're apparently stopping here.

'I'll wait to hear from you,' I reply.

'Are you going to be around town much?'

'I'm not sure. Probably for a few more days at least.'

Oliver has stopped on the yellow zigzag lines, so I don't hang around in getting out. He doesn't waste time, either, as the moment I close the door, he pulls away.

The rain couldn't have got as far as Macklebury as the pavements are dry outside the school. It's a little warmer – although that isn't saying much. Any hint of snow has melted away and, as weeds poke through the edges of the walkway, it feels more like the small town I once knew.

I set off towards Evie's house but, within a few seconds, I'm outside Antiques World. The rusting A-frame board sits on the pavement outside, although there is no accompanying half-eared Baker cousin outside this time.

I'm almost past when I stop and turn. It's a large warehouse-type building with a shuttered garage-style door at the front. It's hard to pinpoint precisely why but there's something about the files in Richard's cabinet being out of alphabetical order that I've not been able to get my head around. It's not only the order, it's that the two businesses run by the Baker cousins – this one and the vape shop – were next to each other.

I head into the building. There is nobody out front, although it's impossible to miss the CCTV camera that's attached to the nearest wall, with its lens pointedly aimed towards the door. Aside from that, there are tall shelves placed short distances from each other, which create long corridors that run the length of the warehouse. There is the vaguest sound of voices from somewhere in the distance but I head into the aisle on the far left, where there's nobody in sight.

Each shelf appears to be packed with very un-antique-looking items. On the first section of shelving, there is a hi-fi that's so old it has a double tape deck built into the front. Next to it are boxy speakers that are remarkably similar to the ones Dad used to have in our living room. Before the days of wireless and Bluetooth, it was cables stuck together with black electrical tape and then stapled to the wall, plus huge wooden boxes with corners sharp enough to amputate an arm.

Past that, there are three rusting fans, a couple of ugly lamps and a ceramic jug. It looks a lot more like junk than it does antiques – but that might be why this is a long way from my field of expertise.

I continue along the aisle, noting much of the same and, as I get towards the end, the voices get louder. There are two men talking to one another, their voices echoing up and around the narrow, packed aisles. I'm largely hidden behind a stack of rotting wooden chairs but I peep through a gap across to the opposite corner, where two of the Baker cousins are sitting on stools watching some horse racing on a television that's pinned to the wall above.

It's hard to figure out who's who – and I didn't have a great grasp over which cousin was which in the first place. One of them is definitely missing part of his ear and I try to remember if that means he's Simon, who was named on Richard's documents as the owner of this place. The vape shop was owned by Terry, which, assuming he's there, would likely make the other man in front of me – the one with a beard – Luke.

If that's true, then it's Luke who offers his phone to Simon, who lets out a low whistle. 'Who's this?' Simon asks.

'You've gotta get on Tinder,' Luke replies.

'We're way too old for all that.'

'You wouldn't be saying that if you had someone messaging you these pics.'

Simon looks closer at the screen and then lets out another whistle. 'Is she from round here?'

'Close enough.'

'You met her yet?'

'We're talking about this weekend – but I used that old photo of when we were in Kavos and—'

'Are you joking? We were teenagers then.'

Luke smooths down his hair and sucks in his gut. 'That's the problem. Do you think she'll notice?'

'That you're twenty years older than your photo? Assuming her eyes work, yeah, I think she'll notice.'

Luke takes his phone back and scrolls through a screen or two. 'Might try meeting her anyway. What's the worst that can happen?'

His cousin doesn't respond directly to that, though he does pull out his own phone. 'You should send those to Pete,' he says.

'Nah, he prefers 'em younger, don't he? Twenty's plenty for our Pete.'

They go quiet for a while as they continue to stare up towards the racing. I figure I've seen whatever it was I came here for, or at least had a look around at the kind of business it is, so turn to go – which is when I manage to catch my shoulder on the stack of chairs. There's a thump, an ominous rattle of wood on wood and then, as I hold up both hands to protect myself from being buried underneath them, the chairs wobble back and forth before settling where they were.

What I have done is alert both cousins to my presence. By the time I've established that I'm not going to be buried under a pile of chairs, they are at my side, each eyeing me with curious disdain.

'What are you doing here?' Simon growls.

I step away from the chairs, towards the exit – which is a good thirty metres away. The last time I saw this pair, they had cornered me outside Paige's flat.

Both cousins are bigger than me and, with his damaged ear, there's something unquestionably intimidating about Simon especially.

'Having a look around,' I reply. 'I didn't know you worked here…'

The two cousins swap a glance that says nothing kind.

'Hear they've finally caught your mate,' Simon says with a smirk. 'They'll be coming for you next.'

'Why?'

'You and him found that kid's body, didn't you? Probably in on it with him.'

I ignore the jibe and continue to back away. Both men continue to follow me along the aisle.

'We know your sort,' Simon calls. 'Coming back here and sneering down at us. Think you're better, do you?'

I'm crab-walking sideways – half heading to the exit and half listening to Simon. I should keep going all the way to the exit but I don't. I stop and face up to the pair.

'Are you sure Richard's not more connected to you…?'

Simon and Luke stop a few paces away from me, both seemingly confused.

'Huh?'

'I heard he does your accounts – and the ones for your cousin, brother, whatever at the vape shop. I thought I should probably mention it to the police. They might have missed something…'

I've done things in my life that are impossible to explain afterwards. One time, I picked up a baking tray from the oven without gloves. The skin blistered and burst and I could barely grip anything for a good two weeks. I couldn't explain then or now why I did it.

This is another thing that feels like that. Absolute stupidity.

Simon moves so much faster than I would have predicted. Before I can shift, he has me by the throat and is pinning me to the nearest wall. I try to flail but he's much stronger than Pete. I grip his forearm and there's no give at all. It's like he's holding a small child, with the small child being me.

His teeth are bared as fury snorts through his nose. He hisses a response, with flecks of spittle spraying onto my neck. 'You should watch yourself.'

As quickly as he grabbed me, he lets me go.

I'm coughing and gasping as I back away, trying to put distance between myself and the two men.

'Keep going,' Simon says, sounding amused now. 'I really wouldn't stick around this town if I were you.'

# THIRTY-FOUR

I hurry away from the antiques place at a speed which would have Paige struggling to keep up. My heart is pounding once more – but it's not only with fear. Mentioning Richard doing their accounts, and especially the police, was a trigger that I hadn't expected. Simon Baker might have thought he was warning me off – and perhaps he was – but he was also telling me there was something worth looking at. I'd be interested to know if the antiques and vape shop were two of the businesses Richard apparently poached from his father.

It is as I'm thinking of what I saw in Richard's filing cabinets that I remember something that had fallen from my mind in the rush and worry over finding that rock in his flat.

I need to get on the internet – and not just through my phone. My laptop is in Canada and Evie's not around for me to ask to use hers. Something tells me she wouldn't want me to anyway.

The answer appears in front of me like a mirage in a desert. Macklebury's library was a place where Paige and I would spend a fair few hours when we wanted to get away from our houses but when it was too wet to be outside. We would scan through the weirdest sci-fi novels and then show each other the strangest parts. It might be a phantom memory but I think there might have been a time when we started to write our own.

As if it has swapped roles with the church, there's a large sign outside that reads 'save our library', which is accompanied by a web address.

I head inside, where there is a wide counter and a barrier blocking any further way in. The barrier itself is already an upgrade on the system from when I was last here – where there was simply a woman who would ask to see a library card. If she was off working elsewhere, people could simply walk in.

The woman here now is younger than I would have guessed, which likely says more about my prejudices than anything else. She's certainly younger than me, with pure black hair and piercings through her nose and top lip. She asks if I'm a member and I say that I was… twenty years ago.

That gets a gentle laugh and a smile as she says there might be a chance I'm still in the system. She types my name into her computer and then laughs properly as she twists the screen so that I can see it.

My membership has understandably lapsed – and the last time I borrowed a book is more than twenty-two years ago.

'I think that's a record,' she says. 'For me at least.'

'I don't owe any sort of late fee, do I?'

There's another laugh as she peers towards the screen again. 'Two million pounds,' she says.

I take out my wallet: 'Credit card okay?'

'You must have a better limit than me.' She taps something on the keyboard and then turns her attention back to me. 'Do you want me to reactivate you, or…?'

'I only want to use the computers.'

'I can set you up with a temporary pass that will get you through today, if that's enough?'

I tell her that it is and she puts some details into the system before printing me out a barcode that I use to swipe myself past the barrier. She directs me towards the computers and then leaves me to it.

The library itself is so much more modern than anything I remember. There are posters up advertising reading groups and kids' writing workshops. Some author is making a visit next week and there is a sign giving details about free computer literacy courses. It's all a far cry from the standard book-borrowing service of when I was young. It feels so much more like a community hub.

I use the login and password I was given to get onto the computer system and then load a browser window. After that, I open the photos on my phone and find the one of the poker tips I found in Richard's desk drawer, on which someone – presumably Richard – had written a string of numbers and letters in the corner.

Something about financial issues has been bugging me ever since Oliver told me about why Richard and his father had fallen out.

It's the simplest question and yet surely the most important. *Why?*

Richard wanted to become an accountant because his father was. I thought, perhaps harshly, that it showed a lack of imagination or desire – but it was also a respect for what his dad did.

So why would he steal clients?

It also ties in to his connection to Mr Wilson – because whatever argument they were having was *also* about money.

It seems likely that the numbers and letters written by Richard are for a password. I thought the fact it was written on a random page of poker tips was one of those conveniences, in the same way that many people taking a note would reach for the nearest scrap of paper. But what if it wasn't?

I scroll through the old emails on my phone, looking for something from Richard. Once I've got that, I turn back to the library's computer, where I google 'Online poker'. I click the top link… which immediately takes me to a page saying that the site is blocked because of the library's filtering policy. I try the second poker site from the search – but that's blocked as well.

I'm about to try my phone after all when the man sitting three computers away leans across and offers a conspiratorial whisper as he nods towards my screen.

'Do you wanna know how to get around that?' he asks.

'How?'

'Alt-control-delete and look for a program named F-W. Click it, end the task and try again.'

I do precisely as he says and am immediately met by a webpage that loads as it should.

The man turns back to his own screen, although I'm aware that he likely still has half an eye on what I'm doing. A simple thing now feels suddenly illicit, so I roll my seat forward so that I'm tight to the desk. I use the rest of my body to shield the screen from anyone behind being able to see.

On the online poker site, I enter Richard's email address along with the numbers and letters that were written on the tips page.

It seems so simple – and yet it works.

The screen turns momentarily white and then there's a message that says 'Welcome Back, Richard!' as it lists a host of upcoming tournaments. There are options to 'play now' and 'buy in', with a notice that there's a tournament every night at 1900 GMT.

I'm not quite sure what I'm looking for, mainly because I've never gambled online, but I click on the 'My Account' link in the top corner, where a new page loads that lists Richard's balance as zero.

Richard's full name and address are on the profile tab – and it's there that I find a new label marked 'deposits'.

And that's where things start to come together.

Richard has deposited almost £13,000 into this site over the course of two years. I press to look at withdrawals – but there are none.

It isn't even my account but I can feel the cold wind blowing.

I try the next poker site from the search results – and the same details work there, too. In all, Richard's login works on seven of Google's top ten pages listed for online poker. Every one tells a similar story of zero withdrawals along with multiple deposits over the course of around two years. The lowest amount he's lost on one site is close to £5,000, with the highest being £31,000.

I open the calculator on my phone and type the seven numbers in. It can't be true, so I try it again – except that the number is the same.

Joanne told me she visited Richard's office and saw him sitting there late into the night. She thought he was burying himself in work because of a feud with his father – but the truth is so, so much worse.

No wonder he was stealing clients from his dad.

No wonder he was overcharging at least one of them.

I've not even clicked past the first page of results but it's clear that Richard has lost close to £150,000 playing online poker.

# THIRTY-FIVE

The last time I watched the local news would have been when Dad had it on in the evening. He was a serial news viewer and it was, perhaps, the only part of his daily routine that I remember him keeping from when I was a little kid all the way up to when I left for university. He'd sit in his armchair with what felt like pie and peas every night and shush anyone who dared make a noise as the local news reporters were on screen.

Dad's chair is long gone – and I don't have a pie or peas – but I sit and watch one of my two teenage best friends dominate the headlines.

*'Another twist today with the story of the man who was arrested in connection with the murder of his former teacher last week. Richard Whiteside, from Macklebury, was today bailed in that case – but immediately re-arrested in connection with the killing of schoolboy Graham Boyes, whose body was found underneath a railway arch eighteen years ago.'*

The newsreader throws to a reporter who is standing outside the courthouse. It's dark now, though the empty steps are lit up. She says that Richard was one of the two boys who found Graham's body and it sends chills through me. As far as I know, this is the first time either of us have been officially identified.

I'm waiting for my name to be discussed, though it never is. After that first mention, the fact Graham was found by 'two boys' is apparently forgotten. Instead, the phrasing makes it sound as if Richard was the only person who discovered the body. As if

Richard killed Graham, dumped the body, and then 'found' it later the same day.

There is grainy archive footage of the railway arch and the bush where we discovered Graham. It's all taped off as a bored-looking officer flits in and out of shot. Another image has a close-up of the blood on the ground, plus there are images of the school as it was, and photos of Graham.

It's Macklebury as it *was*, not as it is now. The Macklebury of my youth. My chest tightens and it feels as if I'm back there.

'You okay?'

I look across to Evie on the sofa. We're in her domain, even though it's as much mine as hers. She was typing on her laptop but her fingers are frozen over the keys.

'It all feels very… *close*,' I say.

Evie shifts the computer from her lap onto the sofa and continues looking towards me. 'You don't have to watch this.'

'I think I do.'

She gives it a moment as we watch the television together. A police officer I don't recognise is saying something about investigations being ongoing and asking any witnesses to come forward. I suppose the circle is complete and we're back to everything being as it was eighteen years ago.

'Mum and Dad were so worried about you…'

I keep my eyes on the screen as Evie speaks. I don't think I can face her when she's talking like this.

'When?' I ask.

'After you found Graham's body. You talked to the police a few times but you hardly spoke at home for a month. Everything was either a "yes" or "no". You stopped watching telly, or going outside unless it was to school. Even then you had a few days off with stomach aches or headaches. Mum would have usually shoved us out the door, even if we had black plague, but she let you decide if you were well enough.'

That lump is back in my throat but I manage to say that I don't remember. It seems as if there's an awful lot that I can't recall about my middle teenage years.

Evie is silent for a while.

Even recently, I've been seeing those weeks after finding Graham as an endless interview, with police, family, friends, locals, teachers and others wanting to ask what happened. There was a sense of being under attack, of saying what it felt like people wanted to hear, instead of what I remembered. It happened so often that the truth of what *actually* happened blended with what I used to tell people. I wasn't sure what was what.

And now, after all that, Evie points out that it could all be a construction, too. I spent a month missing school and looking inward.

'They wanted you to see a proper psychologist,' Evie adds after a while. 'Maybe a psychiatrist. I don't know who does what. They were trying to get a doctor to refer you but it never happened.'

'I don't remember that, either.'

'The only reason it didn't happen is because you had exams in the summer. For the first time ever, you actually did the work – and then you got the results.'

There's a sense that my sister is talking about someone other than me. What she says is true but there's something out-of-body about it.

About me.

'It's crazy that he could have killed that boy and then taken you back there to find the body,' Evie says. 'Netflix make documentaries about that type of thing all the time. They'll have a drone up above the town before you know it for the opening shots.'

'I… I just don't think that's what happened.'

'What if it did…?'

It's an honest question, not something my sister is saying to get a reaction. Because, if Richard really *did* do what they're saying he did, then it'll feel as if so much of my childhood was a lie. Finding Graham doesn't define who I am but it definitely defines a certain part.

There is the rock in Richard's flat, his gambling debts, the fallout with his dad, the accounts he was doing for the Bakers. There's something there… and at the centre of it all, maybe, is Paige.

I suddenly realise that I haven't spoken to, or heard from, her all day. Since I got back into the country, this is the longest period we've stayed apart.

'What are you going to do?' Evie asks.

'What do you mean?'

'Any trial won't be for months. Are you going to wait around for it…?'

'I don't think so. I'll maybe stay for Christmas and… um…'

I can feel my sister staring, wanting to tell me that I have to make a decision. If my life is no longer across the Atlantic, then it has to be somewhere else.

The moment is broken as Evie's phone buzzes angrily from its spot on the sofa. She snatches it and jabs at the screen before turning back to me.

'I'm going out tonight,' she says. 'Late plans. Same friend I'm staying with over Christmas. I'll probably be out overnight tonight as well.'

She closes the laptop and slots it into its place underneath the coffee table, before she heads past my seat. She pauses for a second, standing over me, and there's a moment in which it feels as if she might crouch to hug me. I'm almost ready for it – except she then continues on and out of the room. Moments later, I hear her footsteps on the stairs as she heads up to her room.

The television news has moved on to another story but it's hard to pay attention. I check my phone but there are no messages or calls. The only person who's contacted me all day is Oliver – and it would be quite the stretch to think of him as a friend. I hover over

Paige's name, wondering if I should ask how she's doing – except that I probably know. She'll be in her flat, with her pills… with those messages to Wilson arranging days and times.

A quiz show is on the screen when Evie next appears in the living room. She's in a dress and looks so unlike my sister that it's hard to take her in. Or, more to the point, she looks so unlike *the vision I have* of my sister. It is perhaps only me but I wonder if an older sibling ever quite sees a younger one as something other than *younger*.

She has a small suitcase and says she'll see me tomorrow if I'm around. I tell her to have a good time and then she's off. The front door closes, her car engine fires, and then I'm alone in the house in which I grew up. Not that she has any obligation to tell me – or that it particularly matters – but I have no idea who Evie is visiting, whether it's a man or a woman, if they're friends or 'friends'. I didn't even think to ask.

And that, perhaps, is my biggest problem.

The house rattles as the central heating fights against the outside cold. A pipe clanks angrily from somewhere above and then the window bristles from the wind.

Or did it?

I mute the television and listen as, moments later, there's a gentle *tap-tap-tap* on the window. I open the curtains and look out towards the darkened street. There is no street light directly outside the house, with the nearest orange glow coming from three doors down. I can't see much more than the rippled gravel that covers the driveway. The tree in the front garden of the house across the road is unmoving.

I close the curtains again and return to the seat. I've only been back sitting for a few seconds when there's another unmistakable trio of taps on the glass.

There is no wind, let alone enough of a gust to clatter a window.

I hurry through the house and open the front door, standing in the frame as the cold scratches at my face.

'Hello…?'

My voice is swallowed by the silence of the night.

'Hello…?'

I put on my shoes and then step outside. There is nobody by the windows at the front of the house and, when I look in the other direction, no one near Paige's mother's house.

I take a few more steps along the path until I'm halfway along. Lights are on inside Paige's mother's place, although there's nobody at any of the windows.

There's nobody anywhere.

Except there is.

I'm about to head back inside when there's a scrunch of boot on gravel. I twist towards the sound but it's already too late. I don't see a person, only a blur – and then something big and powerful slams into my side.

# THIRTY-SIX

Pain shoots along my side as my hip connects with the unforgiving gravel, closely followed by the weight of whoever has tackled me. There are other feet crunching across the gravel, more than one person here. I'm not a fighter but I know enough that only bad things can happen if a person gets pinned on their back. My legs are intermingled with someone's arms and I flail away with my feet as I push myself up towards a standing position. It's only as I slip and reel backwards that I feel a swish of air close to my face and hear a guttural snort of exertion. Without meaning to, I've somehow avoided a punch that was aimed at my head.

There's no light, or at least nothing that actually helps. The street light from three doors down is too dim and the ones in Paige's mother's house aren't stretching across the divide between houses. I'm battling shadows, where the constant crunching of gravel gives me more of an idea of where people are than my eyes.

A man grunts 'pin him down' just as someone else launches themselves towards me. I'm on my feet again now, backing away but unsure if I should run towards the house or the street. A blur flashes towards me and I swing a punch of my own that connects with a lucky splat on something that flattens underneath my fist. There's a groan and a person clatters into the gravel with a loud splash of stone on stone and a string of swear words.

It might be the first time I've ever deliberately punched another person. When I was beaten up on my way home as a kid, those bigger boys appeared so quickly that I didn't get a shot in before the kicking began. I went into survival mode of shielding my head, something I'd never been taught and yet came naturally.

As I continue backing away, I realise that I never understood how much it hurts to punch someone. As soon as the shot landed, my fist erupted in more pain than my side. I try to unclench my fingers but they feel stuck in position. I can feel the bones cracking – not that I have time to focus on that because the chomping of the gravel hasn't stopped. There has to be at least three people surrounding me.

Someone grabs at my arm and, as I try to shrug that person off, someone else snatches the other. Their pudgy fingers squeeze my arms as their collective strength drags me down. I try to fight and flounder but there's no point this time – not now there are two of them. Small stones dig into my back as the men use their knees to pin me tight to the ground.

I know who it is now.

There's still very little light but the two people jamming me down are close enough that I can see the half-ear on one and the bulk of the other.

It's Simon Baker from Antiques World and Terry Baker from Vape World.

They haul me up until I'm standing but each keep an arm hooked underneath my shoulders, meaning I can't move my arms.

The other two cousins appear now: Pete and Luke side by side, surrounding me along with the other pair. Luke's face is mashed potato with ketchup. His nose is flat and an explosion of blood is dribbling across his lips into his beard. It takes me a second to realise that it must have been him with whom my lucky punch connected… although I'm no longer sure whether it was that lucky.

He snarls with fury, which sends more blood flowing from his nose across his white-yellow teeth.

His punch is *not* lucky. He winds up and takes a short run at it as he buries his fist into my stomach. Pain explodes up through me as I cough and wheeze, trying to catch my breath. If I wasn't being held up, then I'd be on my back.

Luke readies his fist for another blow and I brace myself, waiting for it to come. Just as he's about to launch himself at me a second time, Pete holds an arm across him.

'Give it a sec,' he says.

It could be him showing mercy but it doesn't sound like it.

My throat is husky as I wheeze for breath. Fifteen or twenty seconds must pass until Pete decides I'm in a fit state to talk.

'I heard you've been getting in my business,' he says drily.

I try to reply, to deny that I have any interest in him, but the only sounds that come are a series of throaty gasps. Pinning him to that wall next to Paige's front door was a very, *very* silly mistake – although mentioning money in the antiques place might have been worse.

'Didn't I tell you to keep your nose out?'

I manage a nod but that's the best I can do.

'Maybe I wasn't clear?' Pete looks sideways to Luke, whose face is still drizzling blood. 'Do you think I was too subtle?'

'I always say you're too kind.'

Luke's response is as if he's trying to speak while underwater. He tries to wipe away the blood but only succeeds in smearing it further across his face. His nostrils are splayed flush, like a defeated boxer's. His stare never leaves me.

'Do you think he needs a clearer message?'

There's definitely no subtlety with Pete this time – and Luke gets the message loud and clear as he arches forward and launches another punch into my stomach. He hits so hard that my gut is in my mouth. I gag and froth, unable to breathe.

A second or two passes in which I'm not sure what happens. One moment I'm on my feet, the next I'm on the ground and being pulled back up by Simon and Terry, who lock my arms again.

'What do you know about Richard Whiteside and his business?'
Pete speaks calmly, as if he's asking where I want to go for dinner.

I try to reply but the only thing that comes is a series of spittle-infused bubbles. 'I...'

Pete's eyes narrow and it's as if he takes my inability to speak as a decision not to. He angles his head sideways, which is the only indication Luke needs to wind up for a third punch.

I ready myself as much as I can, given that I can't move my arms. I tense my stomach – except, before another blow can come, a door slams. The grip on my shoulders slackens and then, from behind, there's a wailing, screaming howl.

Before I know what's happening, I'm dumped face-first on the gravel, only narrowly managing to get my hands up to protect myself. There are small stones in between my fingers – and, though I'm creased over and still gasping for air, I am free.

I roll slowly onto my back and turn towards what sounds like a cartoon witch cackling. The Baker cousins are still standing over me and one of them swears a moment before there's a *thwick* of stone on stone. A moment later and one of the cousins reels backwards, holding his head, as he unleashes a volley of F-words.

I'm slowly getting my breath back as I look up and realise that Terry is now bleeding as well. He has a hand to his head and pulls it away to reveal a smear of red that's pooling into his eyes.

I stretch higher, trying to pull myself up, though only succeed in accidentally grabbing someone's wrist. Pete bears down over me and I quickly pull my hand away, feeling the snap of what feels like a watch strap as I do.

There's another click of stone on stone and then, all of a sudden, the cousins spread out, leaving me in the open.

Paige's mum is next to the low wire fence that separates her property from Evie's. She's barefooted in a loosely tied dressing gown that flaps as she bends down to pick up stones from the gravel that she launches one at a time towards the now retreating

Baker cousins. She's howling and laughing to herself as she reaches for more stones: 'Get out of it!'

More rocks rain down on the four men, who are now actively running away. I watch them disappear along the street and over the road, where they dash underneath a street light and then race into the nearest alley.

Stones continue to *chip-chip-chip* onto the road as Paige's mum cackles to herself. She reaches for another handful and then notices that her targets have gone as she tosses them with disappointment back onto the ground.

'Bah!'

I push myself up to my feet. My side aches from when I first hit the ground and it's hard to stand straight given the pain in my stomach. I turn to face Paige's mother, who makes no effort to fully fasten her dressing gown. I'm not sure where to look but I do manage a pained: 'Thank you'.

She doesn't reply, which is when I notice there's still a rock in her hand. It's impossible not to picture the one her daughter found in the back of Richard's toilet. A weapon in its own right. A blunt object.

For a moment, it feels as if she's about to throw it at me. She arches her back and raises her hand… and then she drops the rock back onto the ground with the rest of the stones.

'Thanks,' I repeat.

Nothing. Instead, she turns and scuttles towards her house. A moment later and there's a loud *slam* as her front door bangs closed.

I gulp a mercifully deep breath and then turn to take in the street. I half expect rubbernecking onlookers, or perhaps even a return of the Baker cousins. Instead, it's still. There's nobody there.

Another breath. The past few minutes feel like a dream, though not a good one.

I turn back towards the house, where the front door is still open – except, as I spin, something colourful catches my eye. Something out of place in the dark.

As I trudge across the gravel again, I see spots of blood and I find myself hoping it will rain tonight, else I'll have some explaining to do with my sister.

I figure the blood is what caught my eye… except there's something else.

Crouching hurts and I feel like a *really* old man as I squat.

It wasn't a watch strap that I accidentally snatched from Pete's wrist. It's something much more sinister. Something I've seen before. Something that should be innocuous.

A braided, colourful bracelet.

# THIRTY-SEVEN

It's late. Too late to be standing at a stranger's door. Worse than that, too late to be knocking on this *particular* door.

The house that had the barking dog in the front garden hasn't changed too much since Paige, Richard and I used to walk past it on our way to school. What *has* changed is my perception of the place. Back then, I was intimidated by the high hedges and anxiously loud dog. Now, it feels like the cosy detached cottage, next to the church, on the edge of town that it likely always was.

I hesitate before ringing the bell and have to whisper 'just get on with it' to myself.

I hope Paige was right when she told me who lived here.

The bell offers a satisfying ding-dong that rings from the inside of the house. I shiver on the doorstep, trying to ignore the pain in my side.

A light comes on in the hallway beyond and then there are footsteps. There is the sound of three locks unbolting – and then Ms Hill stands in front of me. It takes her a second to realise who I am as she blinks. I only then realise that she's likely eyeing the cuts and bruises on my face.

She quickly starts to close the door with a sharp: 'No, thank you.'

'It's about your daughter,' I say.

The door stops three-quarters of the way closed as she peers through the gap towards me.

'I'm really sorry about everything,' I add quickly. 'About the school, about the Co-Op. I wasn't trying to be weird, or—'

'What about my daughter?'

'Does she have a boyfriend?'

I realise how this sounds a moment after I've said it.

I speak even more quickly this time – 'Not like that!' – but the door is already closing a second time.

'You should leave,' she says, offering far more diplomacy than I deserve.

'It's important,' I say. 'I'm not asking for me.'

'What's my daughter got to do with you?'

'Nothing… it's just… do you know Pete Baker and his cousins?'

Ms Hill's grip on the door slackens a little as the gap widens.

'You must remember them from school,' I add.

'Of course I remember. Everyone in this town knows the Bakers.'

'Do you think there's a chance your daughter could be seeing Pete…? Sorry, I don't even know her name.'

She starts to close the door again as her frown sharpens. 'Pete? Of course not.'

I take the bracelet out of my pocket and offer it to her, just about getting my hand into the gap between the door and frame before it closes.

'Did your daughter make this?' I ask. 'I've only met her once and I saw her wearing a lot. I know I could be way off.'

Ms Hill nudges the door further open and then reaches to take the bracelet from me. She lets the door creak wider, seemingly not bothered about keeping me away any longer as she twists the bracelet around her fingers.

'It's one of hers,' she says quietly. 'She always stitches her initials into the pattern. She's been making these since she was eight or nine.'

My old geography teacher turns into a confused, worried parent in front of my eyes.

'Where did you get this?' she adds.

'I had a run-in with Pete Baker earlier. He either dropped it, or he was wearing it.'

I don't tell her about one of Pete's cousins saying that 'twenty's plenty' for him – or that he 'prefers 'em younger'.

She eyes my face again – the cuts and bruises – and then looks back to the bracelet.

'I don't know your daughter and I don't really know Pete Baker,' I say. 'I just wanted to leave this with you and, if it's something, then it's something. If it's not then I really, genuinely apologise for interfering.'

Ms Hill nudges the door until it's more or less all the way open. It exposes a long hallway that leads towards what seems to be a kitchen. There are coats hanging along the length.

'Do you really live in Canada?' she asks.

'Yes.'

'I thought the whole thing in the car park might've been a performance for whatever reason.'

'I really do live in Canada – and I also remember the project you had us do about the North American climate. None of that was made up. I think Paige and I got a bit carried away because our friend had been arrested and, well… sorry.'

She nods slightly, not exactly accepting the apology but not turning me away either.

'We argued,' she says quietly.

'You and your daughter?'

A shake of the head. 'She's called Grace – but no. I argued with Keith about Grace the day before he was killed.'

It takes me a second to realise Keith is Mr Wilson. The entire reason I'm back in Macklebury.

'Why did you argue?'

'I was supposed to be at the teachers' reunion last Saturday. I'd been looking forward to it for a while but I didn't go in the end because I was still so angry at him. He came round the night before. We hadn't been getting on for a long while. After he split with his wife, he thought me and him would get together – but I didn't want that. I was happy with whatever it was we had – but he didn't want to hear that. He tried to use Grace against me, saying that she should live with him. It was all a bit…'

She doesn't finish the sentence. Instead, she rests her head on the door frame.

'We would argue about all sorts of things, so the fact we argued last Friday wasn't such a big thing at the time. I thought it was just Keith being Keith.'

'What did he say?'

'That I should keep a closer eye on Grace and that she'd end up falling in with the wrong crowd if I wasn't careful. I thought he was doing his usual thing of trying to undermine me. I was trying to tell him that she's seventeen and that he doesn't understand because he doesn't live with her and because a seventeen-year-old girl thinks – and wants to act – like an adult. He was saying that he's taught enough kids to know when there's a problem. We ended up yelling at each other. I said things, he said things, and then…' She stares at the bracelet in her hand. 'I thought he was just being a dick.'

'Maybe he was…?'

Ms Hill looks up and catches my eye. 'He definitely was – but that doesn't mean he didn't have a point. Thing is, we're so used to arguing that I suppose I didn't listen. I thought he was talking about me – but maybe he was talking about Grace…'

'Do you think Grace might be seeing Pete Baker…?'

It's the second occasion I've asked – and, this time, she doesn't reply with instant dismissal. There's more resignation now.

She takes a breath and slumps against the door frame.

'She has a boyfriend but I don't know his name and she's never wanted to give too many details. I figured I wasn't much different at her age. As long as she was putting the work in at school, I thought it was okay…' She swears under her breath, at herself as opposed to me. 'Do you have children?' she asks.

'No.'

'You'd think I'd have some idea given the length of time I've been teaching. It's never the same with your own, though. My dad used to be a teacher and he'd always say the same about me. Here I am after all these years and nothing's changed.'

Her phone beeps and she stops to check the screen before returning it to her back pocket.

'That's her,' she says. 'She's out with friends but, if I'm honest, I don't know who exactly that is. She could be with Pete Baker right now. I don't know who she's seeing.'

She sounds defeated. It must have been a really long week for her, before I knocked on the door.

'When you talked to the police earlier in the week,' I say, 'did they ask about Grace?'

'Why would they?'

'That's kind of my point. They'd have no reason to ask, or make any connection – but if she *is* seeing Pete Baker and her dad found out about it…'

Ms Hill eyes me again, putting the same pieces together herself. 'I need to talk to Grace…'

'After that, you might need to call the police.'

She stares at the bracelet and then clamps her hand closed.

'I hope those heal soon,' she says, nodding towards my face – and then she closes the door.

# THIRTY-EIGHT

Paige doesn't answer when I ring the bell next to her door. I've already pressed it half a dozen times before I remember the wires at the back are disconnected. I try the door, though it's locked. I message her and then call.

No answer.

I move backwards on the pavement, staring up towards her window, where a faint light shines from beyond. I consider throwing stones up, like some 1980s romcom – except I feel fairly certain my aim is nowhere near good enough and I would end up hitting myself in the head with rocks.

There's been enough of that tonight, although the thought occurs that, if I'm after someone with a good aim at throwing stones, I should go and get Paige's mum...

There's no need for that because the door opens and Paige stands there, eyeing me carefully. She's in a thin top and tight jeans, shivering against the night.

'What happened to you?' she asks.

'Got in a fight with some stairs.'

There's no hint of a smile. 'I don't need lecturing tonight,' she says.

'Can I come up?'

She half turns inwards and, for the first time since I got back, it feels as if I'm about to be rejected by her.

'It wasn't some stairs,' I add. 'It was someone's fists and the gravel outside Evie's place.'

Paige steps forward into the light and looks at me more closely this time. 'Has someone patched you up?'

'Like who?'

'Did you come straight here?'

'More or less.'

She hovers in the doorway and it feels as if she's about to say that I have to leave.

'I won't be long,' I say.

'It's just—'

'It's important, Paige. I wouldn't be here otherwise – and I'm not going to lecture you.'

She sighs and looks both ways along the street before heading through the door and nudging it wide so I can follow. We go up the stairs and along the corridor together. Her door is on the latch and she pokes her head inside before holding it open. She closes the door behind me and then we stand awkwardly in the area between her kitchen and the sofa.

'I need to ask you something,' I say.

'I just—'

'You've got every right to be mad but I need to ask. When you left the other night, your phone was on the counter. I saw some messages with you and Mr Wilson…'

Paige gasps and reaches instinctively for the rectangular bulge that's in her pocket. 'You had no right.'

'I'm not defending myself.'

'So what are you doing?'

'I guess I'm asking why you've been in contact with him.'

We stare at one another and then Paige moves across to the sofa and sits. She cradles her head in her hands.

'I don't feel well,' she says.

I cross the room and take the spot opposite her on the chair. I don't reply to what she's said, partly because I suspect it's a way of avoiding the question.

Paige groans a little and then looks up. 'He was giving me private tutoring,' she says. 'I wanted... *want* to go back and do a degree. I've been thinking about it for years. I was looking into Open University courses and trying to get to a point where I could start. We had some sessions and he was good with me. Then I lost my job and didn't have the money. I had to stop going but he said we could "come to an arrangement". I obviously said no. We've not had a session in almost five months.'

Paige wrenches her phone from her pocket and jabs at the cracked screen, before she turns it around to show me the messages she and Wilson had exchanged. I'd not noticed when I spied on the messages before but she's right. They haven't been in contact for months. That's why his name was nowhere near the top of the list.

'You acted like you didn't know him,' I say.

'So what? Would it have made any difference if I told you he was tutoring me months ago? If I told you that it stopped?'

I start to reply and then realise that she's right. It wouldn't have made any difference at all.

'Did you tell the police?' I ask.

'What's to tell? That he's a creep? He was having at least one affair for more than a decade. They already know.'

I suddenly realise why Paige was so keen to talk to Ms Hill in the school car park. Why she jumped in to push for information. When it came to Wilson, Paige wanted confirmation, assurance even, that it wasn't only her. That he really is... *was* a creep.

I press back into the chair, realising what an arse I've been. When I saw Paige had been messaging back and forth with him, I immediately thought the worst – and didn't even bother to ask her about it.

'Is that why you're here?' Paige sounds aggrieved and it's hard to blame her. She half-turns towards the other side of the room, where the bathroom and bedroom doors are closed. 'I thought you *weren't* going to lecture me...?'

'I'm not. Sorry… I wanted to tell you about the daughter Wilson had with Ms Hill.'

'What about her?'

'She's called Grace and I think she might be seeing Pete.'

Whatever Paige might have been expecting, it wasn't that. She mouths 'what?' and then frowns as her mouth bobs open and closed. I have her attention now.

'She's only, what, sixteen? Seventeen?'

'Seventeen,' I say.

'Why do you think she's seeing Pete?'

'A few things. I overheard one of his cousins talking about how Pete likes younger women. Then he came to Evie's house tonight with his cousins. There was a confrontation and, well…'

I tail off and my face tells the rest of the story. When I checked myself over in the mirror before leaving for Ms Hill's house, there were two cuts close to my eye and a scratch underneath my chin.

'Why was there a confrontation?'

'It's hard to explain.'

'Was Evie there?'

'Just me.'

Paige's eyes narrow. I consider telling her about how her mum saved me but it doesn't feel like a detail for now. It feels surreal enough as it is.

'Are you okay?'

There's concern in her voice and she pushes herself up from the sofa as she crouches in front of me to take a closer look at the marks.

'They don't hurt, if that's what you're asking.'

She points towards the cuts by my eye. 'This one's pretty big.'

'I think I'll live…'

I mean it as a joke but I'm not sure Paige takes it as such. She sits back down and crosses her arms.

'There was some sort of bracelet on Pete's wrist,' I say. 'I accidentally pulled it off him. I saw Grace the other day and it was exactly like the ones she wears. I spoke to Ms Hill… to *Fiona*. She said that she argued with Wilson the night before he died. He wanted her to keep a closer eye on their daughter. She thought he was having a go at her parenting but it might have been that he was trying to warn her about Grace seeing Pete. I think he knew – and he wanted to stop it.'

Paige takes this in with a gulp. 'What are you saying?'

'You know what I'm saying.'

'You think Pete killed Wilson?'

It sounds much less convincing when Paige says it. Not as real as it has been in my head.

'I think he might be capable of it,' I say. 'He came to my sister's house with three of his cousins to give me a kicking.'

Paige is silent.

'You *know* he's capable of it…'

She glances away, partly looking towards her bedroom door and then twisting to face the floor. I let her sit for a moment.

'Do you know if he was seeing her?' I ask.

Her tone is defiant: 'Why would I know *that*?'

'You know him better than me.'

'I don't know him *like that*. We're not *friends*.'

'But you run when he calls.'

Paige clasps her head in her hands and pulls at her hair. She lets out a low grunt and then looks to me through blazing eyes. 'What about you and the guy who cuts your hair? Or the girl who serves you in a shop? Do you know their life stories? Pete sells something I buy. We're *not* friends and I *don't* know who his girlfriend is. Why do you keep bringing it back to this?'

She looks towards the front door and I should probably take the hint. There's a moment where everything stops and, seemingly, she can't quite bring herself to kick me out.

'Are we being honest with each other?' I ask.

'I've *always* been honest about who I am. I literally put it on the table in front of you and asked if you'd accept me as a friend.'

There is a quiver to Paige's voice and I look towards the table, picturing the two pills she laid there. The only thing there now is the vodka bottle from the other night, with a small amount of clear liquid in the bottom.

I'm not sure any of this has gone how I wanted but I came to ask a question and I suppose now is the time.

'When we were at Richard's flat, you called me through to the bathroom. The rock was in the cistern and I suppose I wondered…'

She doesn't let me off. She wants me to say it. 'Wondered what…?'

'I wondered if you put it there.'

Paige's eyes are so full of hurt that I can't look at her any longer. She tells me the truth without needing to say a word and, suddenly, it's me who doesn't want to be in this flat. It's not her, it's me. I can't handle the crippling betrayal in her voice.

'You can't think that of me…'

I shake my head. 'Not really… maybe. I've not known you in a long while.'

Paige gulps and I can hear the lump in her throat. It's so raw and pained that I can almost *feel* it. 'I've not changed that much.'

'I think I have.'

'I *found* that rock in his flat. I didn't *put* that rock there. Why would I?'

I want to give her an answer but I can't. I don't know why I thought what I did, other than that Paige is an addict and I couldn't get past that. In my sheltered world, an addict is bad. It's black and white… except it's not.

She isn't done. Paige glances towards her bedroom and then turns back to me. She lowers her voice. 'Richard's *everything* to me,' she says. 'That's why I called you. I don't believe he killed anyone. I thought you could help.'

'What do you mean he's everything?'

Paige bites her lip and checks over her shoulder again, as if there's someone standing behind her, even though there isn't.

'He saw what was happening between me and Ollie.'

'What was happening?'

The chills are back.

Paige rolls up her sleeve and scratches her arm. Her voice is still barely a whisper.

'I couldn't leave,' she says. 'Ollie didn't just want a wife, he wanted a *house*wife. He wanted his mum. He wanted a family, where I'd pump out the kids and raise them, while he'd go to work. The problem was that he couldn't, well… y'know…'

I don't at first. I almost say that I don't understand – but then I do.

'I thought it was me,' Paige says. 'We tried more and more things but it wouldn't work. Then he suggested being with other couples and I figured it might help – except he wasn't interested in *me* anyway.'

'What do you mean?'

Paige stares at me, as if telepathically sending the answer because I'm back in the car with Oliver, who is talking about his dad.

*He hates gays and protestors and foreigners*

*He hates gays and protestors…*

*He hates **gays**…*

'I thought it was because of me…'

Paige's voice cracks. She checks over her shoulder another time and then sighs long and loud.

'But you were married for years…? More than a decade.'

'I know!'

She falls back into the chair, sighing and pulling her knees into herself. She's pale and I can't work out if she was like that when I got here.

'Is that what got you onto pills?'

A shake of the head. 'You make it sound so simple. That one thing leads to another, leads to another. It doesn't work like that. He didn't *make* me take anything. I *wanted* to.'

'But—'

'Stop!' Paige shouts the interruption and then follows it up with a sharp: 'I've told you so many times that I don't need saving. I don't *want* saving.'

It feels as if it would be dangerous to reply, so I don't.

Paige breathes deeply and snottily through her nose. Her throat is rasping and, when she speaks again, her tone is husky.

'Ollie controlled the money, so I couldn't go anywhere. I wanted to leave but I couldn't. *That's* why Richard means everything to me. He got me away. He gave me the money to leave and put down a deposit on this place. He gave me a key to his flat and told me there were only two – his and mine. He said it would be safe if I needed it. *That's* why I had his key and *that's* why I really didn't want to find that rock. It was just there. I didn't want any of this to happen. I *told* you we could put it back where we found it.'

It's suddenly clear why Paige called. It wasn't about me, it never was, it was about Richard. She's desperate to repay him for the help he gave her – and that's totally understandable.

'After I left, Ollie told everyone I'd been sleeping around for money and that he'd kicked me out.' She catches my eye. 'You heard that from someone, didn't you?'

No point in denying it. 'From Martin…'

'You never asked if it was true.'

'I suppose…'

I turn away, feeling *tiny*. I should have asked. I saw my friend as a poor little junkie, incapable of making her own choices.

'I *wanted* you to ask. *You*, of all people. We were best friends.'

There's a lump in my throat now and the shame that fills me feels as if it'll never leave.

'Why wouldn't you tell people the truth…?'

I sound pathetic.

'*First*, because I shouldn't have to – and *second* because people had already made up their minds. Look at Ollie's family and look at mine. Nobody's going to believe me.'

She's right – and it's awful. Paige called me here to make things better and I've made them worse.

'I'm so sorry…'

I'm not sure what I want from her. A simple acceptance of the apology wouldn't feel like enough. I don't know what to say to make things better. Words probably aren't enough.

'*Shush*…' Paige gulps. 'Stop trying to save me. I made my choices. I love him…' She raises her voice until it feels like it's twice the volume. Not quite a shout but not far off. 'I *loved* him. But Ollie and I ended up not being the people we thought we were. We changed – and then we changed again.'

There's something about the way she says this that feels more forced than anything else. Considering what he's put her through, it seems incredible that Oliver has been such a big part of her life over the past week.

Perhaps longer.

'Richard lost a lot of money playing online poker,' I say. 'Probably six figures. I think that's why he fell out with his dad. If not directly, then because he had to go chasing business to make some of it back.'

Paige appears rocked by this. She leans back into her chair and then presses forward again. 'What do you mean? He never seemed skint.'

'Maybe he's not – but I think he's been doing the accounts for Pete and his cousins. They run an antiques place near the school and a vape shop in town. Maybe some other places, too.'

'What's that got to do with anything?'

'Mentioning those accounts is what got me into trouble tonight – because when Pete sells to you through those kids, it's always cash, isn't it? He can't just put that money in a bank. He needs everything to look legit – and I guess a twenty-two grand oak table or a sixteen grand writing bureau is one way to do that. Except do you think Pete and his cousins are smart enough to launder money themselves? They'd need an accountant to do the dirty work. Perhaps an accountant with gambling debts, who can't say no.'

There's a small intake of breath as I see it sinking in for Paige, the way it's been sinking in for me.

'But he gave me five thousand,' she says even more quietly than before. She looks around the room. 'That's why I'm living here. Why I can afford rent. I said I'd pay him back but he refused to let it be a loan and said it was mine.'

'If Richard was taking money from the Bakers, then I suppose it *is* yours…'

She whispers, 'No…'

I'm not necessarily right – but it could also explain why he overcharged Wilson for what sounds like a simple piece of accounting. Perhaps he was doing that on a wider scale? Partly to recoup his own poker losses, or partly to give Paige the money she needed to get away from Oliver.

'He did all that for me…' Paige looks as if she's standing in the middle of a road with a car bearing down upon her. 'I never should have looked in that cistern. Never should've shown you the rock, let alone let you call the police.'

'Do you think he did it?'

Paige and I look to one another and, perhaps for the first time, I ask myself that question as well as Paige. Neither of us answer but neither of us need to.

We don't believe Richard killed Graham.

'He might be okay,' I say.

'But what about the rock?'

I take a breath. In through the nose, out through the mouth. A lot of time has led up to the moment that's about to happen.

'There's something I've never told anyone.' I can't look at Paige as I speak. My stomach grumbles and growls in disapproval. 'I didn't tell my parents, or Evie, or you. The only people who know are Richard and the police… and whoever killed Graham.'

'What?'

'There was something done to Graham's body that was never revealed publicly by the police. They asked us to keep it to ourselves, so it could be used against the killer when they found him. I've kept it to myself ever since.'

'*What?*'

I open my mouth and then close it. It feels so wrong to finally say the words all this time on… except that it's a night of truth.

I tap my side. 'There were teeth marks right here. Whoever killed Graham didn't just whack him on the head with a rock. They bit him, too. I don't know why. If the bite mark is nothing like Richard's, then his solicitor will be able to use that.'

Paige is as white as the walls behind her, those eyes wide and wild. She looks terrified.

'Are you okay?'

Paige shakes her head slowly, gulps, and then rolls up her top to expose her belly.

And there, on her side, is an unmistakable rounded purple scar in the shape of a bite mark.

She whispers it even more quietly this time. A horrific, unexpected reprise. 'We tried more and more things…'

'Oliver…?'

His name leaves me as a whisper as Paige gulps again.

'You don't understand…'

But then I do. I understand why she's been checking over her shoulder all this time, because standing in her bedroom doorway, having apparently heard everything, is Oliver.

# THIRTY-NINE

I'm on my feet before I know what I'm doing. Oliver is staring at me and I'm staring back. He's not moving.

'You…?' It's all I can manage. 'All this time…?'

Oliver continues staring until his gaze flicks to Paige. She's still sitting on the sofa, holding up her top to show the scar.

'I was confused,' Oliver says. 'I thought I might be… you know. But I'm not. I like women.' He nods to Paige and his voice hardens. 'Tell him what we just did in there.'

Paige allows her top to fall back into place. She's looking at the floor and mumbles something I don't catch, which only serves to infuriate Oliver.

'Tell him!'

Paige continues to look down but her voice is louder now. 'He likes girls, all right? He likes *me*.'

Oliver throws his hands up, as if this is the answer to a quiz question nobody asked. He's talking to me now. 'See?! All this time you've been chasing around after her – but she always comes back to *me*. She can talk about separation, or divorce – but she always comes back. Always has and always will. She's *my* wife – and that means something.'

'But you and Graham…'

'Haven't you ever made a mistake? He broke his arm sledging on Hail Hill and I took him down to the phone box to call for help. I went in the ambulance with him. We got talking. We were mates and then things just sort of… got out of hand.'

And the puzzle is almost complete.

No wonder Oliver married Paige, given his father's attitude.

No wonder they made each other miserable.

'I didn't *mean* to do it,' Oliver says, still watching me.

'To kill Graham?'

'He *made* me do it. He said he wanted to tell people about him… about us. We argued under the bridge. Anyone could have walked past but nobody did. The rock was just there and then he fell. I told him to get up but he didn't.'

'You bit him.'

Oliver glances to Paige and then back to me. He pulls up his own top, revealing a series of bite marks around his sides and his belly. Some look old – like Paige's – but at least a few of them are recent. Perhaps *very* recent.

'You wouldn't understand.'

He's right.

'But you kept the rock…'

He looks to his empty palm, as if the stone is there now. 'You wouldn't understand that, either.'

Cogs spin. Hamster wheels whirr.

'Paige lost her keys. You only found out she had one to Richard's place when I got back. Then you invited us round to look at articles – but you used the chance to take her keys. Then you put them back when we were all in court together. That's why you kept inviting her to do things. You told us at the beginning that your mum said the police might have to go back to do a second search. Richard told me he'd spoken to you about that, too. You planted that rock in case they did. It had to be somewhere they'd have missed the first time but somewhere they might actually look on a more thorough hunt.'

Oliver doesn't answer. He's watching Paige and I know it's true. If the police didn't find the rock, he could get his souvenir back at some point. If they did, then he was finally off any potential hook, even if it implicated his brother.

I wonder why he kept it. Perhaps to stop anyone else from finding it at the time – and then he couldn't bring himself to get rid of it.

Nobody speaks and I feel so very tired.

Paige hasn't moved. She's staring at the floor, mouth partly open.

I have my phone in my hand and have typed the first '9' when Oliver spots what I'm up to.

'What are you doing?' he says.

'What do you *think* I'm doing?'

I press a second '9' but there's then a flash of movement. I look up and Oliver has lunged towards the table and grabbed the vodka bottle. I've seen what's happening too slowly and the chair is still behind me, giving me nowhere to escape to once he swings the bottle.

I have no idea what happens next.

My head probably hits the corner of the chair as I fall but it's hard to know. The room swirls as clouds swarm across my eyes. The side of my face where I already had scratches throbs and my face is covered in something sticky. I can taste vodka mixed with something else… something metallic.

As I try to roll onto my side, the room swirls the other way. Something is standing over me. No, not something. *Someone.* Oliver. He hit me with the vodka bottle.

My right hand hurts and, when I try to move my fingers, small jolting stabs fire through me.

There are glass shards embedded in my palm. I must've put up a hand to try to protect myself.

I swing my legs towards Oliver but he's either further away than I thought, or I simply miss. There's a crunch of glass from somewhere nearby and then Oliver is next to me. Something rocks into the side of my face, a punch or an elbow, and then everything spins again as my head bounces off the ground.

There are stars and someone's moaning.

*I'm* moaning.

I try to swallow but there's liquid in my throat which makes me cough. There's blood. Everything's hazy, though I see the shape of Oliver stand and reach towards the kitchen counter. He's holding a knife now. The sort that's used to chop vegetables: fat and pointy and sharp.

I swing another leg towards him but miss again – and then he steps forward and raises the knife high above his head. I can't move. Everything hurts.

And then Oliver swings the knife directly towards my chest.

# FORTY

Oliver never completes the swing. He collapses sideways, landing with a crash on top of already splintered glass from the bottle. There's another figure standing over me now.

Paige.

Blood spills from her hand and the red seems to help the clouds lift as she sharpens into view.

There's blood everywhere. Her hand, my hand, the floor – and, as he lies unmoving on his side with a large triangular shard of glass sticking in his neck, from Oliver as well.

I use my left hand to push myself up. Except for the bright red blood, everything is shrouded in a grey haze, as if I'm dreaming.

Paige isn't moving. She's standing rigidly in the area between the kitchen and living room, with blood continuing to drip from her hand. I use the counter to pull myself all the way up and then hobble around to the other side, where I grab two tea-towels.

I give one to Paige, telling her to wrap it around her hand – and then crouch next to Oliver.

It's not just that there's a large spike of glass in his neck, it's that the blood is spurting like a small fountain. Pushing the splinter in further feels like a bad idea, so I yank it out in one fleshy movement. When that's done, I clamp the second tea-towel over the hole in Oliver's neck.

He hasn't moved.

'Paige.'

I can barely say her name. My mouth tastes of blood and I can feel it running down my throat.

She's still frozen and I stand, momentarily removing the pressure from Oliver's wound as I move across to her. The tea-towel hangs limply in her hand, so I wrap it tightly around her palm and tell her to hold it in place. Her face is damp as if she's been in the shower and there is a smidge of something greeny-brown around her mouth.

'I don't feel well.'

She glances back towards the sofa, where there's a puddle of vomit on the seat next to where she was sitting. I hadn't noticed her throw up.

'I'll call an ambulance,' I say.

I step across to Oliver first and tie the tea-towel around his neck, pulling it as tight as I dare so as to try to stop the bleeding without actually choking him.

When I stand again, Paige is staring lifelessly through me. Her lips are a light purple. She sways sideways and then gurgles. I'm not sure I'd know what was happening even if there weren't green stars swimming around the corners of my eyes.

'Paige…?'

'I think I—'

She doesn't finish the sentence because her eyes roll back in her head. From nowhere, there's foam in her mouth – and then she falls sideways, already unconscious as she smashes through the glass table with a thunderous clap of impossible horror.

# FORTY-ONE

There's a bench at the back of the church that sits out of sight from the rest of Macklebury. It used to face a row of trees but, for whatever reason, they've been trimmed and the view is now a wide vista of emerald green fields that stretch all the way to the horizon. As the valley dips down, mist hovers low to the ground. Above that, the dewy grass sparkles as the faintest hint of sunshine glimmers through.

Richard slots himself onto the bench at my side and we sit together in silence for a short while. I have so much to say and yet it feels like words aren't enough. Away from prison, this is the first time we've been together as a duo in a long time.

I watch as the mist rolls across the field. There's a man with a dog far below, bounding across the grass with a shepherd's stick in his hand.

'How's the head?'

I turn and realise Richard is watching me. Before I know what I'm doing, I touch the spot close to my eye and run a finger along the raised patch of skin.

'Thirteen stitches,' I reply.

'I had more than that when I fell off my bike as a kid.'

Neither of us laugh. It's not the day for that.

I turn back to the man with the dog. He's marched far ahead of the animal, who seems to be stuck sniffing something on the ground.

It's Richard who speaks next: 'People are already saying it all happened because Oliver was gay.'

'You don't kill a kid because you're gay.'

'*I* know that. It's not me who's saying it.'

'Who is?'

'*People.* Don't you remember what it's like in a small town? There's no Pride parade here. No rainbow crossings, or stickers in windows.'

'Not everyone will think like that.'

I doubt myself almost instantly, remembering those Facebook comments where everyone had already made up their minds.

'It doesn't need to be everyone,' Richard says. 'Not here. But there will be enough to make sure more kids keep it to themselves because they think being gay means being messed up enough to kill someone.'

I let Richard vent. It feels like this is something he's been wanting to say to someone for a while and it's not like he could let it out with his parents.

The man down below has stopped and is calling his dog. The animal's ears prick high and then it bounds across the field at a ferocious pace.

I try to lift my arm to scratch the scrapes on my face but it sticks while halfway up, so I end up lowering it and using the other hand. Richard notices something is up and leans forward to get a better look.

'You okay?'

'I had another ten stitches in my arm,' I say. 'When your brother hit me with the bottle, a big bit of glass got stuck in my bicep. I didn't even notice until the ambulance arrived. No wonder I was seeing stars. Sometimes my arm gets stuck when I'm trying to move it.'

It takes Richard a while to reply and I wonder how much of this he already knows. It's been a stressful, event-filled, three and a bit weeks. It's not even the same year any longer.

'Thank you,' he says. 'I wouldn't be out without you. I'd have been up on two murder charges.'

'I was only here because of her…'

In barely any time at all, the mist has almost cleared. There's a glimmer of yellow from above and, with a lack of wind and no immediate shade, this is the warmest I've felt since I got back into the country.

'Why didn't you tell the police why you were outside the hotel the night Wilson was killed?' I ask. 'If you said you were meeting Pete, it would have cleared up so much.'

'It's not that simple. I'm still in trouble and could go to prison.'

'Is that what your solicitor says?'

'He thinks it's more likely to be a fine but nobody knows. I was hoping I'd get bail and the charges would end up being dropped because I hadn't killed Wilson and there was no evidence that I had. If that happened – and it almost did because I was bailed – then I didn't have to tell anyone about the work I was doing for Pete and his cousins.'

'The police know now, though?'

Richard doesn't reply immediately. He coughs slightly and then continues.

'I told them when all the other stuff about Pete started coming through. They didn't believe me at first – but they did when I admitted to working on his books and showed them the files. They charged me with various financial-related offences two days later.'

'Why were you meeting Pete at the hotel?'

'He always picked the place. He'd drop off some receipts and then I would have to tidy things up. He didn't want to be seen coming to my office or flat – and also didn't want me going to any of his places. We'd meet in various alleys and side streets, where nobody was likely to see. Sometimes it would be first thing in the morning, other times it would be late. There was no pattern – although we probably met outside that hotel four or five times in all.'

I think of the cook at the back of the hotel, at whom Paige fired questions the night I first arrived back. Perhaps she did know him after all. It's a guess, total speculation, but I wonder if he was also one of Pete's customers.

'Does that mean you were there when Wilson was killed?'

'Of course not. Why would you ask that?'

'Because I don't understand what happened.'

Richard sighs and we sit and watch the dog walker finally reach the furthest corner of the field. He hops a stile and then reaches across to help his dog through the gap, before he disappears out of sight behind a hedge.

'Pete didn't show,' Richard says. 'Or I *thought* he didn't show. He must have done – but later, after I'd already left. The police searched his place and found the knife under his bed. He was so confident he wouldn't be caught that he didn't bother to get rid of it.'

'But why kill Wilson?'

'I suppose that's what the trial will be for.'

I realise how bad a question it is. Only two people know – one of them is dead and the other is on remand ahead of a trial. A guess would be that Wilson had left the hotel and spotted Pete outside. Wilson said something about Pete and his daughter, maybe told him to stay away, and that was that. As I found out on my driveway, Pete is not the sort of person to let something go.

'I talked to Ms Hill just after new year,' I say. 'To *Fiona*. She told me that Grace had been seeing Pete for about four months. I have no idea what she saw in him. She had no way of knowing that her dad knew about her and Pete – or that Pete was around the hotel on the night he died. She kept everything quiet until her mum confronted her with it. When she realised what might have happened, they went to the police.'

'That poor girl's going to have to live with that forever.'

'I hope she has a friend she can share with…'

Richard doesn't reply to that. We know as well as anyone that there's comfort in sharing something traumatic.

The wall of the church behind us echoes as an organist runs through a couple of chords. It stops as soon as it starts. A test run.

'Do you think the knife they found will be enough to convict Pete?' I ask.

'It's more than they had on me.'

'What about Oliver…?'

More silence, though it feels different this time. Not a pause for thought, or a natural break. It's as if the atmosphere is sizzling.

'I failed her,' Richard says.

'Paige?'

'I knew something was wrong but he was my brother and I figured that, whatever it was, it couldn't be too bad.'

'You got her away.'

'Too late.'

'She told me you were everything to her.'

Richard twists on the bench and so do I. For the first time since he sat, we're facing each other properly. 'When did she say that?' he asks.

'On that final night. Before Oliver. I didn't know he was in the bedroom but she had either had enough, or didn't care. After we found that rock in your flat, we couldn't figure out what it meant. She was the one who held firm. She said it couldn't be you and that you were everything to her because you got her away.'

Richard rubs his forehead. 'I don't understand why she let Oliver back in…'

I start to reply and then stop because I know. Richard asked me to keep an eye on Paige and I didn't. She was lonely and Oliver was the one person who wanted her, even if it was to prove to himself that he was somebody he wasn't.

'I caused this.'

Richard says what I'm thinking – except that he's talking about himself.

'You didn't,' I reply. 'Your brother did. Pete Baker did. *I* did.'

Richard pinches his nose as his head slumps to his chest. He doesn't dispute any of it.

'How are your mum and dad?' I ask.

'Not good. They weren't allowed to visit Oliver in hospital because of security issues. He's on the vulnerable prisoners' wing now, waiting for trial, so they should be able to visit him soon.' A pause. 'Not that Dad will ever see him.'

I know what's coming next. I wait for a few seconds – and then it does.

'Why did you save him?'

'It didn't cross my mind not to. I ended up tying that towel around his neck and I suppose that was enough until the ambulance got there.'

'What about Paige…?'

I close my eyes and I'm back in Paige's flat. I was talking to Oliver after he came out of the bedroom – and Paige hadn't moved from the sofa. She was breathing so slowly. She'd been sick, though I hadn't noticed.

'It's not as if I didn't try,' I say. 'It wasn't an either-or thing. I didn't know what to do. I thought it was blood loss, or shock, or…'

I can't finish the sentence. When I open my eyes, it doesn't clear the vision of Paige as she fell through the table.

'I didn't know what an overdose looked like,' I say. 'Her lips were this bluey-purple colour. That's one of the main signs. I thought it was shock because of Oliver.'

'You couldn't have made the ambulance get there any faster.'

It's true but it doesn't change what happened. I'm not sure there's anything more I can say. When I looked up the symptoms of Oxy addiction, I should have paid more attention to what an overdose could look like. I might have been able to save her.

It's as if Richard reads those thoughts.

'You saved me…' he says.

Richard is back staring across the field. It's empty aside from a scuttling of movement close to the hedge that runs along the side. Rabbits or squirrels dart out into the open and then scurry back to safety.

'Paige talked a lot about saving one another,' I say. 'She wasn't a fan.'

'Did she tell you she didn't need saving?'

'More than once.'

'Me too.'

'Did you listen?'

'No. Did you?'

I can't answer that because I don't know whether I failed her. It feels like I did.

Perhaps Richard senses this. He reaches across and grips my shoulder momentarily, before removing his hand. The same as Evie did.

'I mean it,' he says, 'you saved me.'

'It's a shame I couldn't save her.'

Richard says something… a few things… lots of things… but I'm not listening. I'm tired of hearing people tell me it's not my fault. Even Evie said it.

The best friend I ever had was lying next to me when she died from an oxycodone overdose – and I had no idea what to do to stop it.

'Haitch…?'

I realise Richard has been saying my name and I blink back onto the bench. 'Sorry,' I say. 'I was miles away.'

'I was asking if you're returning to Canada, or if you're staying here.'

I close my eyes again and see Paige's face. I know I'll never be able to live here again. This town will always be her place. Evie's house will always be the one next door to hers. Then there's Toronto, which feels as if it will always be Liane's place. Neither of them are mine.

'I'm not going back to Canada,' I say. 'I'm going to start again somewhere.'

'If I can do anything to help, just say. Anything. Any time.'

I offer a small smile of thanks but this is something I need to do myself.

'Rich…?'

A woman's voice sounds from the corner of the church and we both turn to see Joanne heading towards us. If nothing else, then at least he is back with his fiancée. I hope it works as well for her as I think it will for him – because he is really going to need someone when his brother goes on trial for Graham's murder. From what the town is saying, they've matched a bite mark to him.

'They want to start,' Joanne adds.

Richard and I stand and straighten our suits. We head along the path that will lead to the front of the church. Joanne asks if I'm all right and then reaches to take Richard's hand.

'We're good,' Richard says, answering for me, before he clamps another hand on my shoulder. 'She'd have wanted us both here,' he says.

The three of us walk together until we're at the front. Joanne and Richard head through the doors into the main part of the church – but I hang back and let them continue without me.

The paperback has become slightly creased in my inner pocket. I take it out and open the cover and read the two names on the front page. Mine is there in untidy blue scrawl but Paige's is curly and beautiful.

She never finished her final sentence back in her flat.

There were no final words.

There's only this.

Her name and mine, written on the same page more than twenty years ago. I flip to the back page, wondering why I didn't do it when she handed me the book. We figured that anyone could write their names at the front of something to show possession – but only true owners could do it at the back.

It's her handwriting alone this time, the same crafted swirls as from the front, but a different message. One I don't remember from the time but that I do now.

> *People change. Then they change again.*
> *Except us. Because we'll be us forever.*
> *– Paige & Harry*

## *The Blame* publishing team

**Editorial**
Ellen Gleeson

**Line edits and copyeditor**
Jade Craddock

**Proofreader**
Liz Hatherell

**Production**
Alexandra Holmes
Caolinn Douglas
Ramesh Kumar Pitchai

**Design**
Lisa Horton

**Marketing**
Alex Crow
Rob Chilver
Hannah Deuce

**Publicity**
Kim Nash
Noelle Holten
Sarah Hardy

**Distribution**
Chris Lucraft
Marina Valles

**Audio**
Kelsie Marsden
Alba Proko
Arran Dutton & Dave Perry
    – Audio Factory
Andrew Kingston

**Rights and contracts**
Peta Nightingale
Saidah Graham